Forever Young & Foolish

Gary O'Donoghue

This book is dedicated to those I have loved and lost.
It is also dedicated to those that I will continue to love.

I would also like to thank those that supported me through the writing of this book, without you it could not have been completed. I hope you all know who you are, as I may require your support again, thank you.

Revenge

The action of hurting or harming someone in return for an injury
or wrong suffered at their hands.

The Oxford English Dictionary

1978

Chapter1

Sean Farrow woke up from his deep sleep; it took a while for his eyes to adjust to his surroundings and the smell that drifted up his nostrils, the smell of sweat, dirt and alcohol filled the air. He rubbed his eyes and slowly surveyed the room looking for answers to where he was. A small speck of light came through the side of the curtains telling him that it was probably well into the morning, if not, then maybe even midday. There was no one else in the room; he could see that now as his eyes adjusted to the light. There was what looked like Chinese food on a table in front of him still in their containers stinking the room out, and there were empty beer cans on the same table laid out as if they were just thrown straight out of a rubbish truck. There was something else on the table, an empty bottle of Vodka and an ashtray full of used cigarettes, which shot another smell up his nostrils making him want to vomit. Sean put two and two together and realised that's where the banging head came from; and the sight in front of him also had him hoping that he had survived another night out with his friend Taylor Docherty.

He sat up, he checked that his wallet was still in his back pocket, it's there, and he checks the contents, it was empty, and then checks for his house keys which would ensure he could at least return to a sane world, there's no keys. He looks for his jacket in the room and sees it hanging over the arm of an adjoining sofa, and he relaxes. He lays there for a while and tries to recall the evening before, he recalls being drunk, he remembers girls, and beer, lots of beer, all this entered his head, he tries to remember more but his situation denies him. It was all still a blur and may take him some time to recall without the intervention of a third party to remind him, he thought to himself.

There's a noise in another room, he can hear it now, he turns his head towards where it came from and he strains his ears to hear better. He hears it again, like a switch being pressed and then distant footsteps, and now he hears what sounds like a cabinet door banging shut, and then the noise of a kettle boiling it's contents of water. Someone's making tea or coffee thought Sean. He remembers a girl, no two girls, he remembers laughing and giggling and returning to a flat by taxi to somewhere in Battersea, where the bloody hell is Taylor, Sean thinks, and where are the girls. The door opened but it seemed like it was pushed. Sean's friend Taylor Docherty walks into the room with his normal self smirking smile holding two mugs of an unknown substance, he looks at Sean with that knowing smile and places one of the mugs on the coffee table. Taylor spoke first.

'Yours went home, didn't want to drop her knickers, she thought you were down right rude, I got the ugly fat one but she banged like a rabbit all night, that's coffee there mate'. Taylor pointed to the coffee in a stained mug on the table, Sean looked down at it and instantly realised that it had come from a very dirty kitchen.

'She ain't got no biscuit's', continued Taylor, 'drink it and we'll fuck off out of here, I've already called a cab from her phone.'

Sean looked up at his friend while rubbing his eyes again, he was still trying to adjust to his surroundings, his hair was scruffy and he could feel his head banging inside like it always did on these occasions.

'Are you taking the piss or something, he said, 'what are we doing back here and where the fuck is here anyway?'

'We're in Battersea, don't you remember talking to the two birds in the pub, bloody hell mate your memories shocking, drink your coffee, it will perk you up a bit, you look like shit.'

Sean picked up the stained cup and looked up at Taylor with a boyish smile, 'so tell me, did you get a shag then?'

'Yeah', said Taylor, ' I always do, and started to tell Sean all the intimate details as they sat there waiting for the sane world to enter back into their heads again. Sean was still feeling the pain in his head and was finishing off the thick black hot coffee, when Taylor got to his feet.

'Come on mate we need to go before what's her name in there surfaces, I don't want to end up getting stalked, hopefully she wont remember my face when she wakes up'. Taylor smiled with that grin that often says I've been a naughty boy again. They both got up from the sofa and left the room. Before taking the stairs Sean decided to take a peek for himself, he looked into the room and could see the bare arse of a women that looked like she was fast asleep, the bed covers showed sexual activity and a pair of knickers could be seen on the floor. Sean resisted going round the side of the bed to see if the face was pretty or not in case he disturbed the resting female, instead he left the room and looked back at Taylor who had that smile on his face again.

Out on the pavement they could see the streets were deserted, it was a typical Sunday morning, the rain started to fall and the entrance to Battersea Park could be seen across the main road. A London red bus passed through on it's way to Chelsea Bridge and the West End, there was a loud bang in the distance from on-going work on a building site nearby and within seconds the sky was full of pigeons. The cab arrives outside the house where Sean & Taylor left a woman nursing a hangover and a guilt trip. They settle into the back seat and survey the scene of Battersea from the windows of the cab knowing many of the sites, roads and surrounding area very well.

Sean Farrow and Taylor Docherty have known each other from an early age in their childhood on a council estate in Balham, South London. They grew up together, went to the same school and generally did everything together as often as they could.

They grew up in the late seventies and eighties and made most of their money from petty crime mainly selling stolen goods from factory robberies, but never hurting anyone. They were typical of their age group in the area, early twenties, boisterous, womanizing and the occasional scrap due to over indulging in alcohol consumption. Sean and Taylor had a sense of morality and respect which others around them had lost earlier on, others that went down the slippery slope to bigger crimes, gangs and individuals with no respect for society. It was the 1970's, there were troubles in Northern Ireland; British rock was at it's peak in Britain and the United States, the British youth were enjoying life, although there was despondency due to the lack of work and good education. Gang culture was still around, but with new drugs on the market gangsters were starting to exploit this and fighting for territory was on the rise.

Taylor directs the cab driver to a café called Antonio's in Balham where he knew the dim lights; greasy food and hot coffee would bring them back to reality. They entered the café and surveyed the interior and the clientele. Same old faces, Sean thought, some old, some young, with cigarette smoke billowing into the air and suspicious eyes looking up at them from behind newspapers as they entered.

'I need a crap a shower and a large meal to get me back to life,' said Taylor, 'going out with you Sean is always an exciting evening', they both laughed.

'I need to get out of this life Taylor, this ain't the life for me no more, it's not me', replied Sean.

6

Taylor laughed; 'I know what you mean, still, until the next time mate.'

Sean surveyed their surroundings again; faces still buried in their newspapers, going nowhere, not caring about anyone or anything, as long as they have enough money for beer, fags and the odd bet, he looked back at Taylor.

'When we were kids Taylor we dreamed of life, when you grow up, what do you want to be, we used to say to each other, Spaceman, Footballer, Film star, pilot, or even a top chef.'

Taylor looked at Sean with what seemed like a long stare, or he was remembering and knowing something, he took a sip from his coffee and then spoke 'well you were definitely spaced out last night, flying as high as a kite you were.'

'Bollocks' said Sean, 'it's all bollocks; we need to make something of ourselves instead of this crap day in day out.'

When they felt the large greasy breakfast had given them medicinal benefits from the hangover they left Antonio's cafe and started the walk back to where they lived. It started to rain, and continued to fall on them both while the sun threatened to come out from behind the clouds, but was just not quite succeeding. Sean felt the rain start to penetrate down the back of his neck and wished he was back home with Tina his girlfriend in a warm comfortable bed, but he knew he still had a little further to go in the London rain.

'I didn't touch that bird did I Taylor?' he said, 'Tina would have my balls cut off if I did, your sisters a lunatic.'

'No Sean you were quite a gentleman, she wanted it though but you kept on about there being no biscuit's in the house, she eventually left disheartened once she realised you weren't going to give her one.'

'Thank fuck for that' Sean said.

They continued to walk in the rain and now both wished they had waited for a bus, or at least called a cab from Antonio's, the rain was getting worse and they decided to wait it out in a nearby shop doorway.

'Don't forget we are going on that building site tomorrow Sean, in Clapham, where Joe Swain is, you know where that guy was found murdered at the bottom of the lift shaft, we've got some machinery to pick up, Joe has organised it.'

'Yea I remember Taylor, Johnny Saunders they reckon, Pete suggested all the fingers are pointing towards him again, as I said, I need to get out of this shit hole of an environment.'

'Well he did mess around with Johnny, you just don't do that round here, the guy apparently screwed him over for some money, but don't worry, Johnny Saunders is a bastard, and he will get his payback some day.'

'Lets hope so Taylor, 'for your old man especially.'

Taylor looked across at Sean, it's not often they talk about his dead father, but Sean Farrow was the only one that he allowed to bring it up.

'Yes' said Taylor for my old man.'

They both stood there in the shop doorway watching the rain, people were starting to head to the Catholic Church nearby with umbrellas poised to catch the falling rain. Cars were going by and as the gullies were blocked torrents of water were being splashed onto the unfortunate passers by, which looked like it was a deliberate move from some drivers, thought Sean. This led to an excessive amount of verbal abuse from the people who were just about to head into the house of God, Sean and Taylor could not help but smile at the scene that was played out in front of them.

'Are you seeing Tina tonight?' said Taylor, still bemused by the sight in front of him.

'I am, yes mate', replied Sean.

'You're a right old lover boy aren't you Sean, what's up with you mate, are you going soft on me or what?'

'It's your sister mate, she's mad about me, I can't help it, I was born with all this charm, not like you, you're like a fucking dog on heat you are, shagging everything that moves. I mean that large arse I saw hanging out the bedcovers this morning meant I didn't need to have a peek at her boat race.'

They both laughed out loud, Taylor lit a cigarette, and pulled the coat collar up around his neck, 'I'll smoke this and then we had better make a dash for it, can't hang around here all day waiting for the rain to pass.'

Chapter 2

Sean Farrow watched the naked body leave the bed and enter the bathroom, the small curved rear still gave him a stirring, he heard her start to sing, she was happy he thought.

Tina was beautiful in body and person; she loved Sean, and adored him but often worried about his misdemeanours with her brother. He had promised to settle down with her and he wanted to, because he knew deep down he loved Tina, missed her when she wasn't with him and he knew he wanted to be with her forever.

Tina was Taylor Docherty's sister, she was young, petite and slim, Taylor wasn't too happy about the relationship early on, he never could get to grips with his best mate shagging his younger sister, so spoke very little about it, and always shrugged it off. Taylor never suspected anything and neither did his mother Patsy Docherty. Sean was always at their home but they never saw it coming as Sean and Tina were good at keeping it at a low profile, but they knew it was inevitable, they both knew that at some point suspicions would lead to capture. That came one night when Taylor went out to pick his mum Patsy up from the local Bingo hall leaving Sean and Tina drinking from a wine bottle at seventeen years of age, when Taylor and Patsy came back they found Sean and Tina curled up on the sofa with their arms wrapped around each other. Taylor wanted to wake them up but

Patsy insisted they be left alone. When Sean and Tina woke in the morning they knew their secret was out. Nothing was ever said about it, and very slowly it became accepted by all. Although Taylor often showed his disagreement, deep down he loved and respected them both.

Sean waited, he felt the stirring in his groin return and when the singing stopped, he shouted out to Tina.

'Come back to bed babe, we can lie in, Taylor won't be here till twelve!'

The singing continued again, it got louder and louder, 'yes she is happy' Sean thought again, and it made him smile.

Tina came back into the room kissed Sean full on the lips and then slipped back into bed beside him, 'I love you Sean Farrow' she said and slid her hand onto his hard cock. They made love again, Tina's mouth smelling of fresh mint, and her body smelling of sex, they gripped hard on to each other until Tina climaxed to a grinding rhythm as their bodies pressed against each other, she held on to Sean until he came too, whispering in her ear, 'I love you, I love you, you dirty bitch.'

They lay there in each others arms panting and laughing, pushing the covers off to get some air, Sean kissed her neck, he kissed her back and her arms, Tina stirred with his soft lips upon her body, she was in heaven and wanted to be there forever.

'Why do you have to go out today', she said, 'why can't you stay in bed with me, we can lie here, listen to some music, make love, do any dirty thing you want.'

Sean laughed, 'Sounds inviting Tina but I have to go, I've promised Taylor we would meet the boys in the pub and have a couple of games of pool'. Tina looked at him with that worried frown. Don't worry, he said, 'we aren't doing anything dodgy, I'll tell you what, during the week you and me will go out for the day shopping.'

'Ok', she replied, 'will you buy me that dress you've promised me?'

'I will, and you will look absolutely gorgeous in it', with that Sean gradually slid down the covers, buried his head between Tina's legs and brought her very quickly to another climax, this time with his mouth.

It was a Saturday, and for Sean and Tina it was always what they would call a lie in, they had a day off from work and it was always agreed as their morning time. Tina looked across at Sean, she knew that any minute now her brother would arrive taking her man away from her, she knew it was going to be a day of beer and a chat with his friends in the local pub for them both. She wanted him to stay with her safe in her arms but she knew he needed his space to function; she could not take that away from him for fear of losing him.

Taylor rang the doorbell tossing his keys inside his motorcycle helmet; he looked up into the sunshine and waited.

Tina opened her front door, looked at Taylor with a concerned look on her face, 'He's in the shower, go up, I will make you a coffee, hope you are not going to get him into trouble, I love him to bit's, just like I love you big brother', she said.

'And I love you too sis, two sugars and very little milk, thanks', he answered.

There was calmness about them both when Taylor and Tina were together, they were just like any other brother and sister, however, brought together by the hatred of one man, the man that killed their father. They never spoke about it, it was in the past and they wanted to forget, but the man was everywhere in South London, and they couldn't get loose from his grip.

Tina looked into her brothers eyes and Taylor could see they were showing signs of worry and care, he waited for what she wanted to say, he knew there was something on her mind.

'Sean says you're going to the pub to meet the boys.'

'That's right' Taylor said, 'we're just going to the pub, I will have him back in one piece.'

'You make sure you do Taylor' Tina said, 'He doesn't need to be involved in any bad stuff, we are going to get married.'

'How sweet', he said.

Sean Farrow walked into the room drying his hair with a towel, 'What's sweet?'

'You two getting married, your wedding surprise' Taylor said, 'now get your gear on I'm parched and some of the boys are already there.'

'What about your coffee?' Tina said.

'No time sis.'

Taylor kissed his sister on the cheek, smiled, winked at her and headed for the stairs. Sean now fully dressed; kissed Tina full on the lips, told her he loved her and would not be long. Tina pulled him into her arms, and smacked him on the arse.

'Have a nice time', she said as he left the house, 'and bring me back a nice bottle of wine!'

The roads were typically busy in London, the motorbike swung from left to right avoiding traffic jams, Sean clung to the bars of the bike on the rear with his black helmet and leathers glistening in the sun that was surprisingly in the sky. Taylor handled the bike with ease, he was used to it and drove through the streets they knew well with Sean tucked in behind him. There was always something about London in the sun, Sean thought as he viewed the scene around him; when it's there take advantage of it, because it doesn't happen that often. As they travelled the streets Sean admired the women with short skirts that were busying themselves along the high street, he could see the faces of people change, just because the sun was shining. He watched as kids were having a water fight on a corner of the street chasing each other with water guns, they were laughing and looked like they were enjoying every minute of getting soaked. He felt happy, at peace, in love and content, however a feeling in the back of his mind that although sunny today, tomorrow may rain and throw up problems he would not be ready for. They turned off the High St and pulled into the pub car park, they removed their leather jackets and helmets and walked to the entrance of the Public House.

The pub hadn't changed much in years apart from space invader machines, gambling machines and jukeboxes, the furniture remained the same, and the décor was cigarette smoke brown with pictures of horses and their groomers on the walls. Joe Swain was in the far corner, pint in hand watching Sean and Taylor enter the bar.

'What time do you call this?' he said.

'Lover boy here snogging my sisters face off is why we're late' Taylor said.

The bar was rowdy, a hard pub, but there was never that much trouble unless strangers threw their weight around. It was a comfort zone for Sean and Taylor, although Taylor was well aware his father was slain viciously in this very pub. This left him fatherless and with memories of a man, who cared, laughed and loved him very much, alongside his mum and sister with a great passion. Only a few are aware of that incident and only Sean understands why Taylor still drinks in this pub, it's his way of dealing with it, his way of saying out loud; I'm drinking in here because my father couldn't. The pub started to fill with the normal faces, associates, work friends, old school friends and those that lived on the estate that they grew up on and others from the local area. Sean and Taylor settled down for the afternoon with Joe and their mates playing pool and sharing memories of the past. They would often discuss things that happened the night before, two weeks ago, a year ago, and there was always laughter, piss taking and beer. It was their man time and they relished it like any normal society does.

Chapter 3

Tina Docherty sat on the edge of the bed and pulled her silk stockings on over her soft smooth legs, she smiled as she leant forward and felt pains inside herself from the active sex session with Sean only a couple of hours previously. She could hear her mother mooching around downstairs. Tina's mother, like every other mother was caring, loving and always there when needed, but Tina was always aware of a dark side in her mothers youth, she was aware but was never fully informed of her mothers past. They had a healthy relationship but there was something missing, something that troubled Tina, she was aware of what it was but was always too worried and too scared to ask, because she may be frightened of the answer. Tina rose from the bed and walked over to the curtains, pulled them to one side. The light shone in through the bedroom with a torrent of rays from the sun, she brushed her dark auburn hair back and let the sunlight hit her face. She looked around the room and again smiled at the state of the bed from the fucking the night before and the early morning love making, she was in love, her body was exhausted but it felt great. She left the room tottering on her high heels and walked down the stairs to greet her mother Patsy Docherty who was standing at the bottom of the stairs waiting and looking up at her.

'You do know it's nearly one o'clock don't you Tina?' she said.

'Yes mother' Tina answered, 'nothing like a good lie in and hot sex on a Saturday morning.'

'Hot sex with Sean Farrow, I've seen more meat on an ants knee cap.'

'Ok mum, slagging off my boyfriend is not why you are here today.'

'I know Hun, I've come to see my precious daughter, make sure she is happy and take her out for lunch, and hopefully we can both meet a real man.'

'You love Sean just as much as I do so stop putting him down.'

'I'm not putting him down; I've known him since he was knee high to a grasshopper, and I'm only kidding, so grab your bag and let's go out.'

Tina smiled, she knew her mother well and how she practically brought Sean up as one of her own when he was a kid running around with Taylor, and there has always been that friendly banter between them both.

The love from Patsy Docherty was like a mother's, ever since the tragic death of Sean's family at an early age, Tina remembered. Sean Farrow was like any youngster at the age of nine when it happened; Sean's father was rushing his wife, Sean's mother to the hospital when the tragic car accident happened. There was nothing that could be done for all three passengers including the unborn baby, Sean's future sister. From that point in Sean's life he was brought up by his Uncle, a respected local man and the closest relative Sean had to a family. Sean gradually looked upon his Uncle as his father and mentor who was a loving Uncle who spent many a time guiding Sean through life, and this guidance always made Sean think at the last moment if he was doing the right thing or the wrong thing, and this made his life choices easier to make. The love and respect for his Uncle was immense so much so that if there was anything said about his Uncle, Sean showed the anger that none of his friends had witnessed before, so much so that they had to pull Sean off many a scum bag in the pub when this happened. Although there was love and respect for his Uncle, nothing could stop Sean spending a lot of time in the household of his best friend Taylor Docherty and his family who Sean leant on for added security. Sean's Uncle passed away when Sean was seventeen, a sad time for Sean who eventually stayed alone in his Uncle's home but spending the majority of his time with Taylor and his family with the added benefit of gradually falling in love with Tina Docherty, his best friends sister.

Tina often brought up the bond between her brother and Sean and still remembers the day. Sean was hanging from the drainpipe by his jacket that was slowly starting to rip. The boys were bothering the neighbourhood again running across the roof of the estate when Sean slipped on the tarmac heated by the sun on the roof and slipped over the edge. Taylor ran to the edge to see Sean hanging there by his jacket, he grabbed hold of Sean's belt and was struggling to hold on to him due to the pain in his arms, screaming at the top of his voice he managed to get attention and hold on until Tina's mother Patsy clambered on to the roof and hauled Sean back up. When Patsy got Sean back onto the roof she slapped him across both legs harder then she had ever hit her own kids, to Tina that was a show of affection because Sean would have died and everyone knew it, and he was loved and would have been missed. Taylor stood there exhausted, his arms were killing him as he had been holding on to Sean's belt for more than ten minutes until his mother arrived, he had cuts and grazes on his arms from the effect of taking the weight and tears in his eyes from the shock of the incident. Tina knew and understood why the boys have never spoken about that time since, but it bonded them together that day, made them brothers. No one knows what they both spoke about that day as Sean was hanging there one hundred feet in the air with Taylor holding onto him, and no one has ever asked.

Tina looked across at her mother who was staring at her in that way that made Tina feel like she was being loved.

'What you thinking about Tina' said Patsy.

'Nothing mum, just stop cursing Sean, that's all, stop cursing him.'

They left the house and admired the sunshine that finally came through the clouds, walked the short distance to the car and started the drive to Oxford street in the city for some mother and daughter bonding and retail therapy. As they drove they saw people spilling onto the pavements from pubs and bars and drinking in the sunshine.

'London is a fine City in the sun,' Patsy said as she turned to look at Tina.

There was no answer from Tina and this was starting to trouble Patsy, her daughter was not the same this morning, something was troubling her Patsy thought.

'What's the matter with you this morning Tina, have you got something on your mind, you seem troubled.'

'I want to know who my father is mum,' Tina replied.

Patsy Docherty lost control of the car and mounted the kerb. A man walking along the pavement had to jump into a garden before nearly being impaled against the garden wall. Patsy gained control of the car looked in her rear view mirror and saw the man waving and cursing obscenities at them before shrinking into the distance.

'Where the hell did that come from?' Patsy said.

'I just want to know who he is, that's all.'

'But why now Tina, why now, you've never asked before.'

'There's something missing in my life I don't know what it is, I've never asked you before because I have respected your privacy hoping that one day you might tell me, hoping one day that you might sit me down and talk about it, but you never have mum, you never have, why is that.'

'Mark Docherty was your father, not your blood father but your father; he brought you up when you were young, that's all you need to know.'

'I know mum and I loved him very much and miss him just like you do, but I just need to know now, that's all I just need to know.'

'You don't need to know Tina, it's best left alone, that's all, best left alone.'

Tina did not speak, but there was anger there in her blood, anger at her mum and anger at life and not knowing where she has come from and why her mum did not want to reveal who her father was. Tina knew there was also pain within her that maybe her mother didn't know who her father really was, she threw that away as she didn't want to know if there was an answer to that question. They both did not speak, and the next conversation they had was not until they reached their destination.

'Coffee or tea' said Patsy, as they sat in a cafe on Oxford Street watching the world go by.

Chapter 4

Curly Broadbridge felt the pain in his feet, and he felt the pain throughout his whole body, but his feet felt the worst. His big toes were cut off on both of his feet by what he thought at the time felt like probably by some kind of metal cutting implement. He could not see anything as the blindfold was still in place; he was sweating, terrified and had already soiled and urinated in his pants. It was silent again but he knew they were still nearby; he shuddered at the slightest noise, as he never knew where or when the next blow or torturing pain would come from.

Johnny Saunders sat and stared at his victim, the smell of shit and piss was in the air. He raised his hand as if to issue another command, and his henchman Charlie Allan struck Curly across the face with a crushing right hand. Curly and the chair he was sitting on went sprawling across the floor, cracking his head on the concrete. Curly started to cry and whimper like a small child begging for forgiveness and protesting his innocence.

'I've had enough of this low life scum', Johnny said, 'cut him up, throw his parts in the river and get the warning around town, and get rid of the smell of shit in here.'

Charlie took the order and did his work with support from his colleague Stan Smith. They killed Curly with a stab to the heart several times, they untied him and dragged his body outside and down to the basement where the dismembering would take place.

Johnny Saunders anger again came flooding into his brain and mind and he shouted another order towards his two men.

'I want this warning out now, I don't want any other fucker trying to roll me over, and when you're done get back here and clean this shit up.'

Curly Broadbridge was a small time crook who put it upon himself to steal some of Johnny's drug deals, and he was mistaken in thinking he could make some money by pocketing larger then normal quantities for himself. Unfortunately word got round on the street and it wasn't long before he was being watched and scrutinized. Johnny was watching Curly Broadbridge, after his henchmen were suspicious of his behaviour, so he was seized and made to pay for stupidity and greed. His wife, who had been wondering where her husband was, soon realised that he wasn't coming back when she received in the post her husbands feet, both missing the big toes. Johnny knew that he needed to put his message out there and make an example of Curly. He wanted to put fear among the community, to let them know that he is still in control.

Johnny Saunders sat at his office desk reflecting on his empire, he sat impassively smoking on a large Havana and tapping away on the table top. He looked out of the window and saw the sun starting to rise, it was early and he had been up all night fucking prostitutes snorting cocaine and torturing Curly Broadbridge. As the sun rose he could see London starting to wake, and he could see the windows of the offices opposite starting to sparkle into life and shadows cast across with mirrored images of themselves.

24

The financial district would soon start the early grind of deals and more deals; however Johnny's interests were not the City's financial dramas but the bankers who spent vast amount of money on white powder. His runners would see to that and Curly Broadbridge fucked up big style, he was an experienced runner who had excellent contacts that made it easier to sell and market his goods. Now Johnny needed another Curly before he started to lose deals to competitors. He pulled out a black book from the side draw of his desk and worked along from page to page for contacts new and old. He needed people that could supply information on those who wanted work and could fit into the City life. He slowly scanned the pages, memories came flooding in with each name perused, bank robbers, drug dealers, small time petty thieves, rapists, muggers, with each name telling it's own story in his head. Charlie Allan came into the room and looked at Johnny.

'It's all done boss', he said.

Charlie Allan was a confident hard Londoner from the North side who had been with Johnny Saunders for a long time, Charlie was someone that Johnny could trust and it showed in the money that came his way.

'Charlie', Johnny said, 'who do you know that can do what Curly was good at but won't have the bottle to try and turn me over?'

'There isn't anyone boss, Curly was a prick but he was good at what he did, he must have stolen thousands from you, we have his contact book though.'

Charlie Allan threw down onto his boss's desk the diary that still had blooded fingerprints on it. It was a pocket size book and Johnny looked at it like the stare from a hungry wolf. Johnny picked the book up wiping away the blood with a handkerchief he pulled from his breast pocket, and at the same time giving Charlie a stare of disgust to receive it in such a state. Johnny looked back out of the window, the sun was now higher in the sky, and people were starting to build up on the pavements, getting off buses and streaming out of Waterloo tube station. He looked back at the book and started to scan Curly Broadbridge's diary.

'I need to find someone Charlie, otherwise I'm going to lose money to my competitors'. He scanned the pages again and certain memories started to flood back into his mind. He poured himself a Jack Daniels from the decanter on his desk, gulped the contents and looked again at page eighteen in the diary that was taken from Curly Broadbrdge. The name in front of him brought back memories that made him shudder not only from the action but the consequence and the reality it brought him. Docherty's name was there in black ink in front of him, Mark Docherty, beside the name was written, driver and support. It stood out like it was in bold and capital letters and different from the rest, but it wasn't, it was in the same writing, colour and size of font, but for Johnny Saunders it ripped through his memory like it was yesterday, and it was then that it flooded back.

Johnny remembered the day; he recalled the aggression, the situation he was in and the start of his claim to fame. The public house in South London was quiet, he was high on cocaine, he was with Charlie Allan and Stan Smith who were also high, they had drunk excessive amounts of alcohol and were still feeling shit and angry over a loss of respect from the night before. A rival Irish gang beat the three of them to a pulp because they chanted God Save the Queen; they took the beating well, fought back with everything they had, they lost, and were now hell bent on getting revenge.

Mark Docherty was a family man who had his own son from a previous marriage who was Taylor Docherty. He had a stepdaughter Tina, who he had always considered as his own, and brought her up from the age of two with his new wife Patsy. He had been at work, kissed his wife and family goodbye in the morning and looked forward to his return in the evening. Mark Docherty was just out for a quiet drink on his way home from work when he entered the pub at the wrong time. He took the full brunt of Johnny Saunders anger as he strolled through the door and went up to the bar. He felt it in the back of his neck, he felt the eyes and the atmosphere, but his Irish pride did not allow him to turn around and head back out the way he came.

Johnny again recalls the day. He wanted revenge and most of all credibility, Mark Docherty was a face and a hard man and that would deliver credibility back to Johnny. When Docherty walked into the pub Johnny had already made his mind up, he checked inside his jacket pocket to confirm he had the butcher's knife within easy reach. Docherty ordered his pint of Bitter, with his friendly Irish charm booming across the public house, which was also for Johnny's benefit. The atmosphere immediately changed and everyone in the pub could feel it change rapidly. It was inevitable that something bad was about to happen and there was no way that it could be stopped, the ball was rolling and the next few minutes were going to be the change of many lives. The atmosphere said it all.

'Hey paddy you're not welcome in this British pub!' Johnny boomed out

Docherty ignored the remark.

'I said, Irish paddy prick, you're not welcome in this pub, leave your drink and fuck off.'

The barmaid went to take Docherty's pint; Mark Docherty grabbed the pint back.

'Leave it Mark,' she said, 'go home to Patsy and the kids, come back another day.'

Docherty smiled at her and drank from his beer glass.

'Mark go home please' she pleaded.

Again he smiled at the barmaid 'It's ok Mandy, I'll finish this and then leave.'

Johnny recalls how he watched the banter between the Irish prick and the barmaid. He felt the atmosphere change and watched the other four people that were in the pub get up and walk out. The pub was now empty apart from himself, Charlie Allan and Stan Smith, the barmaid and Mark Docherty. Charlie and Stan sat silent with smirks on their faces, a nervous smirk, but also one of excitement because they knew what was about to come.

Johnny recalls further and realises that he is now gripping Curly Broadbridge's book harder than is actually required. He remembers pushing his chair back across the floor making that evil scraping noise, which reminds everybody of chalk on the blackboard. It was like the starting gun, the bell before a heavyweight challenge.

'I told you to leave paddy!' Johnny shouts out again.

'Now come on Johnny, sit down and relax', Mandy said.

'Shut the fuck up bitch!' Johnny retorted.

Docherty continued to face the bar. He was side on to Johnny, who continued slowly towards him.

'Now come on Johnny', said Mark Docherty, 'I'm having a quiet pint in the pub, I don't want any trouble, I just want to relax here and then go home to my beautiful wife and kids'.

Johnny felt the blade handle within his hand, which was well hidden within his coat; Docherty did not stand a chance. Johnny's slow pace made it less threatening but the swift movement of hand and blade out of the coat, meant the nine inch steel blade was imbedded into Docherty's side and into his lungs in seconds. Mandy screamed, Charlie and Stan jumped from their seats and joined in the foray, Mark Docherty fell to the floor and the three animals stabbed repeatedly at his body. He had no chance to fight back; he was grappling at knives to stop the onslaught but soon lost energy and life. They continued to stab

29

at his lifeless body screaming anti Irish obscenities, all the pain they experienced from the night before was taken out on Mark Docherty.

Johnny sat impassively in his room still looking at the name, he recalled, the court case. The power it gave him during and after the case, threatening the jury and getting Mandy the barmaid murdered so she could not reveal names. Eventually every one of the Irish gang became a victim of his violence. His empire started to grow, don't fuck with Johnny Saunders was sent around the community. He was getting more powerful because of that killing, but it worried him, the name on page eighteen worried him, and he didn't know why.

From that moment on, Johnny Saunders became more powerful mainly with violence and money. The best men were hired that had hard reputations and could manage those that could easily be bought for the right price. He had Charlie Allan who had always been loyal; he was also great for managing the rest of the team. Stan Smith was an ex-con who was good with his fists and was the ideal person when it came to putting the frighteners on people. Then there was Ray Flynn a hard man that Johnny was never too sure about but was great for the drug trade and knew many associates that he could influence and deal with. One of which was Winston Scott, who Johnny could rely on early on in his career to manage the black drug trade that was growing fast in many London areas. There were also other people that Johnny could always call upon on a daily basis to support his career, these included bent coppers, lawyers and others that could make things happen for him in the drug trade, sex trade, gambling and prostitution and any legal matters that stood in his way.

Johnny Saunders poured himself another whiskey, he lit another Havana cigar and blew the smoke out of the window, he watched it enter London's air space and vanish. He had no worries, he was on top of the world, no money concerns and no one to fear, but there was something niggling away at him. He put it down to the game that he was in, it comes with the trade, he thought to himself, but he couldn't push it out of his mind.

Chapter 5

Tony Clay woke up suddenly with his alarm exploding in his head and inside the room; he moved his arm and slapped the alarm until there was silence. He opened his eyes, but it took him a while to focus. He remembered he had to be up and out early but still turned on his side and spooned his wife Angela. He realises very soon that he's got that early morning erection, and he knew deep inside that would have to wait till later on, or even tonight. Tony Clay got out of the bed with his erection pointing at the ceiling; he entered the bathroom and got into the shower. This brought him back to reality and an end to his hardened manhood.

Tony Clay was a small time crook dealing with petty factory robberies from across the UK and often internationally. He was known as the third party and was renowned for his professionalism but most of all his ability to be quiet, loyal and have a low profile. He would also deal in whatever could get him additional cash for his future plans that was for him and his wife Angela to an early retirement in the Caribbean. He knew this was the reason why he was often called upon to do tasks for Johnny Saunders, although he hated the ground he walked on, he was indebted to him and that haunted Tony Clay. He was twenty-nine years of age and came from a stable background but was easily led at an early age. He wasn't violent; he wasn't a drug dealer or a drug addict but a good negotiator and businessman on behalf of others and himself. It was this profile that kept him busy, however sometimes he knew they were dangerous tasks.

Tony Clay dressed himself in formal clothes, he went downstairs and made himself some breakfast and black coffee; he sat and looked out of the back windows from his two up two down house in Clapham South London. He surveyed his garden and the rain, which was once again falling down and feeding his grass. He thought of Angela upstairs in bed naked, he wanted to go back upstairs but then quickly remembered his two jobs for the day. One he knew would be easy, for Taylor Docherty and Sean Farrow. The other for Johnny Saunders he knew would not be so easy and the one he worried about. Then he thought about the Caribbean and of Angela again upstairs naked, he was feeling horny again, but he knew that would have to wait till later.

He looked in his diary, 22nd August, on the first line, pick up for Johnny Saunders, an address in Hornchurch Essex, pick up a suitcase and bring to another address in South London a day later, with times and contacts all written down. The second line, drive to Tilbury Docks meet a contact and pick up a van full of Italian design Armani suits and deliver to Sean and Taylor to a given address in Battersea, South London. All in all it seemed a relatively easy day but the Johnny Saunders jobs always troubled Tony Clay. The other job was a doddle and he knew that it would not cause him any concern unless pulled over by the police for any reason, but Tony was also an excellent actor and knew he could bluff his way out of any issue.

He finished his breakfast, tossed the used cutlery into the sink knowing that Angela would work through the home and clear up today, once she managed to get out of bed, he thought. He left the house and as usual looked like an insurance salesman as he got into his BMW car, he started the car and entered the narrow side streets of Clapham and eventually made his way onto the main Road to Brixton and then up to Elephant and Castle and over Tower Bridge. The rain was still coming down and his windscreen wipers were working hard to establish a clear view for him as he travelled the short journey through the City and onto the A13 link road that leads to Tilbury Docks Essex, and his first contact. He was now well out of the City and passing Fords car manufacturers of Dagenham on his right side and heading onto Hornchurch, which would lead him from London to Essex, a journey he had done many times before. He thought of Angela the passionate fuck the night before, and how before they had sex she had asked him to stop the work he was doing and how he managed to persuade her that a few more jobs would mean enough money to run away to their dream home. He laughed to himself how she threw her dinner plate at him and how he had to duck out of the way as it flew past him smashing against the wall behind him, he loved Angela and she loved Tony Clay.

He drove past Hornchurch, Essex and knew he would be in Tilbury Docks in about twenty minutes, he would drive to the pub in Tilbury Town and meet his contact Danny McEwan and then the first deal would be completed.

He entered the public house at around midday as agreed and as expected the locals viewed him with curiosity as a stranger in town. He ordered a small Bells whiskey and sat at the bar near the door. Eyes continue to survey him until Danny McEwan entered the bar a few minutes later and the eyes dropped back into their daily newspapers. Danny ordered a pint of Guinness and sat beside Tony Clay.

'Fucking rain, fucks my hair up, I should get a fucking hat,' he said.

'Or fuck off to the Caribbean' Tony replied.

'Fuck that they have tornados, my wig will end up in outer space.'

'Well there is that' Tony replied.

'Everything is in place as normal', said Danny, 'you can leave your car with me in Purfleet, all locked up and safe and you can return when you're ready.'

'I need to be in Hornchurch at two o'clock' Tony replied, 'so the quicker we get this done the better. I take it it's the same deal, I'm only the middle man, I'm giving you the cash agreed with Sean and Taylor and you give me the van, what happens after delivery is between you, Sean, and Taylor.'

'Agreed' replied Danny.

They left the pub together, Tony followed Danny in his BMW through Tilbury Town, through Grays and onto Purfleet, Essex. The contact was waiting as agreed, hands were shook and money exchanged and counted and the BMW stored in the garage owned by Danny McEwan. Tony looked over the van for any faulty lights, bald tyres and checked the tax disc was in date and then changed into overalls to make himself look more like a van driver. When he was satisfied he shook hands again with Danny and drove the van out of Purfleet and back onto the A13 towards Hornchurch.

The house for his second contact was a large house in the posh side of Hornchurch with large metal gates and a long drive. Tony pulled up to the gates and pressed the intercom, the intercom buzzed, Tony said his name, and the gates started to open, he drove up the long drive until he reached some large steps that led up to the main door. He surveyed his surroundings and noticed three Doberman dogs staring at him from about thirty feet away, they did not take their eyes off him while they sniffed the air, as if sniffing for fresh meat, he decided to stay in the van and wait a while until his contact appeared. He waited for about five minutes until a fat bald man came into view from the side of the house, Tony watched as the fat man whistled loudly and the three dogs ran over to his side of the house and retreated into a large shed. The fat bald man then shut the gate behind them. Tony got out of the van.

'Wise move,' said the fat man, 'you'd be surprised how many idiots get out of the van.'

'I'm here from Johnny Saunders' Tony replied, 'are you Ray Flynn?'

'Yeah, I'm Ray Flynn, and I know why you're here, why you in a shit van?'

'It's another job, Armani suits from Italy.'

'Are they for Saunders?'

'No, for someone else, the package I'm here to pick up, is it ready' asked Tony Clay.

Ray Flynn stared at him with disdain and replied, 'Follow me.'

Tony followed him into the house where he entered a large hallway with large mirrors, and vases filled with expensive flowers and the biggest fuck off chandelier Tony had ever seen. He could see right through the house, through the large kitchen dining room area and into the garden where he could see an attractive older lady working in the garden. When he looked up, Ray Flynn was staring at him while he was pouring what Tony thought, looked like a whiskey into a glass.

'Drink?' he said.

'No thanks' Tony replied.

Flynn pointed to the large table in an additional room seen through large glass doors and Tony could see what looked like an expensive silver case with a combination lock on top.

'That's it over there, said Flynn, 'do you know what's in it?'

'No not interested' Tony replied.

'Do you like my wife Tony Clay?'

'No I just noticed someone in the garden.'

Flynn sipped his whiskey, stared at Tony as if he was checking him out, testing him for any give away or signs of nervousness, Tony remained cool and made a movement with his arm to check his watch for the time, Flynn spoke again.

'When you pick that case up Tony Clay and you leave my house, you've never fucking been here, never fucking seen me and we never fucking met, and you've never seen my wife, you got me, City fucking van boy.'

'Got ya,' Tony replied.

'Cos if you do Tony fucking Clay I will go to your two up two fucking down house in Clapham, kidnap your fucking wife Angela, bring her back here and while she's still alive feed her to my fucking dogs, you got that.'

Tony was silent for a few seconds as he needed to take in what he just heard and then replied.

'Yea I got that; I'll just grab the case then, and be out of your way.'

Tony grabbed the case, he noticed the weight, it wasn't heavy and it wasn't light, but his curiosity was taken over by wanting to get out of Ray Flynn's house. After another exchange that he felt he couldn't really say no to without getting his head kicked in, Tony Clay drove slowly out of the drive. He could see in his rear view mirror Ray Flynn on the footsteps of his six up six down big fuck off house checking out and admiring his new free Armani suit, courtesy of Tony Clay enterprises and Sean and Taylor. He will explain that one to them later, he thought.

Tony took himself out of Essex and into Dagenham on through to the City and down across Tower Bridge through Clapham, and then onto his lock up secure garage in Balham. While driving back from his day's work he reflected on Ray Flynn and how the fat fucker knew about Angela and where they lived, it shook him from head to toe. The psychological effect it had on him and how it angered him from within played on his mind.

He arrived back at his lock up at five thirty, pulled in and unlocked the secure doors; he drove the van inside his lock up and surveyed the familiar surroundings. Steel cages were to the far wall with steel shelving to the left and right hand side of the warehouse, it was around two hundred square meters in size. He opened the rear doors of the van and looked at the suitcase, clumsily trying the lock, no, joy, he felt the weight, again it didn't give anything away, not heavy enough for guns but light enough for paperwork or money he thought. He heard a noise outside nearby which brought him to his senses and wondered if he had been followed, he opened the warehouse doors and peered outside, nothing, it was dark, he could not see anything until he saw a dog rummaging around the dustbins. He reclosed the doors bolted them from inside and went back to the suitcase with his senses now more alert.

Tony Clay sat for a while and looked at the crates in the back of the van, he came to a decision; he has two deliveries tomorrow one for Johnny Saunders and one for Sean and Taylor. He grabbed a crow bar from the rack on the wall and jumped into the back of the van, he prized open one of the crates for Sean and Taylor containing the Armani suits and took about ten suits out from the top of the crate, he placed the suitcase into the crate and then put the ten suits back inside the crate on top of the suitcase. He then re-nailed the crate and marked the crate on the side with a red crayon, jumped out of the van and locked up the rear doors. Tony left the storage unit, locked it securely and walked for about ten minutes before arriving at Balham underground Station, on arrival he decided to take a taxi instead of the underground; he hailed a taxi down with all good intentions to go home to his wife Angela.

Chapter 6

Sean Farrow woke with a sweat, he wondered if he was dreaming, he turned and looked at the clock next to his bed and saw that it was four o'clock in the morning. The house phone was ringing, and he wondered who it could be, he came to his senses rolled over and lifted the receiver.

'Hello,' he said into the receiver.

'Is that Sean?'

'Yes, who is this?'

'It's Angela Clay, it's Tony Sean, he's not home and I know he was meeting you today, he's normally home by now and he would ring me if he was going to be late, I'm worried.'

Sean was silent for a while.

Angela became concerned about the silence, 'Sean', she said with anticipation in her voice.

'Yes Angela, I was meeting him today but not until midday, it's four o'clock in the morning.'

I know, I'm sorry but I'm worried about him, it's not like him, and you know I can't call the police.'

Again Sean was silent.

'Tony has not contacted me', he said, 'that's how we work, we make arrangements and stick to that until we meet' I will continue with our arrangement today and meet him at midday and let him know you called, I'm sure he will be home shortly.'

'I'm worried Sean it's just not like him.'

'Angela get some sleep, there's nothing I can do now apart from drive around London looking for him, he could be anywhere, I'm sure he will be home soon, get some sleep.'

'I can't sleep until he's home.'

'Have you tried calling the hospitals in case he had an accident?'

'I've rang the general hospitals they said no one by the name of Tony Clay has been admitted.'

'Ok Angela, I understand the situation but there isn't anything I can, and not at four o'clock in the morning.'

Angela started to cry; Sean could hear her at the end of the line.

'Angela leave it till the morning, if there's still no news I will call a friend who may be able to make enquiries, call me at eight o'clock.'

'Ok I will call you at eight, I'm sorry for calling you so early Sean.'

Sean put the phone down and looked across at Tina she didn't stir but said

'Problems.'

'It's Ok babe get some sleep', he said.

Sean laid there for a while and tried to sleep but he knew he couldn't, he started to worry about Tony's absence himself,

Angela was right, it was not like Tony to just vanish, it's not like him, he thought. He thought about the meeting with Taylor and Tony at midday and the call he may need to make to his police friend. He closed his eyes again and tried to sleep but now knew it was going to be an impossible task. Sean Farrow got out of bed, he put the kettle on to make himself a cup of tea, Tina was still lying there getting all fidgety because as Sean knew, he was disturbing her beauty sleep. He made his tea and sat down on the chair by the phone in his front room, he looked at the phone sipped his tea and wondered if it was wise to make a call now, or leave it until the morning. He made his mind up and pulled his address book out of the top draw of the side cabinet.

Sergeant Pete Murray was on his night shift. His tasks for the evening were the usual involvement on the front desk. He knew he would be filling in forms and accepting the drunks, petty thieves and all sorts of shit bags exposed to the station on a Tuesday evening. But he also knew he was retiring in two weeks and that kept him occupied on just doing his job and completing his time. Pete Murray was busy taking items from a drunks pocket and itemizing them onto a form when the desk phone rang, he ignored it and continued with his task until the drunk tipped his head to the right and vomited on the floor and dribbled the rest down the front of his shirt. This distracted Sergeant Pete Murray who then changed his actions and instead went for the phone that was still ringing on the station desk.

'Streatham Police Station' he said.

'Sergeant Pete Murray Please.'

'Speaking'

'Hi Pete, it's Sean Farrow.'

Although surprised to hear his name and voice, Pete Murray remained calm and professional due to his surroundings. In all the years Sergeant Pete Murray has known Sean Farrow he has never asked for any underhand favours or called at this kind of hour, he looked across at the station clock on the wall, it was 05:25.

'What can I do for you sir?' he replied.

Sean Farrow relayed his worries about Tony Clay and asked for no favours but for Sergeant Pete Murray to make basic enquires and keep a watching brief should anything come up.

Sergeant Pete Murray made small simple notes while listening and replied.

'Leave it with me Sir, I will call should I find anything out, I have your details.'

Sean thanked him and ended the call, Sergeant Pete Murray returned to the drunk who was still being held up by the arresting officer who was making every effort to avoid the vomit.

Sergeant Pete Murray finished his shift at eight o'clock in the morning but before he left the station he made a couple of phone calls that led to no information on the disappearance of Tony Clay. He left the details with the new Duty Officer who he trusted and told him to call him if he found anything out and to treat it as a non-detail investigation, which meant nothing to be written down.

Sergeant Pete Murray has been a police officer all his life, he was loyal, honest and always based his role as a local bobby who knew the locals well. But Pete Murray was aware that the old traditional policing methods were starting to collapse around him as new human rights laws were starting to make his, and his colleagues jobs harder. This was something that he cared about and one that always made him think about people he loved and cared about. He could see the scum, as he liked to call them becoming stronger and stronger and starting to get away with more and more.

He had a loving wife Fiona who he has missed, ever since her death in her late forties, and he has been a lonely man ever since. Pete Murray and his wife lived in the same estate as Sean and Taylor and he remembered how they attended her funeral as young boys. He also remembered that as young boys they used to do the shopping for his elderly mother; they were tearaways, but nice tearaways he thought to himself on his drive home from the station. He had on two occasions had to step in as the pair were arrested as juveniles for shop lifting and being in a stolen car driven by a wanted person, they got off both offences due to Pete Murray intervening and suggesting it was best if he had a stern word with them instead, which he did. Tragically Pete Murray also remembers the sadness of being called to the road traffic accident and was also the first on the scene where Sean Farrow lost his mother, father and unborn baby sister. It was this occasion that also increased the bonding between the pair of them as well as the comfort that Pete gave Sean after that tragic event.

Sergeant Pete Murray turned the key in his two bedroom flat just off Leigham Court Road Streatham, his entrance always sullen and always quiet and lonely, because it felt that way without the presence of his late wife. He entered the living room and poured himself a whiskey, a tradition that he often kept after a night shift to help him sleep. He viewed the pictures on his old side cabinet, his wife Fiona and his mother Jean Murray, he sat sipping his whiskey and thought of his past life, his relationship with Sean and Taylor, his elderly mother Jean living on an estate in South London, lonely and afraid. He recalled why and how he protected Sean and Taylor for their kindness towards his mother in his absence, and keeping a watchful eye upon her, all based on their upbringing to respect others. He smiled and reminded himself to chase up Sean's request when he wakes up some time in the afternoon. He gulped his whiskey down and went into the bathroom to brush his teeth, he pulled down his covers to his bed, made sure the curtains were closed to shut out the light, got into bed and was asleep in minutes.

Pete Murray woke with a start and then felt anger as he realised he forgot to pull the plug out of the phone socket. He looked across at the clock 09:30, bollocks, barely been asleep for fifteen minutes, who the fuck can that be, he thought. He reached across for the phone and picked up the receiver.

'Hello.'

'Pete, it's Jimmy, I thought I would give you a call before you slept, as it seemed important earlier.'

'Too late, already been asleep you wanker,' he heard Jimmy laugh on the other end of the phone.

'Ok, thought you would want to know about what you left me with this morning, it seemed important.'

'What was?' replied Pete.

'Tony Clay, you asked about Tony Clay.'

'Oh yeah, What about him.'

'About ten minutes ago, a report came in about a car chase with a suspected stolen car and while the chase was going on, a body was dumped out the back doors, the police car chasing couldn't swerve in time and went right over the body causing even more damage to the body. It looks like it may have been gang related, as the body appeared to have been tortured, although forensics will need to be involved to ascertain cause of death. Anyway Pete, to cut a long story short, the man was identified as Tony Clay, the man you asked about earlier.'

'Fuck me Jimmy you sure?'

'Yea I'm sure, anyway, why the interest Pete?'

'Missing person Jimmy that's all, now we know why he was missing don't we, see you on shift handover tonight, and Jimmy, see if you can get a bit more detail for me.'

'Ok, oh and Pete.'

'Yeah.'

'Turn your fucking phone off' Pete Murray heard laughter on the end of the phone and ended the call by putting the receiver back down onto the phone.

He sat on the edge of his bed and pulled open the draw to his bedside cabinet, pulled his address book out and found the phone number for Sean Farrow. He dialled the number but it was engaged, he waited for about five minutes and called again, this time it rang. Pete informed Sean all the details he was made aware of from his colleague Jimmy at the Station and Sean listened intensely without butting in.

'Thanks Pete', said Sean, 'I've just been on the phone to his wife Angela, she will be devastated, I will need to call her back.'

'I would assume police liaison officers would be on their way round soon Sean, well that's if they know anything about her existence.'

There was silence on the end of the phone and Pete was aware that Sean was thinking and the information was sinking in.

'What's this all about Sean?' said Pete breaking the silence.

'I don't know Pete, I just got the call from Angela early this morning saying she was concerned, he was a good man Pete, he kept himself to himself, it would be useful to know, why and who killed him.'

'I will try and get some more details about it and let you know.'

'Thanks Pete,' replied Sean.

Pete Murray put the phone down, he sat there with his thoughts, he had been a policeman for a long time and this was his last shift before his his retirement. He had always gone by his instincts, and his instincts have always been right, and they are now telling him, this is not going to end smoothly, there's something big about to happen. He lay back on his bed; he tried to sleep for a while, but he was struggling, he knew he had to sleep because he would be back behind the desk again tonight for the last time, welcoming scum back to the Hotel cop shop.

Chapter 7

Sean closed the door to Tina's flat behind him and zipped his coat up. The wind was bitter this morning he thought and started the walk along the cold damp pavement towards home. His thoughts were wild in his head, why would someone kill Tony Clay. It could be for the stuff he was carrying, our stuff, or something else, it didn't make sense unless he was followed. Tony was a quiet man but he had his scruples about him, Sean's thoughts continued as he turned off at Battersea Park road and down the Hill towards Clapham. His eyes started to water in the wind so he wiped continuously as he walked cursing the British weather again. Sean pulled the keys from his pocket and walked into his apartment wondering if Taylor was up yet. He felt the cold in the flat too, the radiators hadn't kicked in yet he thought as he heard Taylor in the kitchen. He walked into the kitchen to find a tall-legged dark haired girl standing over the kettle with just her knickers on.

'Morning', she said, 'you must be Sean.'

'Morning, and you are?' he replied.

'Karen, I'm Karen, would you like a cup of tea?'

' I'd love one thanks, where's Taylor?'

'He's in the bedroom.'

'Thanks, oh and Karen', he said

'Yes Sean.'

'Nice tits.'

'Thank you Sean.'

Taylor was lying in bed head to one side unshaven and looking like he was busy nursing a hangover. Sean looked down at him.

'Taylor.'

'What.'

'We need to talk.'

Taylor managed to turn his head and look up towards Sean, he looked as if it was hard work to even move, he craned his neck to listen as for some reason Sean sounded serious.

'What about.'

'Our meeting today with Tony, it's off.'

'Off, why's it off?'

'It's Tony, he's dead, he's been killed, and Pete has given me all the details'

Taylor's head slowly tilted straight and looked up at Sean; and there was silence for a brief moment.

'When did this happen?' said Taylor.

'It must have been last night, Angela called me at four in the morning worried about Tony so I contacted Pete, he was on shift and he gave me the details this morning.'

Taylor continued to try and listen, he took in what he could, as Sean re-laid further everything that Pete had told him, he took it all in until eventually he knew all that Sean knew.

'We must go and see Angela', Taylor said 'she will be devastated and we need to find out if he had our gear as well as any information in his wallet about us.'

'Tony was better than that Taylor, he wouldn't have anything incriminating on him to do with us, there will be old bill all over the place and then they will find his warehouse. We need to get to the warehouse before they do, we can pick up our gear, still do the sale and we may be able to bung Angela some money to see her through for a bit.'

Karen the dark haired tall-legged woman walked into the bedroom holding two cups of tea, with her tits still out, Sean and Taylor both looked at her as she entered.

'Clare meet Sean, Sean meet Clare' said Taylor.

'I thought you said your name was Karen?' said Sean.

'It is, your mate called me all sorts of names all night, he's got a shit memory'

Taylor was silent, Sean smiled and started sipping on his tea, got any biscuit's Karen?' he said.

'How do I know where he keeps his fucking biscuit's?' she replied.

'Taylor was looking bemused, 'Karen,' he said, 'Sean and me here, well, we have to go out, so if you wouldn't mind getting dressed and buggering off, oh unless you would like a threesome here with my friend? Sean would you like a threesome?'

Before Sean could speak, Karen replied, 'well the threesome does sound very nice but my hubby will be wondering where I am, maybe next time.'

With that she started to pick her clothes off the floor, got dressed and headed for the door.

'Nice, very nice', Sean said.

'Yea met her last night, in the pub, she had a row with her husband, he fucked off home, I moved in.'

'Nice, said Sean, 'I'll call Angela, and let her know we are coming over, why don't you wash Karen off you and get dressed gigolo.'

It was too windy for the bike so they decided to use the car; Sean drove as they discussed certain options and how they would deal with Angela. It was still early, yet the streets were starting to fill with cars and the big red London buses were full with the daily commuters, each of them looking very glum on their way to work or whatever their journey entailed. When they got there Angela opened the door with her eyes clearly showing signs of tears. Sean and Taylor walked in to the house while expressing their sadness and walked into the front room. Inside there was a man and women clearly looking like they were there to support Angela.

'This is my mum & dad, Angela said, 'mum, dad, this is Sean Farrow and Taylor Docherty, they are close friends of Tony's.'

The introductions were short and sweet. Sean and Taylor could see they were clearly not welcome or liked by this couple. They knew Tony's work was a little different from the normal nine to five and Sean and Taylor thought that they were being tarred with the same brush, which wasn't exactly wrong. Angela's mum and dad made their excuses and left, promising Angela to return later.

'I will make some tea,' Angela said, 'come into the kitchen. The police have not been here yet, but I'm sure it wont be long before they know about me, then they will be asking all sorts of questions.'

'Tony was ok, they wont find anything, they don't know about his warehouse. Have you any idea who may have done it?' Taylor said.

'No, I haven't got a clue, all I know is he got up yesterday morning as normal, he had a couple of jobs to do and then he would be home. He would always come straight home, that's why I called you Sean, it wasn't like Tony to go missing.'

'We know' said Sean, 'Angela we need to know where Tony's warehouse is and we need the keys, if we can go there before the police we can sell what's in there and give you the cash. If the police get there first they will confiscate everything, we will just keep the suits that Tony was picking up for us.'

'Tony was picking up stuff for you?'

'Yes' Taylor said, 'one of the jobs he was doing yesterday was for us.'

There was silence, Sean and Taylor could see that Angela was thinking before she spoke, 'Tony spoke highly of you two, he trusted you both, and he always said if he was ever in trouble that you two would help him, follow me.'

Sean and Taylor followed Angela into the lounge where ornaments stood on the fireplace, the room was like a financial accountants and nothing like a petty criminals hide out. It covered Tony's alibi completely, he was good at his work and they could see that anyone would be fooled into believing that Tony Clay was a good honest citizen.

'Can you move that cabinet please?' said Angela.

The large cabinet stood in the alcove, Sean and Taylor started to move the heavy object out as instructed by Angela, they could both clearly see that the cabinet had not been moved for some time by the dents in the carpet as well as the dust behind it. They could see a safe buried in the wall, so they moved the cabinet further out so Angela could get to the safe.

'Everything you need to know and need is in this safe, the location of the warehouse and a spare set of keys but I don't know the combination.'

'What you don't know the combination?' said Taylor.

'No, Tony insisted it that way, he said if anything happened to him, you two would sort it out.'

'Fucking hell Angela how we meant to get in there?' Taylor said.

'Angela can I borrow your phone?' said Sean.

'Yes it's over there on the sideboard.'

Sean walked over to the phone with Taylor and Angela looking on. Sean picked the receiver up and dialled a number.

'Hello is that Andy.'

'No I'm his son, wait there and I will get him.'

Angela and Taylor looked on as Sean held the phone to his ear waiting for a response.

'Hello.'

'Is that Andy?'

'Yeah, it's Andy who's this?'

'It's Sean Farrow.'

'Who, I've never heard of you.'

'Sean Farrow.'

'Who the fuck is Sean Farrow and how did you get my number?'

'I'm a friend of Pete Murray, I've got a job for you that needs doing now'

'Now?'

'Yes now.'

'What right now?'

'Yes, right now', replied Sean, 'what's this the fucking Spanish inquisition or what', I've got a job for you and you've been recommended, it ain't that fucking hard, is it mate!'

Taylor and Angela continued to look on, baffled by the conversation that was being played out in front of them.

'Alright keep your hair on', eventually came the reply, 'what's in it for me?'

'I need something open, we can discuss that when you get here', replied Sean

'Where's here?'

"Clapham.'

'Fifty quid when I walk in the door, then we will discuss fees when I know what the fuck it is you want me to open.'

Sean agreed with the cost and then gave Andy the address details on the promise that he could be there within the hour and then he put down the receiver.

'Who the fuck is Andy', Taylor said.

'Handy Andy, you know, the safe cracker, well known as Handy Andy'

'Never fucking heard of him,' replied Taylor.

'Oh ok, you must have missed that bit of gossip with Pete, either that or you weren't fucking listening again.'

'Bollocks' Taylor replied.

'Excuse me boys, here's your tea I promised' Angela said.

They waited the hour and then a second hour before they heard the engine of what sounded like a battered old van outside. The doorbell rang and Angela opened the door.

'I'm here to see Sean Farrow, I'm Andy.'

'Yea I've heard, come this way.'

'You said an hour', Taylor said.

'Fifty quid now or I fuck off', replied Andy.

'Charming' said Taylor, 'I take it you've been to charm school Andy.'

There was no response from Handy Andy, Taylor passed the fifty quid over to him and he stuffed it into his overall's pocket. 'Right where is this thing you need open then', he said.

'It's in here' said Sean.

They all walked into the lounge and Sean showed Handy Andy the safe that they needed open.

'Piece of piss', he said, 'I only want fifty quid for this little one.'

With that Handy Andy went back outside to get his tools, leaving the others staring into space awaiting his return.

'Right you can all leave the room while I work, I will let you know when it's open.'

'Bollocks', said Sean, we are staying right here with you until you open it, I don't know you from Adam, you might open it, take what you want, then call us in'

'Which one of you is Sean Farrow?'

'Me' said Sean.

'You got my number from Pete Murray that should be enough of a reference.'

Sean looked at Taylor.

'I'm not fucking going anywhere,' said Taylor.

'Right the lady can stay in the room', said Handy Andy, 'you too scallywags can fuck off in the kitchen and keep an eye out for the old bill, I will call you when it's open.'

'Fuck me I forgot about the old bill, come on Taylor I'm sure Angela can keep an eye on him.'

'Keep an eye on him Angela', Taylor said, while pointing at his own eyes and walking out the room.

Sean and Taylor drank the tea, while keeping an eye out on the street for the police. They could hear the drilling and banging and the occasional swear word coming from the next room. Handy Andy eventually called them into the room after about forty-five minutes. They entered the room and could clearly see that the safe was wide open; they could see an envelope in the safe and a small bundle of notes bounded by an elastic band. Sean put his hand in, handed Angela the bundle of notes and retrieved the envelope.

'Ok I'm done fifty quid and I can be on my way' said Handy Andy.

'Can we pay you later, we barely scrapped the fifty quid together earlier' Sean said.

'What's all that in her hand then?'

'Ok, Angela give him fifty quid, we can sort it all out later' Sean said.

Angela handed Handy Andy the money and thanked him for his work, he apologised to her for swearing so much and started to pick up his tools.

'Pleasure doing business with you boys, I'll be on me way' Handy Andy left the house, threw his tools into the van, started the engine and pulled away from the house.

'Nice man', said Taylor, 'we must use him again.'

The envelope was still in Sean's hand, Angela was counting the money, when Sean ripped open the envelope. Inside was a piece of paper showing the address of Tony's warehouse and another smaller envelope holding a set of keys and instructions. There was a smaller envelope that was sealed with Angela's name on it and Sean passed this to her.

'Nine hundred and fifty quid boys', she said, 'it looks like he kept a grand in the safe for a rainy day', it can help pay for his funeral', she looked at the envelope that Sean had handed her and Sean and Taylor pushed the cabinet back into the alcove.

'We will leave now Angela, we will be in touch when we find out what's in Tony's lock up' said Sean, 'if you need anything give us a call.'

Taylor drove; Sean had the details of the warehouse and guided Taylor towards Balham. They spoke about Tony Clay, a good man, good standing and with a good woman by his side, and why would anyone want to hurt him. They both came to the same conclusion, greed, easy target, it was either luck that they picked him or it was planned. If it was planned that's a harder thing to follow. They both agreed, get to the warehouse take stock of everything, load up the van, sell off anything that's left and get the money over to Angela. They would then sell the suits onto Eddy in Brixton Market. It seemed easy, they didn't want to get involved with anything other than ensuring everything is locked down regarding Tony Clay's warehouse. It had to be just a lucky pick that he was taken out, but why was he taken in a car, tortured as if they were after some information, it didn't make sense.

They continued to drive with Sean navigating to the last turning, a lane led down to a series of warehouses under the arches of a railway line that went from Victoria to Brighton on the south coast. The car managed to avoid some of the potholes in the unmade road but soon the car was bumping along tossing Sean and Taylor around while they searched for warehouse 228. A train went across the viaduct just as Sean spotted warehouse 228 about fifty yards to the right. Taylor pulled the car alongside the large metal doors and they both got out surveying the area with Sean holding the keys in his hand. They could see to the left and right of where they were, they were being watched by others who owned similar dwellings. In particular a large man watching another man carrying out welding work underneath a car that was also occasionally looking up with interest.

'We can either open up now, have a butchers or come back later', Taylor said.

Sean took another look to his left and right, the men he could see were clearly eye balling them and it made him feel nervous, but he knew he needed to act quick before any police started to sniff around. 'We're here now' he said, 'we might as well take a quick look, hopefully they're just curious.'

'Fat and curious, he's a big bastard, wouldn't want to piss him off, he might weld my teeth together', replied Taylor.

Sean walked towards the doors and put the first key in the mortise lock, it opened, he then put the second key into the large padlock, at first it didn't budge but after a few more tries the padlock snapped open.

'Bingo', he said.

They entered the warehouse and there were cages to the left and to the right as well as the far wall. There was also a van sitting right in the middle of the warehouse with it's rear doors locked.

'Don't suppose you have a key for the van doors then Sean.'

'I don't believe I do mate', replied Sean.

'Shall we fuck off and call Handy Andy, been ages since we've seen him', Taylor said.

Sean looked at him with a flippant look, and took another suspicious look outside at the men who were still clearly interested in their presence, 'Lets have a quick look around anyway.'

'I can already see there's fuck all here,' said Taylor, 'it's probably all been moved on and our gear is in the van, hopefully,

I'm going to have a look for a crow bar or something, it's only a fucking padlock.'

They both started to search around the warehouse looking for anything that could help them break open the back door of the van; Sean soon found a crowbar on the hook when all of a sudden from nowhere the big fat guy they spotted earlier confronted him at the warehouse doors.

'Who the fuck are you and what the fuck are you doing here?' he said with a menacing cockney accent.

Sean and Taylor stopped in their tracks; the look on there faces obviously showing they were now contemplating what was going to happen next.

Taylor spoke first, to the annoyance of Sean, 'I might ask you the same question, and who the fuck are you and what the fuck are you doing here.'

A second man appeared and then a third, both holding car mechanics tools, and both Sean and Taylor noticed could quite easily take the head off any man.

'I'm Sean Farrow, we're friends of the man that owned this warehouse.'

'You're Sean Farrow, who's this?'

'He's Taylor Docherty.'

'You got a driving licence Sean Farrow.'

Sean pulled out his driving license and handed it to the man, the man checked it and handed it back. The man looked behind him and nodded to the two men, they nodded back and walked away, to the relief of Sean and Taylor.

'You're friends of Tony Clay are you?'

'We are, and you are?'

'I'm a friend of Tony Clay, what are you doing here?'

'Tony's been murdered, we are here to sort this mess out for his missus'

'Tony's been murdered by who?'

'We don't know.'

'Fuck, poor Angela, so what are you doing now?'

'We need to get into his van so we can sell what's in it and get the money to Angela before the old bill come round here.'

'Tony told me about you two, and that if anything happened to him you would be around to sort things out, he was a good lad, I can help, the keys to the van will be in the air brick over there, just below the picture of Marylyn Monroe', he pointed towards the end of the warehouse, 'hopefully the padlock key will be there too.'

Taylor walked over to the airbrick, pulled out the brick and found the keys for the van.

'There here' said Taylor, 'what's your name mate?'

'Chester.'

'Do you know Handy Andy Chester?'

'Yea everyone knows Handy Andy, why?'

'Nothing', said Taylor, 'right we will take this van Chester, can you sort out the warehouse for us.'

'Yeah, leave it to me, I will empty it out and lock it back up ready for any police visit, say hi to Angela for me and tell her I'm sorry for what has happened, he was a good man.'

Chester walked off leaving Sean and Taylor in the warehouse, Sean got into the car they came in and Taylor got into the van.

'We'll meet up at the lock up and leave the van there overnight, drive fucking carefully,' said Sean.

'Yeah Ok, hey Sean?' shouted Taylor.

'What.'

'Why am I the only fucker who don't know Handy Andy?'

'Fucked if I know' said Sean.

Chapter 8

Johnny Saunders sat in his large leather chair, he was feeling like king of the world, he was sucking on his Havana cigar, Charlie Allan was with him, the room smelt of anger, the volcano was about to pop, and someone had to pay. It was not a good day for someone, Charlie thought to himself.

'Something's not right', Johnny Saunders said. 'I've got a suitcase full of money and I don't know where it is because some fuckers popped the courier.'

Charlie Allan didn't answer, he knew it was not best to at this point due to the fact that his boss was in a fucked off rage, say nothing, he thought, not yet, let him rant and rave for a bit and then come up with something that will calm the situation. He watched as his boss Johnny Saunders sucked on his fat cigar again.

'All that fucking Clay had to do was go to Essex pick up my loot and get back into London and give it to me, What the fuck happened in between, and where's my fucking money?'

Charlie picked his moment well; he waited for another suck on the big fat cigar, and it came.

'I'll ask around boss, everyone is shit scared of you, someone's bound to blag, you own London, no fucker can take that away from you.'

'Fuck me Charlie why don't you stick your tongue down the back of my trousers while you're at it, what you after a fucking raise?'

Charlie said nothing, his plan didn't work, and he just stood there waiting for the next instruction, and it didn't take long to come.

'I want a visit to Tony Clay's house, I want you to find out who the fuck killed him but more than that, he would have had a warehouse of some sort, find it. I want that bent copper John Wall to find out some things for me, we pay him enough, scare the fuck out of PC Plod John Fucking Wall Charlie. I want you to tell him we want info or he ain't getting paid, I want to know the ins and outs of the investigation, suspects etc., we can get information out of people better then they can. Also who else was Clay doing work for, what was it? When was it? Take the boys with you, I want answers by tomorrow.'

Charlie Allan said nothing more, but left the room, he knew his place and headed towards his colleagues who were waiting in the downstairs lobby. Four of them got into the car and headed off to Tony Clays house first, then to lean on the bent copper John Wall. The scene was set out with the same four characters; they were in a car paid to do a job that was basically to scare the shit out of people. They would collect money owed for protection, drugs and gambling, prostitution and sometimes pay out money to the people like John Wall the bent copper.

Charlie Allan was the commander, the most loyal to Johnny Saunders, and he understood him better than anyone. He knew his bosses dark secrets but he also knew his place in the structure after Johnny gave him a beating in a bar one day, all because he said the wrong thing. Stan Smith was a Glaswegian and the driver, he was calm until you entered into his personal space, and was handy with a knife. Ray Flynn was East London through and through and was originally part of West Hams notorious inter city firm, but soon realised he could make more money supporting Johnny instead, he now lives in a big house in Essex. Winston Scott a huge black man, a family man who resides in Brixton, never says a lot, he only had to be there, stare a bit and people would shit themselves. The cigarettes were lit, and the car filled with smoke and chatter, the weather was too shit to open the windows and let the smoke out, so they just sat in the smoke filled atmosphere discussing football, fucking and fighting, and they revelled in it. There was something about getting a kick out of frightening people from them all, you had to be a sick fuck to enjoy that and the car was full of sick fucks, who didn't give a shit about honest people.

Charlie Allan turned his attention to the job when they pulled up on Angela Clay's road. Stan Smith eventually opened the window to get a better view, the cold air came in and the smoke rushed out like a chimney from a busy factory.

'Ok normal routine' said Charlie, 'Stan remains in the car, the three of us will go up and ask the young lady some nice questions, Winston can do his normal staring shit and it should be happy days, then we can track down where the copper is sort him out, early doors and be in the boozer by five.'

Angela Clay was in her kitchen, she had just read the letter Tony had left her in the safe. It took her a while to open it, but kept staring at it, as she didn't want to accept he was gone. It had details of the warehouse and bank account details, which looked like an account in the Isle of Man. She placed the envelope in a side draw and decided to clean, she found it easier to keep busy, and the house had never been so clean, she thought. Tony's stuff was now removed with help from her family and friends, but there were still the photos on the sideboard to remind her of him. She was sad, lonely and depressed but knew Tony would never want her to be unhappy, so she cleaned and kept herself busy. She was rarely at home nowadays she thought to herself, but preferred the company of friends and family to make the day and nights easier.

Angela never saw or heard them coming and was surprised by the doorbell ringing and it made her jump, she went to answer the front door. Fear immediately entered her body when she saw the three men that she didn't recognize standing on her doorstep, she instantly thought that this was not going to be a good day. Charlie Allan spoke first.

'Can we come in Angela Clay? We want to ask you a few questions, sorry let me rephrase that, we are coming in to ask you a few questions' the three of them moved into the hallway and closed the door behind them.

'Who are you' Angela said, 'what do you want?'

'As I said we want to ask you a few questions about Tony Clay, your dead husband.'

Dead was not a nice word, Angela thought, deceased would have been a better choice of words, these are not nice people, her fear escalated and she felt the need to run, but the black mans stare told her she should not try it.

Charlie Allan continued, 'sit down Angela, this may take some time but that's dependent on your cooperation, have you got any visitors today?'

'No, I mean, yes, yes, the police are coming round soon to ask me some questions about Tony's death.'

Angela never saw it coming but the pain was instant as her body fell to the left and she came off the sofa and landed on the floor. She was dazed and her face felt like it was on fire from the smack that Charlie landed on her, and she now knew this was not a nice visit.

'You just lied to me' Charlie said, 'Your not going to lie to me again are you Angela?'

'No, No, I'm not going to lie to you again, I promise.'

Charlie turned to his colleagues who were standing there with evil smirks on their faces.

'Are you making a cup of tea or what Ray?' He then turned to Angela again,

'You got any biscuit's, Angie baby?'

'Kitchen cupboard', she replied, wiping the tears from her face.

Ray took the order and left the room looking for the kitchen, they could hear him opening and closing cupboards.

'Fucking bonus, top bird boss, she's got fucking ginger nuts', they heard coming form the kitchen.

The room was quiet and Charlie and Winston smiled a bit from Ray's last remark.

'We do love a ginger nut don't we Winston' said Charlie.

'Yes boss' replied Winston.

Angela was staring between the pair of them in total confusion, and in her head she was confused by the whole situation, fucking nuts she thought again in her head.

' So Angela, where's Tony's warehouse?' continued Charlie.

'I don't know, he never told me anything about his other work, just his normal work.'

Again she never saw it coming, again the force of the slap sent her off the sofa and on to the floor, and she started crying.

' I thought you said you would never lie to me again' said Charlie.

'I'm not lying, I promise, he would never discuss it with me.'

'Right Angela, there are three questions I need answers to and I need them answered today, you are going to give me that information, with pain or without pain.'

'Question one, where is Tony's warehouse, question two, who else was Tony doing work for and question three, who killed him and why?'

Ray returned with the tea and the pack of ginger nuts he found in the cupboard, he handed the cups to Winston and Charlie, they all sat down, and started to dunk their biscuit's into their tea, all staring at Angela.

'Right Angie Babe', Charlie continued, 'we are going to sit here and enjoy our well earned tea break, I suggest while we do that, you have a little think about your answers, because when I put my cup down if I don't like what I hear, it's party time for my friend Winston here.'

Angela looked towards Winston, his facial expression didn't change, he just dunked another fucking ginger nut biscuit and then demolished it in one go, she was now in a total state of shock, her face was burning and she knew she had to give them the answers they were after. The room was quiet; she just heard the slurping of tea and munching of the fucking biscuit's. She thought about the questions, fear rose inside her, even further when she knew she could only answer two but not the third. Maybe she could make the third one up to give her some time she thought, she was frantically searching her mind but could not come up with anything, Tony was so damned secretive. Taylor and Sean would have cleared the warehouse out by now, that was an easy one, but to give away Sean & Taylor to these fuck nuts would be suicide for them. She then heard the sound of the cup being placed on the coffee table. She looked up, the one that seemed to be in charge was staring at her, and the other two were still eating her fucking biscuit's.

'Shall we start with question one?' said Charlie.

'I will write it down on a piece of paper for you' she replied.

'Good girl, now Question two.'

'What was question two again?' she said.

Another slap from Charlie sent Angela off the sofa again, and the burning sensation on her face returned.

'Fucking hell will you stop doing that!' she shouted as she tried to get back off the floor.

'Question two, who else was your dead husband doing work for?'

'I told you he wouldn't tell me everything about his work, I never knew or met anyone he did that line of work with, that's why I don't know who the fuck you bastards are.'

She was off the sofa again, with a harder slap this time that made her ears ring with pain, she couldn't keep this up, she thought to herself, fuck I'm scared, and I'm in pain, she frantically thought again, Tony would not want this, he would want me to tell them what ever they wanted.

Charlie was looking down at Angela with a face that said he'd had enough and he wanted answers. Angela could see that her answers were frustrating him. Charlie looked across at Winston, 'Ok Winston, show the lady' he said.

Angela looked up at Winston who placed his cup down and stood up, he went for his flies, he pulled out his penis which flopped down nearly touching his knees, she had never seen anything like it, her cries increased in volume and another slap sent her to the floor again.

'Now Angie babe, Winston here is partial to a bit of anal sex, and that, what he's holding in his hand now is going north up your dirt box very shortly if you don't give us what we want, have you got it, is it fucking sinking in yet?'

Angela nodded 'I've got it, I've got it.'

'Question two' said Charlie again.

'He did some work for Sean Farrow and Taylor Docherty', she said, 'just clothes from Europe, you know top designs and stuff like that, but that's all I know'

Charlie turned to Ray and Winston, 'do you know those names?'

'No boss' said Ray.

'Yeah I'm sure I've heard of them', replied Winston, 'their from the South London scene, small time petty crooks, but I will need to ask around.'

Charlie returned his stare to Angela, 'Question three' he said.

'How the hell am I going to know that, Jesus, if I knew that I would be hunting them down myself to kill the bastards that took him away from me.'

No slap came, but this time she would have been ready for it, but it never came, instead the man who seemed to be the leader stared at her, the black man behind was still standing there with his cock out hanging there and the other fucking mental head was still eating her ginger nuts.

'I believe you' Charlie said.

Angela collapsed with relief and the crying erupted again, she lay their sobbing but could sense the three men starting to leave her home. The last thing she heard was 'thanks for the biscuit's, fucking awesome' as the one that appeared to be the leader closed the door behind him. After Angela had managed to pull herself together she called all the phone numbers that she had for Sean and Taylor, but there was no answer. She had no other way of contacting them. She would have to wait till later but she would need to make them aware very quickly that they are being looked for now since she had to reveal their names. She went to the bathroom and looked in the mirror, all she could see were tears of black mascara running down her face and a bright red mark where he had struck her several times, how many times she could not remember. She went back out into the hall and put the chain across the door and pushed across the bottom bolt. She sat down looked at Tony's photo on the sideboard and wept again holding her head in her hands.

Chapter 9

The three men got into the car with Stan Smith still at the driver's wheel, the cigarettes were lit and the smoke started to fill the interior of the car again.

'Did you get any biscuit's?' Stan said.

Fucking ginger nuts Stan, fucking Ginger nuts,' Ray said.

'Bollocks I never get any fucking biscuit's doing this driving shit', replied Stan.

The other three laughed as Stan pulled the car away on route to their next job. The cold wind meant the windows would stay shut and the car would fill up with even more smoke. Stan pulled the car over to the side of the road and Charlie got out of the car. He entered a phone box and dialled a number that was written in his diary.

'Sergeant John Wall please', he said to the caller on the end of the phone.

'Wait here I will get him', came the reply, Charlie waited and could hear what sounded like a busy office in the background, all the hustle and bustle of crime fighting probably trying to piece together enough information on me and to nail me, he thought to himself.

'Sergeant John Wall,' he heard in the receiver.

'Hello Johnny boy, it's Charlie Allan, we need to have a talk.'

'I thought I told you not to ring me here.'

'What would you prefer, ring you there or ring your wife, take your pick.'

'Here's fine, what's it about.'

'The Tony Clay murder, who did it and why?'

'Why do you want to know?' Replied John Wall.

'Lets just say Johnny has a certain interest in the case and wants something back.'

'I'll dig up what I can and meet you next week same place and time.'

'No we need to know tonight, Johnny wants info tomorrow, and I don't suppose you want me to tell him you couldn't deliver.'

'I will see what I can do Charlie, shall we say our usual pub in Norwood, seven o'clock?'

There was tension on the end of the phone as if there was deliberation going through Charlie Allan's head. Eventually John Wall heard 'ok' on the end of the receiver and the phone went dead.

Charlie put the receiver down, bollocks he thought, a late one, still at least Johnny will have some info. He returned to the car, the others said nothing but waited for their next instruction from Charlie.

'I'm meeting him in the pub tonight, Stan you can drive, you two can have an early one after we have visited the warehouse.'

'What no biscuit's and a late one, what have I done wrong?' Said Stan Smith.

'Stan, head towards this warehouse and stop moaning.'

Stan pulled the car away from the kerb and headed towards the warehouse, they drove through the City of London in a smoked filled car until they arrived at the warehouse as written down by Angela. The car pulled up alongside warehouse 228, they could clearly see there where car tracks in the soft soil leading into and out of the warehouse doors. The place was quiet, it was starting to get dark, no other warehouses were open and there was no sign of anyone else around.

'Looks like we may be too late' Charlie said, 'Ray get some tools out the boot so we can see inside.'

It didn't take long for them to realise someone had beaten them to it; the warehouse was empty apart from some old crates and piles of shit cutlery and crockery.

'Johnny won't be pleased boys, lets fuck off and see if I can do better with the copper, Stan, drop me off home, then drop these two off and come back for me at half six.'

The pub in Norwood was deserted apart form a couple of regulars, Charlie spotted John Walls in the corner drinking a pint, smoking and reading the South London press newspaper.

'What have you got for me Wallsy', said Charlie.

'You not having a drink, then Charlie.'

'No, don't drink with pigs.'

'I'm doing you a favour,

'And you get fucking paid for it so tell me what you know so I can fuck off out of here, I've had a busy day.'

'Ok, there's not a lot to go on, it's a weird one, a normal routine patrol was carrying out mundane duties when it decided to pull over a vehicle, they were obviously bored or had a low arrest ratio. The vehicle they wanted to pull over started to speed up and try to get away and before you know it, Tony Clay was thrown out of the car and the police car tried to swerve but ended up driving straight over the poor bastard. They are still trying to ascertain what injuries were from what.'

'What do you mean?' asked Charlie.

'It looks like he was tortured beforehand and then he sustained further injuries from the police car, there is talk that your lot did it to Tony to try and get information from him, so you might get your collar felt soon.'

'We had fuck all to do with it.'

'So why you interested then Charlie?'

There was silence until Charlie decided to ignore the question and speak 'So you have no ideas who did it.'

'No too early, the only thing is you guys and the hold you have over the City, you lot are our only suspects but we have fuck all else to go on.'

'What about a number plate?'

'It was false, so it wasn't Johnny then?' replied John Wall.

'No not us, but we want to find out who it was the same as you, so when you have details on the case, you call me.'

John Wall nodded as Charlie got up from the table, he pulled out one hundred pounds and tossed it on the table, John Wall scooped it up quickly.

'For fuck sake Charlie, what the fucks up with you, don't do that here.'

'Call me when you have something Wallsy, earn your money.'

Charlie left the pub leaving John Wall looking around to make sure no one witnessed what just happened, Charlie got into the car, Stan was in the drivers seat eating ginger nut biscuit's, and Charlie looked at him with a look of bewilderment.

'What you looking at me like that for, said Stan, I got them from the corner shop, while I was waiting for you.'

'Take me home Stan' said Charlie.

Chapter 10

Alison Redland laid there completely exposed to her situation, she was high, drunk and in a state of mind that didn't matter what was happening to her, she just needed the money for her next fix. All she could think about was her past, she would drift off with memories of her mum cuddling her, comforting her and crying with her. Memories of her drunken father violently abusing her mum, and sexually abusing her. It didn't take away the pain, it brought more pain but the alcohol and drugs took care of that. So for now, she thought, she could lay there, do the deed, get the money and live another day and hope that one day prince charming will come for her and scoop her up out of hell. She drifted off further, she thought of where she came from a poor area of Newcastle. She coped at first until her fathers drinking started, then the world erupted for her. An abusive boyfriend followed, obviously thought that was the norm in a relationship, and then the escape and a train to London to start again. Ally Redland had been in London for three months and had already fallen into it's underworld trap; she became a stripper in a Brixton club to survive, because she knew she needed money. She needed to function and forget the past; she needed drugs and alcohol, the combination that could possibly destroy her. She lay there perfectly still while this man did what he did, she felt like an animal trapped in a bad world, it made her feel cheap, disgusting, and hoped one day she could get out of it all and become a normal human being in a sane world. Ally Redland lay there lost in her world and thoughts, she was with a man she didn't know, a man called Johnny Saunders licking cocaine from her vagina and anus.

There was a noise in the distance, a ringing, then the shadow of a man walking across the floor, she could see more clearly now as her head was clearing, the same man that was down on her, he was picking up a phone, she heard voices in the distance.

'It's late Charlie, I'm busy, what do you mean nothing, what was all gone? The warehouse was empty, no suspects but ourselves, Sean who? Someone Docherty, did you say Docherty? Charlie, I'm busy right now, we will sort this out in the morning; take me to the warehouse tomorrow; I want to see things for myself.

She could hear the man put the phone down, he was walking back over towards her, she couldn't move, she felt the pain inside her anus as he entered her, the physical pain was there, but the emotional pain was worse from the tears running down her face.

Chapter 11

Click the camera went, click the camera went again and another photo came out of the Polaroid camera. Sean surveyed the latest pictures, Tina was laying on her back with just her stockings and fuck me shoes on, and in the second one she was hiding her breasts within her hands.

'God your beautiful Tina, and dirty with it', Sean said, 'I prefer this one, it's more erotic', there's something erotic about being able to see your pussy but I cant see your tits.'

'If you ever show these to anyone Sean I will castrate you', she said.

'Babe of course I wont, what do you take me for?'

'I mean it Sean, I'm trusting you, and these are for our eyes only.'

'Yea and the locals in the pub', Sean giggled.

Tina jumped up and grabbed hold of Sean; they rolled around the bed laughing while Tina was trying to grab the photos out of Sean's hands. They kissed passionately; they made love again, with Tina on top, and again with Tina on her back, and then with Tina bent over on all fours.

'Ok, Ok, I'm knackered,' said Sean, 'you win, but I am doing all the work babe.'

'Ok, then let me go back on top' she replied as she jumped on top of him. She straddled her legs over him and she guided him deep into her, she rode his penis deep inside her with her long dark hair falling down onto her breasts and onto his face, she shuddered, rode faster until she had her third orgasm of the morning. They both lay there sweating and stroking each other until she got off Sean and took him into her mouth slowly licking and taking it deep into her throat, and when she sensed the moment, she took it out of her mouth and wanked his firm cock until he came too. They both lay there exhausted, it was a long night and a long morning and Sean could feel it in his muscles and his breathing, he took his time to compose himself, while his semen dribbled into his belly button.

'That was amazing, where would I be without you,' he said.

'When are you going to move in with me Sean', she replied.

'You know Taylor won't survive without me darling, he needs his precious mate to be able to function.'

'Yeah well maybe I need my precious boyfriend to be able to function.'

Sean stroked her body further and held her close, squeezed her so tight as if they were now joined as one, he kissed her and caressed her and she felt safe in his arms. They lay there like that until they fell asleep again due to the exertion of their lovemaking.

Tina woke as the light came through the window, her body was telling her she had overslept, and she quickly came to her senses.

'Shit Sean, wake up, we fell asleep, and Taylor's banging on the front door.'

Sean jumped out of bed went to the window, opened it fully and felt the cold morning air instantly hit his body.

'Alright lover boy' Taylor shouted up, 'you going to let me in or what?'

Sean threw down the keys, 'let yourself in, and while you're at it put the kettle on.'

'Where are you going today Sean?' asked Tina as Sean was busy looking for his clothes.

'Me and Taylor have just got some business we need to attend to.'

'What's it about Sean?'

'It's to do with Tony Clay.'

'Can I come Sean?'

'What do you mean can you come, you never come, ok you have come three times this morning but you never normally come out with me and Taylor?'

'I've got nothing on today and I'm bored, it would be good to spend the day with the two people I love and care about the most in this world.'

'But we ain't got much on babe, and I'm not sure what Taylor will think of that.'

'Well ask him while I go and have a shower. She kissed him on the mouth, 'I'm sure you can persuade him Sean.' Sean patted Tina on the arse and kissed her on the cheek, pulled on his boxer shorts and t-shirt and headed to the door. As he was going down the stairs he could hear Tina singing in the bathroom, he smiled again realising how much he loved her and decided it could be a good thing for her today to spend time with him and her brother.

'Morning Taylor, we have a decision to make, your sister wants to come out with us for the day.'

'What, why? We've got things on!' he replied.

'I know but I thought it would be good for her to spend the day with you and me to see some of the things we do, to maybe enhance some trust in us and understand that we are not bad boys after all.'

'Have you gone soft in the head? She can't come with us Sean! We are trying to find out what happened to Tony Clay, we are just driving around going to his warehouse to try and work out what happened.'

'Look Taylor it's a one off, she's got nothing else on, she's bored, after we're done the three of us can go out for a nice meal, get pissed, whatever we want, chill out and just enjoy each other's company.'

'You've gone soft!' said Taylor.

'But it's just a one off mate, just a one off.'

The day was warm and sunny when the three of them left the house, this enhanced a joyful feeling in the city that matched Tina's excitement, her excitement of being able to spend the day with the two men she loved and adored. The journey took them across town with a wild excitement in the car due to discussions of love, affection and the history between them. They recalled the times of their past and growing up together, they were

86

reminiscing about family members and the upbringing they enjoyed. There was discussion on pain and grief they shared, with the loss of their father Mark Doherty on the day when he lost his life. The atmosphere was joyous, funny, happy, safe and at times sad, but they revelled in the company they were in, even Taylor seemed glad that his sister was sharing some time with his friend and himself who was her brother.

The journey took them through the streets of London they knew so well, even the journey was the same as the night before heading towards Tony Clay's warehouse but the journey was lost in the excitement of the three travellers in the car enjoying time together which did not often happen.

'So when are you two getting married?' Taylor asked.

'We're not, I am in love with you Taylor did you not know?' replied Sean laughing,

'Go fuck yourself, you're not getting in my arse hole!'

'He isn't getting near my arse hole either!' Tina replied laughing,

'Yeah, anyway, so why aren't you going to marry me then Sean?'

'I will one day babe, but I have to look after your big brother for a few more years yet, he is a twat without me!'

The car turned off towards Chelsea Bridge as they made their way down towards Clapham Junction. The traffic was light; the sky was blue and the journey smooth.

'What do you think we are looking for?' said Sean.

'I'm not sure but I think we just need to get a better understanding of what happened and make sure everything is covered up before the police find out what Tony had in his warehouse.'

'Can't we get Pete Murray involved?' Sean asks.

'We can't keep relying on Pete; we should only contact him when it's really necessary.'

'Why are we getting involved anyway?'

'Because that's what we do, we liked Tony, we like Angela and they're the sort of people that deserve better.'

'Yeah you're right Taylor', replied Tina, 'I met them both once and thought they were a lovely couple, it was such a shame what happened to Tony, he didn't deserve it, he would never have hurt anyone.'

The car pulled into Chapel Road and travelled down the long unmade gravel path towards the warehouse unit's. It took them a while to find Clays Unit so they continued circling around until the faint markings of the warehouse could be seen. Sean turned off the engine and noticed the silence apart from the occasional birdsong in the trees.

'Right', Taylor broke the silence.

'Sis, if anybody turns up we are friends of Tony and we are just making sure that his family are well looked after and we have been asked to look after his warehouse for anything that could be sold. If the police turn up we are looking for somewhere to have sex with you!'

'What!' Tina shouted.

'Well what else can we say?' Why are we going into someone's warehouse where someone sells stolen goods, so we tell them we are here to give you one'

'Fucking charming!' Tina says.

'Don't worry sis, no one will turn up, we will be in and out of here very quickly, we are just having a bit of a scout around to make sure everything is clean.'

'And is it clean' repeats Tina.

'This is why we are here sis, this is what we want to find out, come on all this female rabbiting is putting me off my stride, lets get this sorted', Taylor replied

The three of them got out of the car. Sean took the keys out of his pocket and had a quick look around; it was still quiet and still. There was no one else around not even Chester could be seen with his mechanic friends. The sun was still shining when Sean noticed that the lock had been broken on the main doors, he glanced up at Taylor, and Sean could clearly see he could see the padlock had been forced too, they both said nothing. Sean removed the broken padlock and pulled back the doors revealing what looked like an empty warehouse after the removal of it's contents the day before. The warehouse looked bigger now it was partially empty, the ground level still had it's metal shelves and metal storage cabinets which looked sterile and cold due to the emptiness. There was a small upper level that you could get to via a pull down ladder. That level had crates and wooden boxes that could be seen from below which also looked that they have been made sterile from the day before.

'I am going to have a look round down here' said Taylor.

Sean headed for the ladder to get onto the upper mezzanine level. 'I'll go up there to see if I can look into any of these boxes just to make sure.'

'I'll come up there with you Sean' said Tina, 'I might find myself a nice dress! Or if I'm lucky a whole box of nice dresses.'

Sean helped Tina climb the ladder and followed her up onto the mezzanine level. They slowly walked around the top level checking boxes that appeared to be partially opened to inspect the contents.

'So this is what you do on a daily basis is it babe, checking out dodgy warehouses?' said Tina.

Sean slapped Tina's arse 'It pays the bills babe!'

'But will it pay for a marriage licence?' Tina asked, 'with a bit of luck there might be a whole box of goodies up here.'

Sean laughed and continued along the mezzanine walkway with Tina following closely behind, checking each box as she went. They walked round the mezzanine level but all the boxes seemed to have been checked, probably by Chester and his friends the night before. Sean suddenly stopped in his tracks, there was a noise, the noise of car tyres on gravel and the sound of an engine or was that two engines, he could not tell from where he was. He turned and pulled Tina towards him. She was busy rummaging through boxes and saw in his face there was a problem, immediately she stopped and found that she could also hear what Sean was listening to.

'Stay up there Sean' shouted Taylor, 'don't come down whatever happens'

Sean and Tina heard Taylor, they listened and could hear the cars clearer now, it was too noisy to be one car, they weren't driving fast, and it was a slow deliberate pace. Sean could tell that now, and there were definitely two cars. Sean pulled Tina closer to him and put his finger up to his mouth to indicate silence. He listened further, he heard the engines stop, and he heard the doors open and then close, then heard footsteps on the gravel outside. Sean looked around, he didn't know why, but decided he needed a hiding place fast; he felt it was the natural thing to do. He pulled Tina towards him again, pointed to the position he had just created and whispered in her ear, 'get in there now', she listened and did as he said concealing herself within the cardboard shelter. Sean followed Tina behind the boxes and started to pull the boxes around them to conceal their position.

Chapter 12

Taylor stood there motionless. He didn't want to move he just watched the two cars drive up towards the warehouse in a menacing way. He watched as the doors opened and five men exited, alongside a plume of cigarette smoke bellowing from the car. He recognised one of the men and his heart started to beat faster, they didn't say anything, but took slow meaningful steps towards where he stood. Johnny Saunders was the last to enter the warehouse, he was sucking on his fat cigar and the smoke he exhaled was rising into the warm sunshine. There was silence for a while and Taylor felt the fear rise inside of him. He knew he was in a position that was difficult to get out of, he was scared of his father's killer, the man that stood there before him now. There was a feeling of bravery but also anger that entered his body, he hoped in his head that Sean had heard him state that they should stay where they were, he hoped that Sean, and especially Tina would not come down from the place that was concealing them from danger.

Taylor looked at the five people in front of him, he recognised Johnny Saunders and now some of the other men with him also, they looked intimidating, and especially with the silence they brought into the room. The silence made him feel more scared than the fact they were actually there. He stood his ground until Johnny Saunders; still puffing on his cigar threw it to the ground, stepped on it, and extinguished it into the earth.

'Morning Taylor' growled Johnny Saunders breaking the silence.

'Now what are you doing here in Tony Clays warehouse?'

'I could ask you the same question Johnny?' said Taylor.

'You fucking could but you ain't got the fucking authority to do that you cunt!'

Taylor could see the smiles on Johnny's four henchmen; he could see they revelled in his fear.

'I am just checking to make sure that Tony's clear with the police and that Angie, his wife can be well looked after.'

'Angie his wife, can be fucking well looked after, what do you mean by that!' shouted Johnny.

'Just as I said Johnny, I am making sure that any gear left here can be sold off, she has to look after herself now.'

Sean was struggling to hear the conversation from the position he was in, he struggled to hear as he kept his hand over Tina's mouth. He could tell she was scared, he was scared himself, in fact he was shitting himself, not for him, but for his friend Taylor below. He looked at Tina, her eyes were wide and he could sense the fear in her body, so he held her tighter.

'Do you know about my money?' Continued Johnny.

'What money?' Taylor said.

'Tony Clay was picking up some money for me and I found out he was also picking up some suits for you. In that fucking process you got your suits but I didn't get my fucking money, because my courier got fucking topped! So where's my fucking money?'

'I don't know anything about any money Johnny?' Said Taylor.

'Don't call me Johnny you cunt! I killed your dad because he was a fucking Irish tinker bastard! Now where's my fucking money?'

'Look Johnny.'

'I said don't call me fucking Johnny!'

'We haven't got our suits either!' shouted Taylor; we don't care about our suits! We care about Tony and we just want Angie to spend the rest of her life in peace.'

'Well get the fucking violins out for Saint fucking Taylor here, I am fucking angry! I am fucking mad, and some fuckers going to pay for the loss of my fifty grand and I am gonna find out where the fuck it went! Johnny Saunders looked across at the men with him.

'Stan, wait outside with the cars, Charlie, shut them fucking doors.'

The noise of the doors closing terrified Taylor, and terrified even further Sean and Tina up on the mezzanine floor. The fear grew with the knowing realisation that something evil was about to happen. Sean continued to hold onto Tina, and when her eyes met his, he could see the fear in them, but he could also see the tears, he could see the fear, and she could also see the same in his eyes.

'Get that fucking chair over here Charlie!' shouted Johnny.

With that Charlie dragged a chair from the side and found some rope on the floor.

'Get that fucker and tie him to the chair.'

'Now come on Johnny, I don't know anything about any fucking money!' shouted Taylor.

Taylor didn't see the punch coming but he felt the pain as he landed on the floor, and he knew his nose had been broken, he moaned and lay there holding his face until he felt the arms drag him up onto the chair. His nose was pouring with blood and his eyes were watering. He felt the hands grapple at him and he could feel that he was being tied to a chair. It was hard for him to focus due to the pain and the tears in his eyes, and due to the damage done to his nose. He just hoped inside his head that Sean and Tina would stay hidden.

When the blow was heard Sean gripped Tina tighter, her eyes were flowing now with tears. He could feel her tensing up and he was now starting to worry that she would make a noise. He felt scared, vulnerable, trapped and cowardly, but he knew Taylor would want them to stay hidden.

'Where's my fucking money you cunt!' shouted Johnny again Before Taylor could speak he needed to spit blood, he spat it out and the noise of the extraction of liquid could be heard as it hit the concrete floor, he looked up at Johnny who was now standing over him.

'I don't know anything about any fucking money', he said.

The second punch came from the right and Taylor felt the pain and the chair fall backwards as he landed on his back. Within seconds the chair was lifted back up and this time he had to spit some teeth out of his mouth. There was a difference this time; the second punch created a difference in Taylors feeling and attitude, anger poured from his body and he felt braver.

'You're a sad cunt Saunders!' he shouted, 'and I am gonna fucking see you rot in hell you bastard! You killed my father and

I have stood by and never done anything to you, I know fuck all about your money. You can do what you want to me, but I can't give you the answers you're after. If I knew about your money I'd tell you because it don't matter to me, what matters to me are real people; people with respect, and you ain't no real person, you're a cunt!'

The third blow hit him in his stomach and the pain was excruciating, it winded him severely and he lay there searching for his breath, and a pain he had never felt before in his life. Again he felt the chair being picked up and back onto it's four legs ready for the next beating.

'That one's because you called me a cunt! The next one will be because I don't like you, got it!'

Taylor did his best to nod without causing any further pain to his body.

Sean was trying his hardest to listen what was being said below him, and he was also consciously putting into his brain who the five men were with Taylor, he didn't know why he was doing that, and he put it down to his animal instinct. It was then one of the boxes above him came crashing down onto himself and Tina, and with that came an instant fear that ripped through his heart. He looked at Tina and again put his finger to his lips indicating silence, and he could see instantly in her eyes the fear that it brought. It went silent in the warehouse and Sean listened to anything he could hear below, it was then he heard an order from the voice of Johnny Saunders to check out where the noise came from.

The noise of the ladder being pulled down from it's hangers bought additional fear into both Tina and Sean, and they both knew they could only wait for the oncoming investigation, like a game of adult hide and seek, Sean thought. The fear also brought sound as they heard the steps upon the ladder runs as whoever was coming up clumsily took each tread slowly. The mans foot steps upon the mezzanine floor were now also reverberating around the warehouse, and with every step the noise got louder as they got nearer and nearer towards Tina and Sean.

Sean held his breath, as he could sense the man getting closer, there was nothing he could do, it was a game of cat and mouse and the seeker was going to be the winner. He could now see shoes in front of him on the mezzanine floor just outside where he was with Tina, the shoes turned as if they were searching for something. When the cat jumped out, it even shocked Sean and Tina, and the noise it made was like a lion attacking an antelope, and with it the shoes became invisible in the turmoil that was being out played outside of Tina and Sean's hide out.

"Fucking hell!' Sean heard the man scream as the cat ran passed where the shoes had been.

From below Sean could hear Johnny Saunders screaming,

'So what the fuck is it Ray!'

'A fucking cat boss, just a fucking cat, scared the living day lights out me, fucking thing', replied the man.

'Get yourself back down here then you fucking twat, stop playing Dr fucking Doolittle we've got work to do.'

Sean and Tina held their breath; they then heard the noise of the man moving back down the mezzanine floor towards the ladder,

97

they heard the steps on the ladder before they started to breath again.

Johnny Saunders looked at Ray Flynn as he landed back on the warehouse floor; he then turned back to Taylor.

'Now where were we before we got rudely interrupted by puss in boots. Oh yeah you were calling me a cunt. Right the money if you don't know where the money is, guess what, you and your fucking lover boy.'

Johnny looked around the room at his colleagues again.

'What's his fucking lover boys name?' he said.

Charlie looked up at Johnny Saunders, 'Sean Farrow boss.'

Johnny Saunders looked back down at Taylor.

'Well you and your fucking lover boy Farrow are gonna find out where my fucking money is, and you will tell me where it is within two days, because if you don't I will stick a blade right through your lungs just like I did to your fucking old man, you got that Docherty, you fucking got that you cunt.'

Taylor was still, he was looking up at Saunders who was standing there in front of him spitting as he shouted at him. He felt a sadistic tone go through his body and a sense of bravery and anger hit him that he had never felt in himself before. Before he knew it he leapt off the chair and head-butted Saunders straight on the nose with all his force. They both went down and Taylor landed on top of him, there was not a lot he could do, as his hands were still tied behind his back. But the leap made him brave, and the sight of Saunders ear in front of him became too irresistible to ignore as he bit on it with the full force of his jaw and teeth. Taylor could not feel anything else, just anger ripping through his body, he didn't notice the gristle of flesh in his mouth as he was beaten on the back until he was dragged to his feet by the other men, it was then he had to spit part of Johnny Saunders ear onto the ground.

Johnny Saunders got to his feet, he looked again at his colleagues; he wiped his nose with his sleeve and felt the side of his ear that was partially missing. He nodded at Ray who had been dishing out the blows, and then he looked back at Taylor.

'Your two days have gone boy, Taylor heard Saunders say, and in his daze he saw Saunders pull something from his coat pocket. The fourth blow was a cosh across the head, delivered by Saunders himself, and Taylor never saw it coming, and this one he never felt, alongside the other blows delivered, he didn't feel anything anymore, and then his world went black.

Sean looked down at Tina, her eyes were full of tears, he held onto her tight, it was then that he spotted the puddle and instantly knew she had wet herself in terror. She had urinated in fear and the evidence was in front of him, so he held her closer to him. He didn't notice it himself but tears were also pouring down his face. He then heard the chair being pulled up again but this time there was silence and then he heard the words that hit him like a hammer, and he had to hold onto Tina even harder.

'Fuck me boss I think we've killed him' he heard one man say.

'No I think he's just out cold, check him Ray, is he breathing? He heard another say.

He then heard Saunders voice booming around the warehouse, 'so fucking what' look what the cunt has done to my nose and ear, where the fuck were you lot when I needed you, fucking dumb twats.'

The warehouse became silent again while Ray bent down to check Taylor, there was no breathing and no pulse and blood was oozing from the large cut on his head.

'Well' said Johnny.

'We've done it in the past boss but I didn't think we would kill him with those blows?' replied Ray Flynn.

'Well he's fucking dead you twat!! How the fucking hell are we gonna find my money now you stupid cunts?'

'What are we gonna do with him now boss?' said Charlie.

'Fuck him, leave him here, shouted Saunders, 'it will look like something to do with Tony Clay. You bunch of fucking idiots!! What am I paying you for, I need his lover boy found now, what's his fucking name again?'

'Sean Farrow boss' replied Charlie Allan.

'Find him, I want that cunt found, now let's get the fuck out of here, you fucking idiots you cant get anything fucking right.'

Before Johnny Saunders exited the warehouse, he looked down at the warehouse floor, he bent down picked his ear up and put it into his pocket.

Chapter 13

Sean Farrow sat there with the woman he loved and he held her tight in his arms. He heard, as the warehouse doors were pulled open below him, and he felt the cool fresh air enter the warehouse. He felt his eyes go cold with the cool breeze and he felt Tina's shaking vibrate around his body. He knew he had to keep her still and quiet until they were gone and he continued to listen. He could hear footsteps on the gravel path, he heard the car doors open, then shut, he heard the engines start up and the cars pull away. It was then he heard the silence apart from the birds still singing in the trees outside. She was sobbing now and he allowed her the comfort of letting it out, as he felt sure they were gone. He told her to wait there and that he would be back for her. Sean pulled himself up from the boxes and looked over the railings of the mezzanine. He could see Taylor sitting in a chair below him, his arms tied behind his back, his head down with his back to him. There was no movement; he stood there for a while looking at Taylor from above, he looked down at Tina who was looking back up at him. In her eyes he could see pain, while she was searching in his for hope.

'Sean please tell me he's alive?' she sobbed.

It took him a while to move his legs to move away from her, but slowly he managed to walk to the ladder to get down to the next level, it was in a slow pace as the shock was still reverberating around his body. As he got to the ground level he could now see Taylor from a side view, his head was down, and blood was pouring down the front of his shirt. He walked over to him, he touched his shoulder and tried to feel for a pulse, he didn't know how to, but he did what he thought was the way it was meant to be done. Taylor looked in a bad way, there was no movement, but the blood was showing the real tragedy that had gone on. He called out to him in a low voice 'Taylor, Taylor, Taylor' but there was no response.

He got onto one knee to look up at Taylor; he put his hand near his mouth to see if he could feel any breath, there was no breath. He held Taylors hand and tried to feel for a pulse on his wrist, there was no pulse. He cried and he wept, and felt ashamed for not being able to help his friend, he put Taylors hand back down and looked up at the mezzanine, but could only see the boxes that concealed their presence. He got up and pulled the warehouse doors shut and the whole place became dark, he was lost in his world of grief and the uncertainty of what he should do. He was sure that Taylor was dead but still couldn't believe that he had lost his friend within minutes of chatting and laughing with him. He looked up again at the mezzanine, he decided it was time and climbed the stairs using the ladder again and crossed the floor towards Tina. Sean knelt down to where she was sitting sobbing and crying in her puddle of urine. He held her hand and whispered softly in her ear 'we have to leave Tina.'

She looked up at Sean 'Is that with Taylor or without Taylor?'

'It's without Taylor' he replied.

She looked into Sean's eyes and she knew what it meant. Sean allowed her to cry and grieve for a while but was aware he needed to get them both out of there and call Pete Murray as soon as they left, he pulled her to her feet.

' I don't want you to look at Taylor', he said 'you don't need to look, you just need to leave with me; you don't need to see your brother like that.'

She followed his instructions and they walked across the mezzanine floor towards the ladder with Sean holding her on his left side so that she couldn't look down at Taylor. Before Sean descended the ladder he told her again that she doesn't need to look. He descended the ladder to the ground floor of the warehouse and helped Tina down.

'What are we going to do with Taylor? We can't leave him here?' Said Tina.

'We'll talk to Pete, Pete will sort it all out', Sean replied.

Holding her close to him he guided her towards the warehouse doors, but before he had time to react, she pulled herself away from him and looked across at Taylor who was about four feet away from her. Sean tried to grab hold of her to turn her away but there was aggressiveness from her and strength that he hadn't seen or felt before.

'I want to look Sean, you cant stop me he's my brother, I want to see what those bastards have done to my brother!' She went over to Taylor, touched his hair and kissed him on the forehead, and she wiped away some of the blood that was on his shirt and jacket.

'Don't worry,' she said. 'They will pay for what they have done to you here today, I swear on my life.'

Sean took hold of Tina's arm and pulled her away, he opened the warehouse doors and looked back for one last time at Taylor in the chair, and then he closed the door behind him.

Chapter 14

Pete Murray was sitting in his living room, he had the TV on and was watching the BBC news; he picked up the cup of tea he had made a little earlier and sipped from it's rim. He was contemplating again; he was missing Fiona and looking up at her photo on his side unit. There was something different today, he thought to himself, it was as if something was about to happen, he had these feelings now and then and they were often right, but he never knew, what, or if, anything was going to happen, he threw the thought away. There was nothing going on in the news, just some clips about Northern Ireland and potential peace talks, which he had heard a thousand times before, so he got up from his chair and walked towards his balcony doors. He watched as pigeons were pecking away at bread he had put out there earlier, it wasn't meant for them so he opened the doors and watched as they flew away into the air. He felt the breeze hit his face and he rubbed his chin, I need a shave he thought to himself, standing on his balcony and watching the world go by below him. He watched as children played on the new playground that had recently been built by the council, he saw the children playing on the swings and going down the slide, it was good to hear them laughing, it made him feel like there was a world outside his home. He waved at Harry a neighbour he has known for a few years now as he walked through the estate. The phone rang behind him and he turned his head in the direction of where it came from, he thought about his earlier feelings but threw them away again, Pete left the balcony and walked into his living room. When he picked up the phone he recognised Sean Farrows voice straight away, although it sounded different then usual, it sounded distressed and he knew that he would find out why very soon. Sean told him all that had happened that day and Pete felt his body start to shake with sorrow but mainly anger, anger that he had not felt for years, he continued to listen until eventually Sean had explained all that had happened in the warehouse.

'Sean', said Pete, 'where are you now?'

'I'm in a phone box in Balham, Tina's with me, she's waiting in the car.'

'Sean, you need to go home, you need to take care of Tina, leave Taylor to me, I will sort that out, do nothing until I contact you.'

Sean listened to Pete, he knew he would sort it all out, but something was biting at his conscience, 'Pete', he said, 'I couldn't do anything, Taylor didn't want me to, he told me to stay where I was with Tina, I couldn't go down, I was looking after Tina Pete, I couldn't help him, but now I wish I did, now I wish I had gone down to help him.'

'Sean, you had to look after Tina, you did the right thing, don't worry about that, you did the right thing, go home now, as I said do nothing, I will contact you later tonight'

Pete put the phone down, he looked out onto his balcony again, the pigeons were back, eating the bread that was not for them, he threw his newspaper at the windows and watched as the pigeons flew into the air again. He sat down on his chair again, he rubbed his chin, I will shave later, he told himself, he has things he needs to do. He went to his cupboard in the hall and pulled out a pair of shoes, he put them on and grabbed his light overcoat, and then took his keys from the hook by the front door. He left his flat and walked through the estate passing the kids as they played on the swings, they were still laughing, that's good, he thought, but he couldn't raise a smile this time. He walked for about two miles passing a number of phone boxes on the way, until he came across one by a busy four-way junction, he looked around and lifted the receiver and dialled a number that he knew well. The phone was picked up by a detective he vaguely knew, but only occasionally met so he decided to try and disguise his voice the best way he could. Pete Murray explained to the detective that he had some information in regards to the Tony Clay murder case and that they would be very interested in visiting the warehouse owned by him. He gave the detective the address and he could hear that the detective was writing it down but didn't seem to be too interested. Pete needed the visit to take place now so he explained to the detective that there may be another body within the warehouse, he sensed the mood change from the detective on the other end of the line. Pete knew that the question would come from the detective asking him for his name and address, and it was inevitable that it would happen, and when it did he knew it was time to put the phone down. Pete left the phone box, he walked the two miles back to his apartment, he walked passed the new playground noticing that the children had gone and the swings were still, he looked up at his balcony, the pigeons were back and he growled within himself. When Pete returned to his apartment he removed his coat and shoes and placed them in the same place they always went, he walked into his lounge and poured himself a whiskey, he then got his notebook and pencil from his side cabinet and sat in his favourite chair. He needed to write, he needed to get things down, this always worked for him, like when his wife died, he wrote about things he was worried about, he wrote how he could deal with the problems and he felt the issues go away a lot easier. He was doing that now, he was writing, he was planning and he was putting processes together, he listed the problems and ways those problems can be removed, with plans and timelines. Pete felt like the good detective he always wanted to be, he was self-planning and it made him feel good, he poured himself another whiskey and continued with his sheets of paper in front of him.

When Pete Murray woke up he knew he had overdone it with the whiskey, the sofa felt comfortable beneath his body and it felt good, he didn't mind the occasional lapse in his procedures and it felt good to break a few rules now and then. His head now was experienced to whiskey so was not aching but he did have that heart burn feeling that he got if he drunk too much of the stuff. Looking at the coffee table in front of him, he could see the large pile of paper that he had been working on still sitting there. He had done well, he thought to himself, and it was all out of his system now, mind body and soul, and was now in a materialistic form in front of him. Pete lifted himself up slowly into a sitting position on the sofa, his legs and body told him he was not a young man anymore, he looked out of the balcony windows, the morning light was coming through into his room filling it with free light, there was a robin eating bread from his table, Pete Murray smiled as the morning light warmed his face.

Chapter 15

The sun shone through the clouds that were just starting to show signs of dispersal in the morning, a morning that was going to be the start of a bad day. The temperature was a cool July morning with only a slight breeze in the air, it was early but people were already starting to gather in the house, shaking hands with solemn looks on their faces. People were beginning to experience that unwelcome knowledge and uncomfortable situation of knowing the next sentence would be 'it's been too long', 'we only see each other at funerals.'

Tina got up early and was helping her mum Patsy who was already in the process of offering light snacks and tea to those in the house, as well as something stronger for the day ahead.

Sean Farrow lay in his room, his eyes were focused on the ceiling, he was drifting off into memories and trying to understand the deep meaning of life, how things happen and how the opening of doors can lead to disaster or luck. He knew he had to drag his legs out of the bed, he knew the day would bring him pain, sorrow, discomfort and the need to achieve a world record in shaking hands, and winning the Oscar for acting and putting on a brave face. He knew he could do that, he could shake hands, he could smile, and he could greet people because he was good at building that brick wall to hide his emotions. He decided it was time and threw the sheets back, hauled himself out of bed and headed for the bathroom to shower. The hot water hit his head like a hammer just how he liked it, thoughts and feelings entered his brain, there was an energy in them, he could feel it each time these thoughts and memories entered. It was like a message trying to enter but couldn't get passed the barrier that he had successfully put up. He shaved, washed, and then cleaned his teeth thoroughly knowing he had a lot of people meeting to do today. He walked back into the bedroom and spotted the black suit that was hanging up, he looked at it, such a formidable dress sense for a dismal occasion he thought, for some unknown reason he did the sign of the cross, strange he thought but then related it to his Catholic upbringing and threw that one over his shoulder too.

Sean Farrow sat on the bed, he felt lost, and a realisation was sinking in that he was now on his own, he did everything with Taylor. He knew that any issues they would sort out together, but this one, the issue of today, he would have to do on his own. He knew he would have support, but it was all down to him to stay strong and focused for those that were in grief. He had others to think about more so then himself and he had to be strong for that, even so he felt alone, insecure, scared and vulnerable.

Tina entered the room, 'You Ok Sean', she said.

'Yep, I will be ok, get this day over and we can start a new life, how do I look in my black suit Tina.'

'Respectful, you look respectful,' she replied.

'Are you ok, Tina?'

'Yes I'm ok.'

'This day should never have come, it's not right, it doesn't seem real and it's way too early', said Sean.

'It seems real to me Sean because we were there, we know what went on and we know who by, I'm going to feel a lot better when we can do something about that.'

There was a quiet moment between them, as they adjusted their clothing, Sean was tightening his tie up to his neck, something he always hated and Tina was having a last minute check in the mirror, it was like they were both about to step into a boxing ring.

'We can have a little think about that after today'. Sean said, 'it's been playing on my mind what happened and it sounds like you have been thinking about the same thing too.'

'Those bastards Sean, those fucking bastards, if I ever get a chance I would like to castrate the fuckers.'

Sean looked at Tina, there was moisture in her eyes, this would be a hard day for her too, Taylor was her brother, she loved him very much and it was understandable what she had just said, but could she have the anger and bottle to ever carry that out, if the chance ever come he wondered.

'We should go Tina, people will be waiting for us, are you ready for this?'

'No I'm not Sean so I will be leaning on you for support, is anyone supporting you Sean.'

'No, I don't need it', he replied.

'You're a typical bloke Sean Farrow, bury it, put your wall up and then one day it comes up and bites you in the arse.'

'Well if that ever happens I can lean on you darling, come on let's enter the lions den.'

It started at Patsy's house, they were all there, friends, family and acquaintances and some faces that Sean had not seen before. They left the house and got into the cars, those dam cars that would take you to the cemetery where everyone would stare inside, Sean remembered. After parking the car in the small car park in South London Crematorium, Sean and Tina walked along the path towards the cemetery building. The lions den was prepared for them, the faces of the people as they walked passed were full of sadness, pain and sorrow. When the shaking of the hands began with people well known to them, less known people and those they had never even seen before, what also began was the voices echoing in their ears as they walked past.

'I'm so sorry for your grief', he was such a nice boy, I know you will miss him Sean you were inseparable, he was too young to go so early, he will be missed, I'm so sorry Sean.'

'You're next cunt' where's the money?'

Sean stopped in his tracks and looked up at the man that shook his hand and whispered those words into his ear, the man was smiling, he was tall, and had a scar across his left cheek, he gripped Sean's hand firm and maintained his stare and smile.

113

Johnny Saunders sends his best wishes', he said.

Sean maintained his stare upon the tall man, maintained the grip and was searching frantically for something to say.

'Thank you very much' was all that Sean could reply. The grip was hard to release from, until finally the tall man felt it was enough time to get his message across and released his firm grip.

The coffin was heavy, Sean thought, as he lifted it and carried it into the church with Pete, Joe Swain and other close friends. The feeling that his friend was inside was overwhelmingly surreal as he walked the short journey to the front of the church where he would lay his friend down. Releasing his grip on the handles was hard for him, until Pete came round and helped him pull his hands away with care and affection. Sean walked over to Tina and slid into the pew at the front alongside Patsy; Sean parted them and sat between the two holding both their hands.

'Who was that man?' said Tina.

'What man', replied Sean.

'The tall man you spoke to Sean, there seemed to be an atmosphere.'

'I don't know who he was.'

Tina went to say something else when Sean interrupted her 'we will discuss it later.'

Tina was looking at him with concern when the priest began to speak and welcome people to the funeral of Taylor Docherty.

The ceremony was sad and emotional but there was also the

feeling of anger that drifted in the air hovering above the people that gathered in the pews. These people all wanted to be part of the remembrance, they came to show their respect, support and above all disdain for those that tortured and killed Taylor Docherty. Pete Murray was the first to carry out a reading. He spoke about Taylor and Sean, their past and their childhood, the respect and caring they showed in the community, the boyish charm, the devilment and mischievous ways, but also with a respect for those around them. Patsy spoke of her son, how proud she was of him and how he was taken away too early before he could become a family man. The priest spoke of religion, the ability to be strong in these sad times and that God protects us from the evil that carries out such crimes. He then spoke of forgiveness for those who live such sordid lives, as judgment day will fall upon them once their heart also stops to beat.

Sean Farrow looked up at that point still feeling drained by the whole day, he had thought about it a couple of times recently of revenge upon those that he had heard and seen that day torturing and killing his friend and blood brother. But this was different, the priests words were like a message, like an instruction and approval to seek out those that carried out such a barbaric act and to actually get away with it and not feel anything until their heart finally stops beating. Sean was certain the priest's message was delivered to him, he turned and looked behind him, the tall man from outside was now sitting at the back of the church and Sean was slowly starting to realise that this was not going to go away. 'Think straight Sean' was hammering out in his head, 'I need to get today over with and think about what I need to do to keep Tina and myself safe, this will not go away until I find out about this fucking money', Sean turned back to the priest who was finalising his words for his friend Taylor.

The day continued to be the same for Sean and Tina, the meeting and greeting and condolences were delivered and received with sincerity and when Sean looked around for the tall man, he was gone. The wake did not improve the atmosphere, the pub did it's best to provide refreshments and food for those that attended, but for Sean and Tina, it was a case of having to smile, more then a must do. There was the occasional laughter in the pub but the atmosphere still had a sadness about the whole occasion, as if there was something missing, and of course for Sean it was Taylor, when he thought about it, it made him scared that his life would now be a one man show.

'You ok Sean?' asked Pete.

'Yea I'm ok Pete, I need to mingle a bit to have a chat with some of the people I haven't seen for a while, and you Pete, are you Ok?'

'Yea I'm ok too, bollocks to everyone else, here have this scotch.'

'Cheers mate', replied Sean.

'Pete took a swig of his whisky, 'I was sitting on the bench by Fiona's grave at the cemetery, it was then that I saw you arrive Sean, I spotted the tall man approach you, he shook hands with you, do you know who he is?'

'No', replied Sean.

'He works for Johnny Saunders.'

'I gathered that', replied Sean.

'What did he say Sean?'

'Something about money and that I will be next, he was a big fucker weren't he Pete.'

'He's somebody Saunders uses to put the frighteners on people, he has form, been inside for assault, offensive weapons, grievous bodily harm, started his education as part of West Ham's inter city firm, his name is Ray Flynn.'

'Charming, and now he thinks little old me knows where Saunders's fucking money is, fucking hell Pete how the fuck did all this shit happen.'

'Wrong place, wrong time, but the issue you have is to find out what money they are on about and what do you do when and if you know where the money is. These lot are cunts Sean, they won't stop until they get their money, and it isn't only the money it's the loss of respect and the power they may lose if they show any weakness.'

Pete looked at Sean directly in the eyes, 'unfortunately sometimes you have to fight fire with fire.'

Sean Farrow was looking at Pete Murray, he knew what the message meant, he knew what the stare meant and he was taking it all in.

'You do know you're a an ex copper now Pete don't you?'

maintaining his stare.

'Yeah sometimes Sean, sometimes, and sometimes I can be a cunt too if I want to be, Taylor had multiple fractures caused by fists, knuckle dusters and a heavy blunt instrument, no prison sentence will ever be vengeance for that kind of thing, what they need is a bit of the same, if you know what I mean.'

Sean looked at Pete Murray, gulped at his scotch and again looked back at Pete.

'Good scotch Pete', he said with a slight smile.

'You're not alone Sean, come and see me in a few days when all this is over, we can have a chat about old times and another drop of this fine scotch.'

'I'll do that Pete, in a couple of days' Sean replied.

Sean clunked Pete's glass with his own and started to walk away from the bar before stopping and turning around to Pete once more.

'Pete, I can be a cunt too sometimes,' he said.

They both raised their glasses before going their separate ways and mingling again into the crowd to socialise at their friend's funeral.

Chapter 16

Sean woke up with a mouth as dry as a bone, there was nothing he could do but lay there licking his lips, he was dying for a piss but couldn't move out of the bed, 'too much bloody whiskey again' he thought. He could sense Tina next to him and wracked his brain for memories of the night before, did he do anything wrong, did he streak, drop his trousers; end up in a fight, who knows? But when Tina wakes up I'm sure she will remind me of what a twat I have been, he thought to himself. He looked across at Tina, she laid there, she was quiet and looked like she was catching fly's with a mouth as wide as the Dartford Tunnel, blimey she was pissed too, Sean thought, well that gets me out of the dog house if she was pissed too. Sean eventually managed to haul himself out of bed and headed for the toilet for the piss he desperately needed; it seemed to go on for a lifetime, when he heard Tina from the bedroom.

'Get me some pain killers from the cupboard will you babe' she said.

'Why you got hangover love', he replied, 'you should have because you were as drunk as a Scotsman last night.'

All Sean heard was a groan but realised then he had got away with it, Tina was more pissed than him last night, magic, he thought.

'No problem love, tablets and water coming up.'

Sean and Tina lay in bed, Tina still lying on her side, wishing her pain away. Sean was sipping on his coffee and thinking about the day before, he looked out of the window, the sky was grey with dark clouds moving across the skyline and rain was falling hard against the window pane, it made a comforting sound even though it normally brought misery to the streets of London. Sean watched the rain for a while and thought of the day before, his childhood, his friendship with Taylor, Tina laying next to him and how everything was taken away from everyone he loves. He watched droplets of rain gradually fall down the windowpane and settle into a pool of water on the windowsill before spilling onwards to the ground below. He looked again into the sky, a rainbow had started to form, it curved across from one side of the window to the other, he wondered if he followed it would he ever find the start or the end and would there be that famous pot of gold. It was the day after the funeral and a Saturday, he wasn't going anywhere, he was just going to lie in, probably all day and basically do fuck all. Maybe wait for Tina to liven up and have a shag, he didn't know what he wanted, his brain was searching for something and he kept thinking about the so called missing money, what Pete Murray said and the tall man with his threats. He had anger inside of him and questions he needed answering, but he didn't know how or where to start. He would have that meeting with Pete, he thought, that might clear my head.

Chapter 17

Pete Murray was sitting relaxing in his lounge, and thinking about the funeral the day before. He was reflecting what had happened and was trying to piece together the future and how he will handle any conversation with Sean, when and if it would ever happen. It was then that the phone started to ring; he answered it after reaching over to turn the television down.

'Hello Pete Murray', he said.

'Hi Pete how you doing it's Sean.'

'Hi Sean I'm fine thanks' good to hear from you after the funeral, it was a sad day, how are you doing.'

'I'm Ok Pete, I knew it would happen and probably everyone else did too, you know, how I would feel after, it just seems strange without Taylor around.'

'I suppose a bit like losing your right arm Sean.'

'Yeah you could say that Pete, he was a good friend for a long time and we did everything together.'

There was silence for a while, Pete was waiting to find out what the actual call was about, and he had an inkling of what it was but needed Sean to pull the strings, or at least be responsible for his decisions. Sean spoke first.

'Pete, what you said at the funeral yesterday, you know about fight fire with fire, cut to the chase Pete, what did you actually mean?'

'Why don't you come and see me Sean, we can have a drink a natter about old times, when can you get here?'

'Tomorrow's Sunday, what you up to tomorrow Pete, tomorrow's a good day for me as long as Tina lets me out.'

'Bring her along Sean.'

'But I thought we would want to discuss things Pete, you know, fight fire with fire.'

'Tina is a very capable girl Sean when she wants to be, she wouldn't want you gallivanting around without her now she has lost her brother. It will be a general chat Sean, no decisions will be made, if you want to fight fire you will need an extinguisher, I just maybe be able to help. Taylor was like family to me, let's meet tomorrow, seems ages since I last had a roast dinner in the pub, how about the pub by Clapham North Station, around one o'clock.'

'Ok Pete, I tell you what I will pick you up.'

'No it's ok Sean I will get a bus, you know I don't want to put on anyone, see you there at one.'

With that the phone went dead like it was the end of the world, apart from the sound of the dead tone on the phone. Sean placed the phone back down on the receiver, stood by the window and looked out, he was wondering if this was one of those moments in everyone's life where you get to a junction in a road, and if you turn left, that happens, and if you turn right this happens? The cars were going by on the road outside and the rain, the fucking rain started to fall again', he said to himself as he watched it fall outside his window. He longed for the sunshine again and the long summer days, he continued to watch the traffic outside, everybody looked glum, and then the car horns started. Sean followed the sound out of his window, he could see a man trying to undo his window, he could see the rage in his face and knew any minute now he would be successful in opening his window and a stream of obscenities would erupt in the morning air, and then it happened as expected. Sean smiled with his correct assumption of the future. The traffic moved on but the rain prevailed, Sean left the window and turned on the radio, the band Mud was playing Tiger Feet, what a shit song, he said to himself aloud, how the fuck could that get in the charts, do they not know this is the seventies, not the fucking fifties, he much preferred T Rex, Deep Purple and Led Zeppelin, 'I'm a bit of a rocker at heart, I must update my album collection, he thought.

Chapter 18

The pub was gloomy in the background of the afternoon grey skies due to streetlights on the fringes of the housing estate. The typical English south London pub had an aura about it, locals frequented it and the odd stragglers that entered it's interior struggled with the austere atmosphere that would cut any hardened male ego immediately. It was friendly enough, although it had it's volcanic feel to it that at any time it could erupt and swallow everyone one in it's path and often it would unless it was managed by experience bar staff and management. It had a reputation that everything could be purchased within it's walls, it was often said if you wanted to buy an elephant painted pink with football boots on, you would find someone in this pub that could get it for you.

Pete Murray walked along the pavements passing several shops after getting off the bus, he pulled his coat in tighter to keep in the warmth and protect himself from the unexpected wind. He passed the chip shop next door to the pub, which made him feel hungry from the smells exiting it's doors and it made him look even more forward to his sunday dinner. His thoughts drifted to the clientele within the pub, he knew he was respected in the area even though his past career made him vulnerable but he still felt a little nervous as he entered into the saloon bar. Pete noticed the heads turn as he entered, but the odd nod from the locals made him relax a little more, he moved closer to the bar undid the buttons on his coat and started to remove his scarf.

'Hi Pete' said the barman.

'Hi', said Pete as he struggled to remember the young man's name and internally cursed his age and his reduced memory.

'How are you', he said, 'can you get me a double Bells whiskey and ice please?'

'No problem Pete', replied the barman as he turned to retrieve a whiskey glass and continued on with his task.

Pete turned to scan and look around the pub and carried out the odd nod to faces he knew, names unremembered but faces he knew. Some, he thought to himself, he may have even nicked at some point in his career. Pete heard the glass hit the table and started to fumble in his pocket for the right coinage.

'It's Ok Pete, said the barman, Sean has paid for your drink already, he's in the other bar with Tina.'

'Thanks' said Pete and again cursed himself for not remembering the barman's name as he turned away from the bar.

He entered the public bar, more heads looked up, 'no nods this time', he thought to himself. He noticed two younger men playing pool and an older couple sitting on a round table tucking into what looked like their roast dinner, they too looked up at Pete, he noticed a smile from the old lady, he smiled back, but the man continued to survey him. Pete sat down next to Sean and Tina.

'You do know you're the only ex copper that can walk into this pub don't you Pete' said Sean.

'I'm not sure if that's a privilege or a life sentence', Pete replied.

'It's a privilege Pete, they know you're an ex copper but you were a fair one, you were fair to them and their sons, you nicked scum, they don't like scum either', but there's probably someone in here that still might want to smash your face in' Sean said with a smile. Pete smiled too; Tina sipped on her white wine, still worried about the oncoming conversation. All three heads turned as a pool ball went flying across the floor followed by the eruption of laughter.

'What kind of fucking shot was that' said one of the youngsters, followed by 'bollocks' from the other.

'Your fucking shit at this game jimmy.'

'Go fuck yourself and go and get me another pint you twat.'

'Bollocks, it's your round you cock sucker.'

A man walked into the bar, again Sean Tina and Pete turned to the new figure entering the bar. An Irish accent boomed into the room.

'Jimmy, shut the fuck up! said the new figure in the room, 'finish your game and let these nice people eat their meals in peace.'

'But dad', replied one of the youngsters.

'Jimmy', replied the man with a stern look on his face, a face that the boy knew he shouldn't mess with.

Jimmy went silent, the new face in the room looked around and nodded at Pete, Sean and Tina and then at the old couple and left the bar. Jimmy and his friend put the cues down on the pool table, picked up their drinks and left the bar giving a curious look at the table to their left where Sean Pete and Tina sat.

'This pub never changes Pete; said Sean, 'what the fuck did you want to meet here for.'

'It has nice roast dinners, he replied, 'and besides sometimes I still need to feel alive', Pete Turned to Tina, 'you're looking as gorgeous as ever Tina.'

'Thanks Pete', she said.

'Now shall we eat you two, I'm starving.'

The three of them quickly decided that a roast dinner was the best order of the day; Sean ordered at the bar and settled back down with Pete and Tina who were busy reminiscing about the old days. General chat was discussed, as well as the funeral and some thoughts about Taylor before the dinners were delivered, they sat for a while, ate their food and consumed a few more drinks before Pete thought it was a good time to bring up what he thought the three of them were really there for.

'Taylor was a good boy Sean, he said, he shouldn't have died the way he did, there are some bad men out there, and they are not the same as you and me. They don't have respect or give a fuck for the normal average Joe public that wants to get on with their lives with no hassle. Pete takes another swig of his whiskey and Sean and Tina can see the vein on his temple start to throb, not a good sign they thought.

'These men just want to make money', Pete continued, 'and they don't give a shit who they harm in the process, they are a new breed of animal that needs removing, but all the bureaucracy around the police force and human fucking rights is making it hard for the police to nail these bastards. People like you and me, my family, your family and your children shouldn't have to put up with the scum that is starting to get one over on the law. Johnny Saunders is one of those scum that should be put in a cell with a hungry dog, but we could never do that without sufficient fucking evidence.'

Pete took another swig of his whiskey, leaned back in his chair and looked across at Sean & Tina. Sean could still see the vein in Pete's temple throbbing, the way it did whenever Pete was angry, he remembered the times he and Taylor shook in fear whenever they saw Pete's vein throb that way.

'You seem angry Pete', he said.

'I am angry Sean; those fuckers killed one of us, the respected people of this community, someone who looked after my mum on the estate when I was out nicking scum and chastising future criminals, and I can't do anything about it, I'm too old and decrepit.'

Pete Murray leant back in his chair, pulled out a cigarette lit it, took a long drag and continued.

'But then I thought about it, maybe I can do something about it, maybe I still have something I can use to eradicate these cockroaches that killed Taylor, maybe I can use my experience and my contacts during my time as a policeman.'

Sean and Tina still sat there looking at Pete, they didn't speak, the pub was quieter, the older couple had left the bar after finishing their meal, and the bar staff were busy in the saloon bar serving drinks to the locals. The bar became an eerie silence, before Sean finally spoke.

'What do you mean Pete?'

'There are people still in the police force that feel the same way I do, they hate the scum that are destroying London, and they want to get rid of them too especially Johnny Saunders and his gang of illegitimate thugs'. They can't prove he did it but they know he did, they just can't make anything stick on him, and the only way to ensure of his demise is to get down to his level.'

Pete took another long drag on his fag.

'And that's where you come in Sean, that's if you want to get revenge on the people that took your friend away.'

Tina spoke for the first time, 'What Pete, you want Sean to deal with Johnny Saunders and his gang on his own, are you mad, what kind of stupid scheme are you on about, this could get him killed, this is bloody crazy, what fucking planet are you on!'

'Tina, he won't be on his own', he replied, 'you're going to help him, and so am I, I'm going to give you all the details and information you need to kill those fucking bastards.'

'Sean take that fucking whiskey off him', she said, 'he's bloody pissed.'

Sean never spoke, it was as if he was taking it all in, he took a swig of beer from his glass and shuffled around a bit in his chair like a nervous boy who was just about to enter the dentist chair.

'Sean' Tina was looking at him with her eyes wide in a baffled confused look.

Sean looked across at Pete.

'And how will you do that Pete, how will you help, and secondly, why is Tina involved', he said.

'Sean', again Tina yelled as if she was in a dream and not comprehending what was happening. Sean ignored her and continued to focus on Pete Murray's face searching for the next answers.

'As I said Sean I have experience as well as some old friends in the force that can be very useful to us, they can provide us with details, addresses, locations, names, numbers, contacts and maybe some form of protection if we need it. And Tina, well she was there, she was there when they killed Taylor, she heard it, like you did Sean, what they did to him and you both couldn't do anything about it without risking your own lives.' It's a bit like me, bloody frustrating not being able to take the Fuckers down, get them to court and then they walk free because we forget to have a search warrant or forgot to sign a bit of fucking paper or some bollocks.'

'Us, what do you mean us, we aren't the fucking mafia Pete, this is me and Tina you are talking to not Bonny and fucking Clyde, and yes we were there and it still hurts me that I was not able to jump down like superman and take them all out and save Taylor!'

Sean looked around the pub, he realized he was raising his voice, he felt Tina's hand on his leg and then the squeeze, the reassuring squeeze that she knew how he felt.

'What if you had the opportunity to be superman and take them out', Pete Said.

'What if I did all the leg work, what if I got the details and you just had to turn up and be superman.'

'You want me, no wait a minute; you want me and Tina, Superman and Bloody Wonder Woman to kill Johnny Saunders and his gang.'

Pete took another drag on his fag, leaned forward in his chair and flicked ash into the ashtray.

'Yeah.'

Again silence, Sean turned away from Pete and looked at Tina.

'Is he for real, I think you're right Tina, we need to take that bloody whiskey off him.'

'He may have a point Sean.'

'What, what you on about, do you know what he is asking us to do, you were going ape shit about it a minute ago, now you think this may be a good idea, shall I take your bloody drink away too?'

'He may have a point Sean, be honest, we have thought about getting revenge but it never became reality because we didn't have the means or the bottle to carry it out, it just hovered in the air. Maybe Pete can give us that opportunity, if we can do this safely with Pete's support and guidance, maybe it won't be so bad. I would get a kick out of getting those bastards back, wouldn't you?'

Again silence, Sean's chin was nearly touching the floor, Tina leaned across, softly put her hand under his chin and lifted it to close his mouth.

'And that's why I asked you to bring Tina along Sean', said Pete.

Sean turned and looked back at Pete, 'you're both fucking pissed.'

'My round I think' said Pete, 'we have more things to discuss' and he got up and wandered back towards the bar, leaving Sean and Tina staring at each other, sitting at the table in an empty bar.

Chapter 19

Pete Murray looked across the River Thames; he felt the slight wind on his face as he watched the boats travel up and down the choppy waters in and out of London. Chelsea Bridge was to his left and Battersea Bridge to his right, he looked across at Battersea Park, it was quiet and too early for people to be wandering around he thought to himself. He pulled his scarf up higher around his neck, it was a cool morning and he felt the wind whistle down his neck. He continued to survey the boats, the small and the large boats all carrying different cargo, which was mostly carrying coal, timber and the odd boat full of crap and rubbish. He noticed Chelsea Bridge to his left was starting to get busier with traffic when he felt the presence of someone behind him.

'Morning Pete', he heard and turned to see his friend he had come to meet standing there.

'Morning George, you gave me a start creeping up on me like that.'

'Old habit's die hard Pete, nice to see you, it's been a long time, I was worried when you called me, but pleased at the same time.'

'So how are you George?' said Pete.

'As well as can be expected, what with me bad back and losing my hair.'

'We are all getting old George, it comes with the passage of time and all that running after robbers has shot my knees to pieces.'

'Tell me about it Pete, but you're looking well mate.'

The two men stood there with their coat collars pulled up around their necks and their hands stuffed deep inside their pockets. The early morning chill that came off the river made them feel the need to keep the cold away.

George Patterson was a friend of Pete's from the force and was still serving with the police; he wore a trilby hat that made him look like he'd come straight out of the forties. Pete knew he was a good friend and one that could be trusted and that's why he asked for this meeting, if anyone can get the information he needed it was George Patterson.

'I'm sorry to hear about what happened Pete, you know, about Taylor Docherty, I know you were close to him.'

'I was George, he was a good kid, did you manage to find anything out for me George?'

'Yes,' said George, 'a couple of things, you know we have a few people on the inside and undercover, well it turns out Johnny Saunders lost some money and someone stitched him up, and we think your boy got mixed up in it somehow. We think it was someone he knows, or one of his enemies, it's a bit sketchy at the moment but someone close to him would have known his deals. Rumour has it he had some money on route from Essex, from a drugs deal or for a drugs deal and the courier was Tony Clay. Then a routine police traffic vehicle stop and search ended up with a car chase and this Tony Clay was hauled out the side of the moving car and the police car ended up running over his head, poor bastard, they couldn't avoid it apparently, according to the officers involved. It appears Tony Clay was tortured before hand and we spoilt the fun by turning up before they killed him. We still have no idea who was driving the car or who tortured him.'

Pete Murray continued to listen, he was pleased his friend was there, he was pleased that he had gone out of his way to help him, but so far, he had nothing, he needed to hear more.

'Go on George', said Pete, while pulling his coat further around his neck.

'Johnny Saunders is still looking for his money and he is pretty pissed off according to our sources. As I said it looks like Taylor was caught up in it and Saunders's anger was taken out on him at Tony Clays warehouse'. We have nothing to go on but it has all the hallmarks of Saunders, we have two murders, your boy and Tony Clay and my boss is pissed off that we are still not breaking any ground, Saunders and his mob have come up with good alibis as usual.'

'You've questioned them?' Said Pete.

'We have Pete, but we have been digging around for evidence and come up with nothing so far, we have checked their alibis, they all look kosher but they've probably paid people off for the alibis or scared the shit out of them to stop them talking.'

Again there was silence while Pete took in the detail, some office workers walked by so they waited until they were far enough away so as to not be heard.

'Did you get me the details I asked for George?'

'I did Pete but it wasn't easy, questions were being asked, what do you need to copy these files for etc., but I'm owed favours Pete, so people just looked the other way.'

'Then I owe you George.'

'You owe me fuck all Pete, we go back a long way.'

George Patterson looked around to see if anyone was nearby, and the cold wind caught his face, satisfied he reached into his coat pocket and pulled out an envelope, he handed the envelope to Pete, who took it and slid it into his inside coat pocket.

'I really appreciate this George, you got time to chew the fat, just for a bit, for old time's sake.'

'For a bit Pete, but then I have to get back, duty calls and all that bollocks.'

They both sat down on a bench overlooking the river and discussed the past, all the memories came back for Pete and it made him smile for a while. He had a long police career and George was part of that for a considerable time, they shared thoughts, experiences and history, and it was good to relive those moments for a brief period.

'One thing I need you to try and set up for me George' said Pete

'What's that?' replied George with a concerned look on his face.

136

'A safe house, they are going to need a safe house, if Saunders is looking for his money, he's also going to be looking for Sean Farrow.'

'Fuck me Pete your not asking for much are you, how the fuck am I going to swing that one, you know the paperwork involved in that, it has to be signed off, neighbours have to be checked out, financial costs, fucking hell that isn't going to be easy.'

'I know George, what can you do.'

There was a silence between the two, Pete was looking across the river and George Paterson was staring at Pete. George looked away and then he also looked across the river, he was thinking in his head, the work involved, the secrecy, the people he would have to convince and influence to pull it off, he knew it would be hard, unless he thought, unless they could come to a compromise, he turned to Pete.

'If I can pull it off Pete, they would have to move out at very short notice if I needed it, no fucking around, none of this 'just a few more days bollocks, as soon as I make contact they get the fuck out of there as I will only have a couple of hours notice that someone else needs the safe house.'

'You're a fucking diamond George, I knew you would come up trumps.'

'A fucking mug Pete, a fucking mug is what I am. I will be in contact soon when I've sorted it, but don't get them measuring up fucking curtains before I fucking say so.'

Pete laughed as they got up from the riverside bench and said their goodbyes with a firm handshake. As he watched George leave, Pete touched his inside coat pocket before he moved off to make sure he still had the envelope, he decided to leave it there and review it later where he could digest the information with a whiskey or two. He felt the wind drop and then the air change from a morning chill to a comfortable warmth; he pulled his collar back down from his neck and watched the boats on the river one more time, as he did he also noticed joggers starting to appear across the river in Battersea Park, what the fuck is all that about, he thought to himself. He turned his back on the park joggers and the river wall and headed back towards Chelsea Bridge where he needed to get his bus back home.

When Pete arrived home he poured himself, what he thought was his first whiskey, and the one that would warm him up from his morning meeting with George. He sat in his room and couldn't decide if it was too early or not, he looked at the glass he had just poured, then he looked at the clock on the wall, and then over at the picture of his late wife Fiona on the side cabinet. He knew she would not approve, so he put the glass of whiskey to one side. The envelope that he got from George was sitting on the coffee table in front of him, he lent forward and picked it up and slid the letter-opening blade through the glued edges at the top. He peered inside and he could see there was about eight or nine pages inside and he slowly pulled them out of the envelope. They were all type written and on each corner there were photographs attached by a paper clip. He surveyed them for a few seconds and looked back down at the whiskey, he picked it up and gulped it's contents feeling it warm him up inside immediately, and instantly he could sense the disagreement from the photograph on the side cabinet.

He picked up the top two pages and surveyed them; there was information on both sheets about Johnny Saunders and a photograph of him in the top right hand corner. The pages contained, names, addresses, date of birth, criminal records, family history, associates and any other information required to be able to put surveillance out on someone. It even included, false names they have used, addresses they frequent, and favourite restaurants and bars and girlfriends they have and visit. All of the other sheets were similar all with the same detailed information, all with photographs, some were mug shots and some you can see had been taken from surveillance. Scum, Pete thought to himself, dirty scum, with no care about society or people, there just in this world to make it best for them, dirty fucking scum. Pete put the papers down and poured himself another whiskey and again gulped the contents down. Christ, he said to himself, someone or some department has been watching these bastards. He soon realised to himself that he doesn't care where the information came from, but there was enough detail here to make things a lot easier for his plans.

For the next four hours Pete surveyed all the paperwork and made his own notes on separate sheets. He realised he had already come to the decision that he would hang on to the information and manage the way forward. It would be his choosing how the operation of pay back for Taylor's murder would go and he wanted to be part of it. He was fed up with the new policing methods that were now becoming part of the police procedures, all based on peoples rights shit and beside, he thought to himself; he's not a copper anymore. He would meet Sean Farrow and hand over the first and then control the situation, it was best this way to protect Sean, he could also ensure colleagues in his past that felt the same as him could protect or turn a blind eye. He had decided on the first victim, it would be a soft target first, less aggressive, easier to find and less of a worry for Johnny Saunders to get suspicious about, and if successful it would give Sean more confidence for the next. Pete looked down at the paperwork in front of him again and the photograph in the top right hand corner, he had decided Stan Smith would be the first victim and then he poured himself another whiskey.

Chapter 20

The London streets were different tonight Sean thought, people were hanging around having conversations while drinking and smoking outside public houses. It had been a warm day and people were still enjoying the late evening sunshine, it seemed to cast a spell over the entire population, he looked across at Tina, except Tina he thought, she was away with the fairies in her own world, she looked stressed but in a calm way.

'You ok babe?' he said.

She looked up at Sean.

'Yes, just fucking scared that's all, never killed anyone before.'

'Me too, I mean scared, and never killed anyone either, you want to back out?'

'Yes, but no, yes because I'm shitting myself and no because he's a cunt and needs to die.'

'It's the angel, devil thing,' Sean said.

'What do you mean?'

'Devils and angels on our shoulders, the devil is saying do something bad and the angel is saying do something good.'

'The devil's winning at the moment, but the angel keeps butting in,' she replied.

They sat in silence for a moment, until Sean spoke.

'They made you piss your knickers in fright, they tortured your brother, we heard it all and I couldn't do fuck all about it, the guilt rips me apart every minute of the day, I need payback to get rid of my demons and the devil on my shoulders is going to help me.'

Again they sat in silence while driving through the city streets; it was eleven twenty at night, chucking out time from the pubs. They had a list of three pubs that Pete Murray had given to them, pubs that Stan Smith frequented and they were slowly driving from pub to pub in hope of finding their first target. For three nights they had planned it, not much of a plan, but they had a plan, find him, follow him and when he was alone Sean would smack him across the head with a cosh as hard as possible, he was a big fucker so the first hit had to be hard and on target. Tina would then dowse him with the petrol and Sean would throw the match and then run like fuck. They had rehearsed it in the living room with a bucket, the cosh, a bucket full of water and a box of matches, Sean would swing the bat, Tina would open the can and pour the water into the bucket, Sean would light a match and drop it into the bucket of water. It seemed to work ok; they increased in speed and became confident the more they did it; they got it down to five seconds, five seconds to kill the bastard. But Sean remembers his unsuccessful attempt trying to persuade Tina not to join him, he could do it on his own he told her, but she was adamant she would be there and part of the plan. Sean looked across at Tina and wished he had won the argument by not allowing her to take part, he squeezed her hand, and it was sweaty.

'I have demons too Sean' she said.

Sean remained silent and continued driving slowly down through Streatham High Road he then took the next junction towards the last pub of the evening, in Clapham. The evening became darker, there was no moon and people were starting to leave the pubs on the high streets and gather around taxi ranks or move onto the nightclub in the high street. Sean turned into the South Circular road, working his way slowly towards the pub on the junction of the Avenue before slowly driving past the pub on his right.

'There!' Tina shouted out as Sean moved slowly along the road.

'Where?' he replied.

'Outside the pub, four men drinking and smoking on the benches behind the large pot plants.'

Sean looked across towards where Tina was indicating and then into his rear view mirror and pulled into a side street opposite the pub.

'Where' he replied again, looking out towards the pub.

'To the right of the entrance behind the pot plants', she replied.

'How do you know it's him?'

'I don't. It's just intuition,' she replied.

'We have to be sure; we don't want to bash some poor Tom, Dick or Harry's brains out on fucking intuition Tina.'

'Fuck off Sean, just wait here a minute! she shouted.

Sean looked across; he could make out four men laughing, smoking and drinking but could not make out their faces.

'We're too far' he said.

'Just wait here, we need to make sure but from a safe distance.'

They sat and waited, the longer they waited the more lonesome and scared they got. To calm her nerves Tina had drank a bottle of wine before they left the house, but Sean drank nothing, he wanted to remain in control, he was calm, but like Tina, he was shitting himself, but he had to be strong for her.

'One man's getting up' Tina said.

One man among the group was rising, they both watched the situation change, as he leaned across and started to shake the other men's hands and pat one of the men on the back. He walked away from them leaving laughter behind and waving his hand in the air, he started to cross the road directly in front of Sean and Tina's car.

'Fuck Sean he's heading this way,' Tina yelped with fear in her voice.

Sean looked across and could see the man swaying as he walked, clearly from the alcohol he had consumed, but he was still stable enough to cause concern, Sean thought. He was walking directly towards the street they were parked in, when he was about ten feet away, Sean grabbed Tina and kissed her full on the mouth, inserting his tongue like some wanton teenager so that their faces were obscured, Tina understood and returned the kiss praying the man would walk by uninterested, until.

Bang! The man was banging on the window on the drivers door where Sean sat, Tina's instant reaction was to pull away from Sean and look up in fright.

'Give her one for me mate!' the man shouted right by the window, he laughed and got closer to the window, he shouted again, 'give her one for me!' he looked at Tina, who could see the mans laugh fade to a realisation that he may have recognised her. He laughed again, moved away from the window and started to walk and stagger up the road.

'He fucking recognised me Sean, he fucking saw me', she said.

Sean quickly looked across the road, the three men were all looking over, they looked like they understood what had happened and were laughing at their friend's antics. Sean then looked behind him; the man was swaying up the road still, hopefully on his way home.

'Was it him?' Sean said.

'No, but he recognised me I'm sure.'

Sean looked behind him again, the man was gone, he didn't back up, he couldn't have recognised Tina; he would be still here asking them questions.

'What do we do now Sean?'

'We wait', he replied, 'for all they know we are just a couple of gropers, not someone who's just about to burn their balls off.'

Sean looked back again, definitely gone, he thought.

They waited for a further twenty minutes when a car pulled up beside the men, a man got out and spoke with them, the three men stood up and started walking towards the car. Sean and Tina watched as the last man stopped himself from getting in the car, looked left and right down the road, he leaned back into the car as if talking to one of the men inside the car. He exited the car slamming the door behind him and the car pulled away. The man left on the pavement could be clearly seen now, the street lamplight shone directly on his face and broad shoulders.

'It's him isn't it Sean.'

'Yes,' said Sean.

'Oh shit Sean, yes, it's on.'

The man stood on the pavement as they watched; he looked up the road again looking left and right, and then looked at his wristwatch.

'Stick to the plan Tina and we will be ok,' said Sean, 'it would be best if he went right, there's a couple of alleyways that way and he may cut across the park, if he goes left we may need to abandon it.'

They watched the man, he still pondered as if not sure which way to go.

'Go right you fucker go right', Sean said in his head.

The man swayed, looked again at his watch and turned right.

'Bingo' said Sean.

'Oh fuck,' said Tina, 'I was secretly hoping he would go left.'

'Stick to the plan Tina, stick to the plan', he replied.

Tina got out of the car carrying her bag with her, as rehearsed she crossed the road and went up the side of the pub into the estate and circled around the back of the shops, she knew she needed to get in front of Smith. Tina pulled into a shop doorway and slipped her trainers off threw them into her bag and pulled out her fuck me shoes and put them on, then she pulled out a blond wig, lit a cigarette and slid slowly out of the doorway walking towards Smith who was about one hundred yards away. It's funny she thought as she walked slowly towards him, all her fears had gone, pure rage was running through her body, she wanted revenge and she was walking towards it right now.

Sean got out of the car, he pulled the cosh and knife from out of the bag and tucked it down his trousers and shut the boot. He turned to the right and crossed the road so he was about one hundred yards behind him, he looked up, Smith was still swaying but still ok on his feet, he stopped again and looked at his watch, he turned, and he looked at Sean, he continued to look at him for a short period but then turned on his feet and carried on his way.

Tina could see Smith getting closer, she put her best prostitute walk on as the gap between them shortened, Tina spotted Sean far behind, and she saw that Smith had spotted Sean, the plan was already fading. Tina continued to walk, he must fall for it, he likes prostitutes, Pete said, and he's known for it, it's his weakness. Tina stopped by a shop doorway; she took a long puff on her cigarette, not because she needed to, but to assist with her disguise, because he was now very near, near enough to touch.

'You looking for business darling?' she said as she took another puff on her cigarette.

Stan Smith stopped; he looked Tina up and down.,

'How much?' he replied.

'All depends what you're looking for?'

'Full sex?'

'Full sex is fifty quid', she replied.

'I'm a copper thirty quid or you're nicked.'

'You aren't any copper', I can smell them a mile away, and you don't smell like no pig' she smiled.

'It's now twenty quid then or your fucking nicked.'

'Alright, alright, thirty quid full sex, fucking pig, I've got kids to feed, follow me'

Stan Smith looked behind him, the man he had noticed had gone, where the fuck did he go to, he thought to himself.

Tina looked at him, 'You coming or what!' she shouted.

He turned back round and she escorted him to a nearby alley, it was dark depressing and smelt of piss, on entering the alley, Smith looked back once more.

'Thirty quid up front before I take my knickers off', she said, looking at him.

Stan Smith laughed and passed her the thirty quid after getting it out of his wallet.

'You better be worth it whore', he said, 'take your knickers off and bend over that dustbin.'

Tina started to lift her skirt, she started to remove her knickers when she saw the dark shadow of Sean approaching up the alleyway, she felt relieved but also got an over powering feeling through her body like a rush of adrenalin that something exciting and dangerous was about to happen.

The man started to manhandle her; he stunk of beer, fags and stale breath, and just as his hand groped at her between her legs, Sean released the first blow with the steel cosh to Smiths skull. Tina heard the metal hit bone and Smith let out a cry and fell to the floor pulling Tina down with him and landing on top of her and across her legs, with her bag falling away to the side. Fuck, Sean thought, this is not going to plan, he watched as Tina tried to pull away from under Smith, he started to hit him again and again but the giant of the man meant he was just dazed, he was trying to get up and kept falling back down onto Tina as Sean could only hit soft tissue. Sean went for his knife it was not there, so he hit again with the cosh. Smith was trying hard to protect his head he was dazed but not fully down, Sean was panicking, Tina was screaming 'hit him, hit him' Smith was recovering, Sean could see his strength returning as well as the affects of alcohol leaving him due to his struggle for life.

'Cunts, cunts' Smith was screaming, 'I'll fucking kill you, you cunts.'

Sean continued to bash away with the cosh but was starting to panic, run he thought to himself, but realised he couldn't run, Tina's was trapped, it's not going to plan, he thought, it's not going to plan, fuck, what happened to the planned five seconds, fuck, Sean is screaming in his head. It was a mess, a frenzy, Tina was still trying to pull herself free, and her bag was to one side, Sean was bashing away at soft tissue again and Smith was gaining the momentum, Sean could see him reaching into his pocket, it was all in slow motion. Fuck thought Sean, as he saw steel shining in the light from the street light, he knew what that meant, a knife, he has a knife, he then saw it swish across and his eyes followed the light until he saw it embed itself into his leg. The pain was instant and excruciating and Sean fell instantly to the floor like a blow from a steam train.

'Fuck Tina he's stabbed me!' he shouted, as he managed to pull himself onto his rear and backed away to a wall and lay against it, breathing hard. Sean was in shock, he could feel it deep inside as he looked down at the knife sticking out of his leg, but in slow motion again, he could see Tina rising from underneath the man.

Tina was free, she managed to pull herself free when she saw the man stab Sean who she could see was now leaning against the wall looking at the knife in his leg. Tina looked towards Smith who was now getting to his feet, he was getting back in control and as she moved forward she was instantly punched by him knocking her sideways and back down.

'You bastards are going to die for this', she heard, 'you think you can mug me you fuckers.'

The man was now walking towards Sean with an evil grin on his face, Sean knew this was it, the end, he had no more power he was helpless. The man was now leaning over Sean, the first punch caught Sean in the jaw, the second one Sean managed to stop the blow with his arms, all Sean could think of was what a complete fuck up, and it never went to plan at all, now I'm fucked and can't protect Tina. It was then Sean felt a searing pain in his leg, Tina had pulled the knife out which made him scream in agony, he looked up to see the mans face, and within a second he saw Tina lift the blade and thrust it into Smiths neck from the side, his face showed it, he fell back away from Sean, blood was squirting from his neck, and he was trying to hold it back but the pressure was too much, it was pouring out the side of his neck out of the gaps in his hands, and to Sean it was all still in slow motion. Sean was beaten, he was in pain and breathing heavy from the initial fight and he was still leaning against the wall, stabbed, punched and dazed. He watched as Tina dropped the knife and ran to her bag, she then pulled out the petrol can, he saw her undo the lid and start dowsing Smith with the fuel, she was screaming something at Sean, he can see her mouth opening but nothing was coming out, what is she saying, he could not understand what she was shouting, until noise and stability returned to his ears.

'The matches, where the fuck are the matches!' he heard her shouting.

Sean now realised what she was shouting put his hand in his pocket and pulled out the matches, now covered in blood from his wound, he handed them to Tina, she struck one, it did not light, she struck another, this also did not light, Smith was still holding onto his neck, he knew the wound was fatal and was trying to get up off the floor again, she struck the third match, it lit, Tina threw the match as he was rising, the alley way lit up like a erupting volcano, as Smith was alight screaming, Sean could feel the heat from where he was leaning against the wall. Smith was still trying to get up, he was trying to get to Tina, but eventually fell back down at her feet in flames. Tina ran to Sean, 'we need to get away' she started to pick Sean up who was dazed but needed support to stand; she took him to the entrance of the alleyway.

'Wait here, keys, where's the keys Sean', she shouted.

'Right pocket', he replied.

Tina grabbed the keys from Sean's pocket, 'Wait here I'm going for the car', she said.

Within seconds she was gone while Sean waited at the alleyway. He turned and could see the man lying on the floor still burning, he could smell burnt flesh and hair.

'That ones for Taylor you cunt!' he managed to say in a laboured shout.

Tina returned, picked up Sean, dragged him to the car and opened the rear door, Sean fell into the back seat, she returned to the alleyway and picked up anything left behind including her knickers and the knife, got back in the car and pulled away.

'You ok', she shouted at Sean, 'hold tight onto the wound, use your sweat shirt as a tourniquet.'

Sean pulled his sweatshirt off and tied the arms around his leg and pulled tight to help stop the bleeding.

'I'm ok', he said, 'drive normally we don't want to attract attention, I think it's stopped bleeding but it hurts like fuck.'

'Lay down, keep your leg in the air', she replied.

'What the fuck happened there that never went to plan did it, I'm hurting everywhere, are you ok, are you ok' he repeated.

'Exhilarated' she said, 'but my jaw hurts.'

Tina continued driving at normal speed until they reached home, Sean was speaking fast as if in shock.

'We need to get rid of the car, we need to burn it, I have contacts, my god how many times did you stab that fucker, he wouldn't go down.'

They got to the safe house; drove the car into the garage and Tina helped Sean out of the car and into the flat. She undressed Sean, cleaned and dressed his wound the best she could, after both deciding the hospital was not a good option.

'It went through the side of your thigh' she said 'and out the other side, looks like it just went through the muscle no major arteries, you will live but it will hurt for a while.'

Tina washed Sean down and then had a shower, when she came into the bedroom Sean was laying in bed, she got in beside him and caressed his body, stroking him all over and kissed his body. Sean was surprised when she got on top of him and rode him until she came; then she laid down beside him and fell asleep. Sean could not sleep with the pain but also the smell of burning hair and flesh still in his nostrils. He lay there thinking, kill one was done, it didn't go to plan, so I must make sure kill two goes better.

Chapter 21

Johnny Saunders sat in his garden, he was relaxing and reading the morning papers, he was in a calm mood, but was reflecting on his current situation. The situation that he knew he needed to take control of again, Johnny was aware that once you start an empire the hardest thing is maintaining control. You have to get respect, above all from those around you, your enemies that want to take you down at every opportunity; and he recognized that as his best trait. There is also those that work for you, he thought, those that need to be controlled with fear or money, in which Johnny Saunders knew he had both, money to control the people, his people, and the corrupt do gooders, and he also knew he had fear, and as long as he paid his people well, he could control the fear. He lit a cigar, his first of the morning; he drank some coffee, and surveyed the papers.

'Body of local man found in a warehouse, beaten to death and appears to be related to another London gangland killing'. Johnny continued to read, it was an old newspaper article, but he liked to keep this one, because it troubled him, it troubled him because he still hadn't found his money, and he still hadn't found Sean Farrow. It was starting to grate on him, he was worried about the money, although it was a lot of money, but someone was taking the piss out of him and he didn't like it, he knew he needed to take back control or his rivals would see him as being soft. At first he didn't notice the doorbell as he was too engrossed in his thoughts, and then he heard it again and wondered why Isabel was not getting herself to the front door as quickly as she should do.

'Isabel, get the fucking door will ya!' he shouted.

He heard the scurrying of feet as the doorbell went again; there was a pause when Isabel the maid eventually came into the garden.

'There's a gentleman to see you Johnny.'

'And who might that be Isabel?'

'The one with the big scar across his face, the one I don't like, mind you I don't like any of your visitors', Isabel said.

'He's not a gentleman Isabel, but you can show him through.'

Johnny Saunders thought of the news he had been expecting, the news that Ray Flynn may have brought all this way to him, the news that they have either found Sean Farrow or his money. He looked to the sky and followed a bird that had left a tree in his garden, it landed just by the edge of his swimming pool; it drank water from the edge of the pool and hopped around in the garden like it owned the fucking joint, Johnny thought. Johnny grabbed his coffee cup and launched it at the bird, the coffee cup landed nearby with a crash and the bird scattered into the air unharmed, but probably shocked by the missile projected towards it. Bit's of china flew across the patio spilling it's contents of coffee staining the pool area like an oil slick.

'Fucking bird, think's it fucking owns the place, Isabel get me my fucking air rifle!' Johnny shouted.

Ray Flynn followed Isabel into the garden area, while Johnny was still cursing the bird; Isabel quickly surveyed the situation standing there with her hands on her hips.

'For Gods sake Johnny look at the mess you have made, what do you think I am a slave or something?'

'Yes', said Johnny smirking.

'Sometimes your anger gets the better of you, it's only a bird.'

'One fucking less bird if I had my way, now clear it up, I pay you to look after me and shut the fuck up, I'm sure there's plenty of Spanish tarts out there that would want your job.'

'Arsehole', said Isabel in her Spanish dialect as she started to get the equipment out to clean the mess up.

Johnny looked up at Ray Flynn.

'Well sit down, you're making the place look untidy', He then looked across at Isabel as she wandered off, 'did she just call me an arsehole Ray?' He said.

'Yes boss.'

'Fucking Spic, I'm best to get shot of her and get myself a proper maid. Well what news do you have for me then?'

'Bad news boss, it's not good.'

'What kind of bad news, is it about my money? Because I don't want any more fucking bad news about my money.'

'Worse news boss, no money, no Sean Farrow, and Stan.'

There was a break in the conversation as Johnny sipped on his coffee and Ray waited for him to finish, 'what about Stan?' asked Johnny.

'Dead boss, he was found down an alley, stabbed in the neck and.'

Ray stood there not knowing how to finish the sentence, he noticed Johnny staring at him waiting for him to finish, and the frustrating break in the conversation could be seen on his boss's face.

'And what', said Johnny eventually, 'fucking spit it out Ray.'

'Well, he was set on fire boss.'

'Set on fire, what do you mean set on fucking fire?'

'Looks like it was planned boss, not one of them prostitute issues he always got himself into, it looks like it was planned and carried out by someone who followed him and knew where he might be. I've been asking around but there's little to go on, there was some blood at the scene which was not his so it looks like he got one of them before they doused him in petrol and set the poor fucker on fire.'

'Where was Charlie when all this was going on?'

'We was having a drink boss, we all went our separate ways after, I don't think Charlie knows yet, I haven't been able to get hold of him.'

'What's the old bill saying, and what's Wallsy had to say for himself?'

'I've asked John Wall, he knows fuck all, he says it looks like there seems to be some kind of cover up, he reckons he can't get any detail on it at all.'

'Ray, John Wall is my bent copper, he works for me, I pay him good money to find out stuff for me, he needs to start fucking delivering. This looks like someone's trying to fuck me around and muscle in, we need to go street to street and find out who, and put a fucking stop to this, and Ray?'

Ray Flynn was watching Isabel cleaning up the mess, he could clearly see that as she bent over hc could see the tops of her stockings, he quickly looked back at Johnny who was starting to lose saliva from the side of his mouth, not a good sign thought Ray, time to start backing away.

'Someone has nicked my money', said Johnny 'and now they've killed one of my men, I need to find out who, and something else Ray, where the fuck is that Sean Farrow, fucking find him and you might find my money.'

'boss I'm right on it, I'll get hold of Charlie and sort it all out, me or Charlie will get back to you as soon as we have some positive news.'

Ray Flynn turned and started to leave, but before he did he had one more glance across at Isabel who was still sweeping up and cursing Johnny at the same time, and Johnny was starting to curse her back. At this point Ray thought it was best to leave on his own accord and not to disturb the happy couple in their happy home, although not a couple. He knew he was right, there was something going on, and who would blame Johnny, 'I'd love to give the Spanish bird one, Ray thought to himself.

As he left Ray Flynn smiled, and when he got to a safe enough distance from the house, he was happy the conversation went the way it did, there was far less mention of the money then he expected, it appears Johnny is more concerned with getting Sean Farrow and finding out who may be starting to rip him off. Ray Flynn left feeling more confident as he walked out of Johnny Saunders house; he was feeling more cock sure of himself that Johnny had not suspected him of trying to steal his money by killing Tony Clay. The smile left his face, Tony fucking Clay, even after all the beatings he gave him he still didn't reveal where the money was, why the fuck was Clay so insistent on being a martyr, thought Ray, he would still be alive today, probably with only one eye mind you and I would be fifty grand richer. This troubled Ray Flynn, even up to the time he had to throw Tony Clay out of the of the van because the stupid old bill decided to play cops and robbers that night. Ray Flynn left Johnny's house and pulled out of the drive, he wanted the money more than Johnny, after all Johnny had loads of money, he didn't need it, he could keep both parties happy by blaming Stan Smith for the murder of Tony Clay and stealing his money, it could put him in the clear. But Ray knew it was too early to mention this, that would put suspicion on Ray, he had to find the money first and then blame Stan Smith and plant some evidence or proof, he could arrange it all in good time, he thought, all in good time.

Isabel finished clearing up the garden; she looked around and felt happy with her work, as it was now back to normal she thought. She looked across at Johnny, he was in his thinking mode, he was quiet and this was the time she disliked him the most, he is going to want to take it out on her in the bedroom again later she thought, that made her uneasy until thoughts of the extra cash he throws her way after made her feel better.

Johnny Saunders chewed the end off one of his cigars and spat the end onto the floor and lit it, he sat back into his chair adjusted the cushions and thought about what Ray Flynn had just told him. Was he feeling vulnerable, no he thought, it's a set back so he wasn't feeling vulnerable. He thought about Stan Smith, he didn't allow himself to feel low about anything but he thought about Stan Smith, he had known him for a very long time and yet when Ray told him what had happened, it didn't register at first, but now it's starting to sink in. Stan Smith fucking burnt alive, Johnny let it sink into his mind and tried to imagine the scene, and then he tried to think who it could be, who would want to kill one of his men and in such a brutal way. Johnny Saunders realised that's what was troubling him; it wasn't the loss of the money, or a friend, but the unknown, first the money and now Stan, but he didn't know the answers, that's what was troubling him as he sat and thought. He looked across his garden and again looked up into the trees when the sound of bird song entered his ears.

'Isabel, I thought I asked you to get my air rifle! He shouted.

'Yes Johnny right away, coming up your majesty.'

Isabel hurried to the cupboard next to the swimming pool changing rooms, she found the air rifle, and she loaded enough pellets into it's cartridge and then hurried back to Johnny. She left him in the garden and went back into the kitchen and started to prepare dinner for the master, as that's what she called him in a sarcastic Spanish way. She watched Johnny from the kitchen window, he was sitting there still contemplating, he was in his thinking mode, she then saw the bird leave the tree in the garden, she saw it land by the swimming pool edge, she watched as it started to drink, and she saw Johnny raise the air rife, she saw him fire, she saw the bird fall to the side, and she watched as it twitched for a few seconds and then went still.

'Fucking bird, thinks it owns the fucking place, well not any more' she heard Johnny say.

'Fucking arsehole' Isabel said to herself.

Chapter 22

Sean poured Tina another glass of champagne and watched her face glowing as she surveyed the bubbles. They were sitting in a quaint English village pub on the outskirts of Essex and had just eaten Camembert cheese with warm crusty bread. The pub was typically English, in an up market area, the locals were all city gents with their wives or family enjoying a Sunday afternoon being looked after by the local landlord. The pub was busy and the landlord was doing well with a car park full of expensive cars, however, the person that Sean and Tina waited for was missing, this was the second time they had sat and waited for Ray Flynn.

Sean poured himself another glass of champagne and looked at Tina. He thought of her sitting there with her summer dress on, stockings underneath that sexy dress, knickers that barely covered anything and fuck me shoes that would dig into his back. He felt the urge in his crutch and how he would like to take her outside into a field, put her up against a farmer's fence and fuck her from behind.

'I love you Tina', he said.

She smiled.

'I love you too Sean, you dirty git, I know what you're thinking, I can see it in your eyes.'

'Well if we can't end a life today we might as well try to start one.'

Tina smiled nervously as if the joke was too much near the mark.

'He's not coming again' Tina replied.

'Well if he doesn't we've had a nice afternoon again eating well and drinking champagne.'

They both looked out into the gardens and the car park, the sun shone through the clouds and although a warm day it was the time of day when as light fades, it brings a cool breeze and the light jackets and cardigans have to be worn to keep away the chill. Cars were starting to leave and the pub was becoming emptier, they sat while the waitress started to clear away their table and asked if they had a nice afternoon, Sean replied 'yes thank you' and then ordered a black coffee with a whiskey on the side for himself.

'We may need to come back again Sean', said Tina.

'I can't for a while; I need to make some money to pay for this lot.'

'Shall we order another bottle of champagne?' she said.

'No we need to be sober enough if he turns up, let's just wait a while more,' replied Sean.

'If he doesn't turn up after we've finished our coffees and drinks, we will go, and I will let you take me up some country lane for a good seeing too', she replied with a grin on her face.

Sean loved her for that, the spur of the moment thing, and the way she tosses her hair with slight embarrassment when she talks like that, and then he felt the stirring in his groin again.

'Ok deal', he said.

Tina called the waiter over and ordered another bottle of champagne, smiling across at Sean and poking her tongue out at him with a smirk.

'We have to blend in Sean', she said.

'I'm going to stick to the whiskey,' he said, 'we need to make sure this happens right this time and not like the last time, when I ended up with a blade in my thigh, you need to make sure you're ok.'

'Sean I'm drinking because I'm shit scared, we're just about to smash another blokes head in because of what they did to Taylor, allow me a little relief.'

'I'm not denying you the relief, just want you to be switched on, that's all, unless he doesn't turn up and I take you up the country lane, you can drink yourself pissed because then you're a dirty bitch' Sean laughed and Tina smiled.

The coffee arrived, Sean knocked back his whiskey, and Tina sipped on her champagne and then they both looked out and surveyed the car park again. They sat in silence and watched as the odd car pulled out of the car park, there were just a few more tables with diners on and four or five people standing around the bar area. A car entered the car park, inside a male driver with a bald head and a female passenger beside him could be seen, with no other passengers. Sean and Tina remained silent as they both watched the car enter, the car pulled in and the man and woman got out of the car.

'It's him', said Tina.

'I know, fuck it's on,' Sean replied.

Sean called for the waiter, asked for the bill quickly and cancelled the champagne, on it's return he paid cash and they left the pub from the opposite door to the one the couple had already entered, and were now sitting at the bar, laughing and giggling with the locals.

Sean and Tina got into their car and pulled out of the car park, they drove for about ten minutes down through local villages and then into country lanes. They continued through the lanes until they came to a lane surrounded by trees and entered into a car park frequented by dog walkers and ramblers. They sat for a while in silence, a couple came into view and headed towards a car nearby, Sean and Tina watched as they opened the boot of their car, took off their walking boots and put on comfortable shoes, got into their car and pulled out of the car park. Sean and Tina got out of the car, went to the boot and Sean retrieved a ruck sack and threw it in the back seat, Tina got in the back and started to undress and put on dark comfortable clothing, Sean joined her and did the same beside her. They threw the other clothes into the boot; Sean threw the rucksack over his back and locked the car doors. They started to walk towards a tree-lined path, saying nothing until they got further away from the car.

'Let's hope we don't look suspicious starting a walk at this time of day' said Tina.

'There is no one about, anyway if there was they would have just thought we were going for a quick fuck', replied Sean.

They walked down a long muddy track with trees and bushes either side for about fifteen minutes, not saying anything, just walking and looking ahead. There was a couple of farms to the right with livestock still in the fields and the night sky was starting to draw in with the cool breeze starting to pick up. They didn't pass anyone or hear anything apart from sheep bleating and a dog barking in the distance. They continued walking until in the distance to the left between the trees they could see the roof of a building. They stopped for a while, and Sean looked at Tina, before again walking on until they were in line with a large wall hidden behind bushes and trees. Sean looked around from where they came and up ahead of the path before they both moved silently off the path and entered the undergrowth in the direction of the large wall. They moved quietly so they did not stir the dogs that they knew might be on the other side of the wall. Once they got to the wall Sean removed the rucksack from his back, sat down with his back against the wall, Tina sat down beside him, they sat in silence until Sean spoke in a low voice.

'Ok, I whistle, we wait, throw the meat over the wall, we wait, and when it's quiet you lift me up to the wall to check the dogs, if it's all Ok I lift you up, we drop down, run to the back of the house, I smash the back window and enter, you wait outside and keep an eye on the dogs, you wait for me outside, unless the dogs wake then you wait in the conservatory' Tina looks at Sean and nods her understanding. Sean stands and opens the rucksack, he retrieves two brown paper bags and unwraps the parcels to expose the meat, he looks at Tina and kisses her on the mouth. He retrieves a black ski mask and puts it on, pulls the cosh and knife from the bag and tucks them into his trousers; Tina puts on her ski mask.

'Ready', said Sean.

'Ready Sean,' she replied, 'Sean', she says again.

'What.'

'I love you.'

'I love you too babe', he replies while looking at her, he then looks up at the wall, he whistles, they hear nothing, he whistles again, and in the distance they can hear dogs barking. They listen as the barking come nearer, but it's more of a curious barking than a, I want to eat a fucking robber, barking, Sean thinks. He throws the meat over the wall, and they can hear the paws of the dogs pounding on the ground and their panting as they got nearer, Sean and Tina can sense now they are just over the wall. Sean recalls in his head what Pete had said, 'there will be two Doberman dogs, trained to guard the house', hope he's right, he thinks, and there's just two, and the meat has enough poison in it to make them less responsive or hopefully fucking dead.

Over the quietness of the night they can hear the dogs starting to eat at the meat with the odd frenzied fight between them as if they are fighting over the biggest piece. Sean and Tina wait as the dogs do what they do best and pig out on the meat.

'Greedy fuckers aren't they' Tina whispers into Sean's ear.

Then there's silence, Tina holds out her hands and Sean puts his right boot into her cupped hands, they both count to three and with a heave Sean is lifted up until he grips the top of the wall and hauls himself up onto the top of the walls edge. Perched there he looks down and see's the two dogs lying on the ground below him, one dog is out cold the other manages to turn it's head and look upwards at Sean before dropping his head back down into a surrendered position. Sean sit's himself up onto the wall and puts his hand down to pull Tina up, he does so with ease as she also grips the top of the wall and pulls herself up. They both look down at the dogs and then across the lawn to the large house. Immediately Sean eases himself down and then helps Tina to the ground, they both run to the back of the house turning every now and then to keep an eye on the dogs. When they get to the back of the house, Sean grabs a rock from the garden and smashes the back window of the conservatory, lucky, he discovers, like all stupid bastards do, the key was on the inside of the door so all he had to do was unlock the door from the outside, he turns the lock and enters the house. Tina waited outside on the corner of the house watching the dogs, which were still knocked out on the lawn by the far wall. Sean could not believe his luck, not only was the key in the back door but the main door to the house within the conservatory was not even locked he just turned the handle and the door opened, he listened, he could not hear anything. He knew that if he stopped for a while he would start to panic, so he entered the house quickly and looked for the basement door. The house was large, big downstairs rooms, big paintings on the walls, expensive furniture, all neat and tidy. Sean walked slowly around the main room which led from the conservatory to the hallway, he was fucking scared, he thought, what the fuck am I doing here, and then he saw the photo on the side cabinet with a picture of the fat cunt who killed his mate, tortured him to death, he stared at it for a moment and then left the room looking for the hallway. He entered the hallway which had a large staircase with a large chandelier hanging down from the ceiling, all bought with drugs and violence Sean thought, he looked across at the stairs which led up to a landing which went off to the left and right. He found the door under the stairs which he knew led to the basement, he went over and opened the door, it too was unlocked, fuck me he thought, and this bloke nicks things for a living, you'd have thought he'd know better. He entered the basement and found the stairs in the dark, he found a switch to the left and turned it on, he could see the stairs more clearly now and looked down below which looked like a typical basement with boxes, shelves and it had a large collection of bottled wines. He switched the light off. Sean proceeded down the stairs; he waited down below until his eyes adjusted to the light and then found some boxes in the corner, no ones going to want to move boxes at this time of night he thought. He moved some boxes silently to one side and then crouched behind them, pulled them back into himself and waited in silence, been here before he thought to himself, but this time

170

I'm the fucking killer. It was damp, and silent and he thought of Tina outside, he shouldn't be doing this with her, but he understood, it's her pilgrimage just as much as his and she wanted this just as much as him. Does this make them sadistic killers or does it make them revengeful killers, he thought, he came to his conclusions; he wouldn't be doing any of this if Taylor was still alive. He looked at his watch, Ray Flynn has been in the pub now for one and half hours, this could be a long wait, hopefully it's just a couple of drinks with a meal and then home. Sean stayed in that position for another two and half hours, moving to his left and right to be more comfortable and to get rid of the cramp. Every now and then he would check that he had the cosh and the knife in an easy to get to position and sometimes pulling it out and gripping the handle to ensure he understood it's weight. It was then he heard a dog or maybe two, he's in the basement so it's walls are muffling the sound but it's definitely dogs, shit he thinks, Tina, the dogs are awake sooner then anticipated. He is now thinking fast, do I move from this position, back out of the basement, do I stay here and wait longer, the next noise makes his mind up for him as he can hear a car on the gravel of the drive, he wait's. He can hear above him now, the front door opening and shouting in the hallway.

'I saw you looking at him all night you slag and don't say you weren't.'

'Look Ray you're paranoid again with too much beer, I wasn't looking at anyone'

Sean hears a slap and then a muffled cry.

'Don't call me paranoid you whore you were bogging him all night, don't you ever fucking back chat me.'

'I wasn't, I was just saying.'

'You fucking bitch, I'll show you.'

Sean struggles to hear but in his head in this dark room he can make out that Ray Flynn has hit his wife again harder this time, he can sense he is dragging her across the room in some way to the front room, he can hear her screaming, fuck Sean thinks what do I do, he pulls himself out of the boxes as silently as he can and climbs the stairs to listen. He can hear sobbing and the moans of a man that is entering a woman, grunts, groans and sobbing, he is in a position that he did not expect, he could go in now and save the woman but that would fuck up everything, he wait's, the moaning and groaning stops, the sobbing continues only softer.

'Now fuck off to bed you bitch.'

Sean hears shuffling and the wife above him crying as her footsteps hit the stairs above him. He goes back down the stairs, he has to wait, Flynn may be drunk and will fall asleep, it will be easier, but he also needs his wife to fall asleep, another wait, bollocks he thinks. Waiting is time to think, time to shit yourself further, time to think about the dogs, what the fuck happened there, he thought, they should be dead. The cellar door above him opens, he jumps off the stairs in silence and gets behind wine racks that are full up with wine, and he wait's. He can hear someone searching for the light switch above, the light comes on, and the room is lit up as someone starts to descend the

172

stairs. Sean can see Ray Flynn's feet first and then his legs, then his fat arse covered by his fat pants, then his bare back with extensive tattoos and the thick neck, and then his balding head. Flynn stops at the bottom of the stairs and looks around the basement, he shivers in the cold and dampness of the underground room.

'Fucking bitch', Sean hears him say, 'fucking slag taking the piss out of me, I need another fucking drink.'

Ray Flynn turns and looks directly at Sean's position and starts to walk towards the place where Sean is standing behind the wine rack, Sean can see in his eyes, there is no recognition that he is there, no awareness in Flynn's eyes as he heads towards Sean. He looks directly at where Sean is as if surveying the area and deciding which bottle to take, Sean is static but with a sweaty grip on the cosh, and quietly searching for the knife, is Flynn looking at him, in this light he is not sure. Ray Flynn is standing there for a moment, as if looking straight at him, it's then he pulls a bottle of wine from the rack and looks at the label, Sean is looking directly at him, Flynn is looking at the wine bottle label but then Sean sees something else change in his eyes and it's then Flynn raises his head and looks directly at Sean, there is no time. Sean is immediately pinned up against the wine rack as Flynn pushes the wine rack towards Sean, he is screaming and forcing the rack against Sean's chest, Sean is too slow to react but manages to push back as best he can, bottles smash to the ground and Flynn has the power to crush Sean in, but as the bottles smash down Flynn's bare feet start to tread on broken glass. The noise is terrific, from the smashed bottles on the ground to the screaming from Flynn as he treads on the broken glass, this allowed the pressure to be released off of Sean and he manages to get free from the crushing wine rack, he looks immediately at Flynn who is starting to pick wine bottles up to throw at Sean. Sean, seizes his chance and smashes the cosh down on Ray Flynn's head, he falls, he hit's him again and again across the head, his head is bleeding, his feet are bleeding, 'go down you fucker, go down! Sean screams. There is red wine all over the floor, mixed with blood, and he can hear the dogs barking, Flynn is also screaming in this cellar of a hell hole, the dogs, fuck the dogs, Flynn's wife, fuck, fuck, fuck, Sean starts to grab at anything, the cosh has gone with all the fluid around it's handle, gone out of his hand, he reaches for a bottle, and he can see Flynn is reaching for another bottle, Sean grabs a bottle first and manages to smash it across Flynn's head, he's down again 'stay down you fucker, stay down!, Sean screams. Sean falls to the ground exhausted, Flynn is laying in wine and blood moaning but alive, Sean can't move, he's exhausted and breathing heavy, he hears footsteps on the basement, stairs, he can't move. He looks up and sees Flynn's wife descending the stairs holding a shotgun, fuck he thinks, it's all over.

The wife looks at Sean who has still got his mask on, she looks at the basement floor and the scene of her husband laying there in wine and blood, and she looks at the cosh lying at the foot of the stairs in front of her.

'Is he alive?' she asks, looking at Sean directly.

Sean is silent, he looks at Flynn, who is breathing and moaning and any minute now will wake up and fucking kill him. Sean nods, 'yes he's still alive.'

Flynn's wife, looks down at the cosh, she looks at her husband who is starting to come round, he looks up at her, he smiles and looks at Sean, the evil gratifying smile that tells Sean he is in trouble.

The wife descends the last step still holding the shotgun pointed at Sean, again she looks at the cosh, and she kicks the cosh in the direction of Sean.

'Then finish him off,' she says in a gratifying voice.

Sean sees Ray Flynn's facial expression change as he tries to get to his feet, Sean manages to grab the cosh and hit's him across the head with all his force, and he hit's him again and again, until Flynn starts to fall. Flynn grabs hold of Sean as he went down, the struggle and force of the man was intense for Sean and he couldn't do anything but fall down with him into the blood and liquid. They were both staring into each other's eyes gripping on for dear life and trying to reach for anything nearby they could use as a weapon. Sean could see Flynn reaching for a bottle that was spinning nearby, he was nearly getting a grip but the blood on his hands was making it difficult and it spun towards Sean's reach. Sean grabbed at it, got a firm grip and smashed the bottle down onto Flynn's head, with it's red contents exploding onto them both. Sean could see Flynn was still not out from the blow, he saw his large neck in front of him, he still had a grip on the stem of the bottle and thrust it deep into Flynn's neck and throat, and again red liquid exploded into the room. Sean felt Flynn's grip release from him and as he did he fell back onto the floor besides Flynn who was now gurgling through the blood fighting to take his last breath. Sean was breathing heavily and couldn't move for exhaustion and fear, he looked across at the woman at the bottom of the stairs who was staring down at him and her ex husband. There was something sadistic about what he had just done, he thought, bashing a bloke's brains out while his wife looked on. The bastard deserved it, he deserves to be laying there dead in his own blood and wine, it was payback for Taylor, and in a weird way, Sean thought, it was payback for the wife. He was dead Sean could see that, as he looked across at Flynn who's chest was now motionless, as he laid there eyes open to the ceiling in surrender, and so did Flynn's wife, as she stood there still pointing the gun at Sean.

'Go' she said, 'leave the house before I change my mind.'

'What about your dogs?' replied Sean?

'Go' she said again.

Flynn's wife went up the stairs still pointing the gun at Sean, Sean followed, and once outside the basement, again she told Sean to leave. Sean left the hallway and entered the large living area, he could see the footprints left from his shoes, wine mixed with blood as he left, he entered the conservatory where he could see Tina lying in the corner crying and unable to move, he picked her up, she held him.

' I thought you were dead' she said.

'I'm ok, we've got to go Tina, and we need to run.'

'The dogs, they're outside, they're not dead', she replied.

Sean could see the dogs outside the conservatory windows, they were barking like mad with teeth full of blood from the meat, and they looked like dogs from hell, he thought.

'We need to outrun them', he said.

'Fuck Sean we can't do that.'

'We have to.'

At that point there was a whistle, a loud whistle and a women's voice was calling the dogs, the two dogs ears pricked up and they both ran from the back of the house to where the calling was coming from.

'Now Tina now', shouted Sean, he hauled her up and they both exited the conservatory door and ran as fast as they could along the edge of the garden to the wall where they had entered, Sean could see both dogs running in the opposite direction, until he saw one of the dogs turn and spot them, Sean watched as the dog started to return with teeth preparing for the kill.

'Faster Tina, faster!' he shouted.

They reached the wall and Tina quickly put her arms down for Sean to get his foot inside, it was then she saw one of the dogs returning with the second slightly behind. Sean put his foot into Tina's hands and Tina hauled as best she could while Sean jumped and tried desperately to grab the top of the wall, his feet were slippery due to the wine and blood and his feet slipped out of Tina's hands, they tried again with the dogs bearing down on them. Tina managed to hold his foot still but his hands grabbed and grabbed at slippery brickwork as he tried to get a grip which seemed to be much more difficult the second time, he heard the dogs, getting nearer and nearer, he thought of Tina below him and grabbed at the brickwork a second time, this time there was a grip and he hauled himself up, and pulled himself up onto the wall. Sean sat upright on the wall looked across the garden to see the two dogs about ten feet away at full speed and teeth bearing ready for the kill, he put his arm down Tina grabbed his hand and she was hauled up just as the first dog was in biting distance, both dogs were jumping at the wall as Tina and Sean sat on top of the wall, Sean looked across at the house, he could see the lone figure of a women standing at the back door with a shot gun in her hand, she seemed to look impressed that we survived her dogs he thought. They both dropped down to the other side of the wall panting, leaving the dogs on the other side barking like mad butchers, they then heard another whistle and calm returned to the Essex countryside again.

'We have to move Tina, we can't stay here.'

They both got up and ran out of the undergrowth onto the path and ran down the footpath tearing off their masks as they ran, passing the farms and the fields to the left that were visible with the moon shining down on the old buildings. When they got to the car they hauled the rucksack into the boot and drove out of the car park.

'What happened? Is it done? Are you hurt?' said Tina.

'Yes it's done; let's get home first', he replied.

There was silence on the way home; they travelled across town from Essex back to the safe house, which was their new home for a while. When they got home, Sean filled the rucksack with the clothes from the back of the car, he locked the car and they both walked around the block to the front door. Once inside Sean relayed everything to Tina, what happened in the house, and what happened in the basement and how Flynn's wife became part of the unusual circumstances. Tina sat there and listened to the whole story, Sean could see in her eyes the astonishment of what had happened, and how it must have been hard for her to listen to all the commotion in the basement and be transfixed to her position unable to do anything. They both showered, Sean scrubbing hard at the wine and blood on his hands, he walked back into the bedroom where Tina was sitting on the bed, and they both sat in silence for a while.

'I will get rid of the car in the morning' said Sean,

'Sean, someone called the dogs off', Tina replied, 'allowing us to escape, a women's voice calling the dogs.'

'I know, I can only think his wife wanted us away from the scene to make it seem more like a robbery gone wrong or a gangland killing, what ever it was, she found an opportunity to have him dead too and she took it.'

'Sean, I'm not sitting in some dark corner again, next time I want to be involved, for my own sanity.'

They slept easy that night; they didn't make love, as it seemed to be something fading away as other things was consuming their desires. They held on to each other all night, and slept with the realisation that they were doing good, even though they knew it was a bad thing what they were doing. They knew they could be seen, at least by themselves they are doing good, it will rid them of their demons, and the guilt they felt for not being able to help Taylor the day he died.

Chapter 23

Johnny Saunders threw his betting slip onto the ground and spat out his cigar butt, he then cursed the dog that he had just lost a bet on.

'Spastic fucking dog', he said, 'did you see that Charlie, fucking thing looked like it had a fucking jockey on it's back or it had three legs'. Johnny continued to rave on about the slow dogs that he had bets on, he was with Charlie Allan and they were at Wimbledon dog racing track, South London.

'I did boss, I need to go and see Billy boy, he assured me the races were rigged and these were the dog's that would win.'

'Billy Boy, what's he got to do with my dogs?'

'He gave me the dogs names last night, said they would come in, hundred percent certain he said.'

'Fucking certain, he's taking the piss, fucking certain to rob me the Irish tinker cunt, sort him out for me Charlie.'

'Yes boss.'

Wimbledon dog track was busy, the bars were full and the money was flowing between hands on and off the track. Johnny Saunders was a betting man but now a mad man, he had bet a lot of money on what he thought would be dead certainties to win and this was starting to add to the problems he felt he was starting to get. He ordered another double Whiskey at the bar, drunk it straight down and watched some beautiful women walk by.

'Where's Ray, Charlie?' he said.

'He's at home I think boss.'

'There's something not quite right there Charlie, I'm starting to feel that Ray maybe doing a Curly Broadbridge on me. I mean the money, there was two things that Clay had to do on that day, get my money from Ray and pick up suits for Farrow & Docherty, and then it all went tits up.'

There was a roar in the crowd as another race started, Johnny and Charlie looked down and in the flood lit arena they could see the greyhounds running out of the traps, they could see the sweat on the animals, the steam from their mouths and the hare travelling at full speed on the electric rail.

'I don't think he would have the bottle to do anything boss, I think he's pretty loyal, but I can look into it for you.'

'Yeah Charlie do that, just to cure my curiosity, what about you Charlie, have you got the bottle to do it?'

'Yes boss, I've got the bottle but I wouldn't do it, I know where my loyalties stand and I'm happy with how and what you pay me, besides you would find me and cut my fucking toes off.'

Johnny looked into Charlie Allan's eyes.

'I admire your honesty Charlie and that's why I trust you, and yes I would cut your fucking toes off, and your cock.'

They both laughed, although Charlie's was more of a nervous laugh then Johnny's.

'And what about Sean Farrow, where are we with that one.'

'We can't find him anywhere, we've asked around no one knows where he is, we've been to his home, asked his friends. His girlfriend is missing too, you know Tina, Mark Docherty's daughter and Taylor Docherty's sister, we haven't come up with anything, even John Wall has been making enquiries but nothing.'

The dogs went round the track again, and the people were jumping up and down screaming and throwing their arms in the air, the winner ran past the post panting and the trainers ran out to retrieve their dogs. Johnny Saunders looked down at his betting slip, again he screwed it up and threw it to the floor, 'fucking spastic dog' he said.

'I had fifty grand taken from me Charlie, I need to know who's got it, I'm a little fucked off why no fucker can find it for me or why no one can find Sean Farrow, who is he, fucking Houdini, find him Charlie.'

'I will boss.'

'The other thing Charlie, this tinker, Billy Boy, does he know who he's dealing with, does he know I've spent a lot of money in his place and not had a good return, I want him sorted too, why haven't I heard about him before today.'

'He's not a tinker, he's Scottish, came down a few months ago, brought some money with him from up there and started to set himself up down here, he's got a bit of reputation that he's not scared of anyone. His father came from South London and moved up to Scotland, Glasgow, when Billy was young, his mother was Scottish and missed home I think, that's why they moved up there. He started off same old shit nicking cars dealing drugs etc. and then started to get a bit of a reputation as a hard man, so he built a bit of a family around him and some parts of Glasgow became his own. He moved to London for the rich pickings someone told me.'

'Scottish tinker then, does he wear a kilt?'

'No boss.'

'Smash his fucking head in then, set up a meeting with him, no fucking sweaty sock is gonna muscle in on my territory, why didn't you tell me about this cunt'

'I did boss, you were high on coke at the time, shagging a whore, not sure if you took it all in.'

Johnny Saunders looked at Charlie, he lit a new cigar, he took a long puff before exhaling it into the air, he thought about Stan Smith he thought about his lost bets, he thought about this new Scotsman in town, and then he thought about Charlie Allan's last comment. Charlie didn't see it coming but felt the blow from the bottle on his head, he felt the warmth of the blood hitting his neck, and he felt the pain in his back as he hit the bar and then the floor, he was dazed, he looked up and could see Johnny Saunders leaning over him, holding the top of the bottle. He was still dazed, he could see Johnny shouting words but could not hear anything, and he could see people looking down at him. They all had open mouths and looked shocked, very slowly he could hear the roar of the crowd beginning to come back into his head, he felt for his head, it hurt and he was stunned and there was a sticky warm substance on his hand. He felt hands pulling him to his feet, they were strong arms, the noise was getting stronger, he could now hear the crowd screaming more, he could see Johnny in front of him pointing at him and slowly the words came into his ears, ' don't ever talk to me like that again you cunt, you got it Charlie, you fucking got that Charlie.'

Charlie nodded but felt the pain in his head as he did so, he felt the arms start to release him, he looked left and then right and recognized the two men as being close associates of him and Johnny, they looked serious and troubled, he thought. Charlie started to get his thoughts together and stability in his legs, he could see people had left the bar area and those that were still there were looking at him, he regained himself and brushed himself down, he felt a hand on his shoulder and one of the two men handed him a hand full of napkins to stem the flow of blood from his head. He was regaining himself and sat down on the nearest table, he could see that Johnny was pulling over two more chairs and Winston Scott and another black friend of his sat down around the table.

Charlie Allan was still coming around and was trying to listen to the conversation which was coming in and out of his head, he listened intensely and at the end could summarise what he thought he heard and what Winston was telling Johnny.

'Ray Flynn has been killed at his home, looks like an attempted burglary gone wrong.'

Charlie Allan looked up to see Johnny, he could see his eyes were focusing on what he had just heard, and he looked at Winston.

'Are you sure Winston, where did you get it from?' Johnny said.

'From John Wall, boss.'

Charlie looked up, the bar staff were clearing up the shards of glass and spilled beer from the floor; they looked across at the table that Charlie was sitting on in disbelief in what had just happened.

'From John Wall, Ok Winston, thanks, what else can you tell me?'

Winston looked towards Charlie who was still holding napkins to his head to stem the flow of blood, and then he looked back at Johnny.

'Well boss, John Wall said a few things, apparently Ray and his missus went out for a meal at their local and the locals said they seemed normal and then they left. He also said that the dogs looked like they were drugged and the back door window was smashed in, and it looked like there was a massive altercation in the basement, you know where he kept all his booze, that's where he was killed, bludgeoned with some kind of blunt instrument, and bottled in the neck boss.'

'And', said Johnny.

'Well Wallsy also said that nothing was stolen and that, Ray's missus slept through the whole fucking thing, sticks cotton wool in her ears to help her sleep apparently. When she got up to get a glass of water, she searched for him and found his body in the basement and called the police.'

Johnny stared at Winston and then looked around the bar area, as he did he noticed people staring in his direction and then they all quickly looked away as if not wanting to be part of the mad mans entertainment. He reviled in that thought, they are still scared of me, and he looked back at Winston and then Charlie who was still holding the napkins to his head.

'This all sounds a bit dodgy boys, first Stan and now Ray and alongside my money vanishing at the same time, this ain't right. The other thing, everyone around me is a suspect at the moment, including you guys', Johnny then looked across at Charlie, 'Charlie remember what I said about Ray, well I want you to visit his missus and search the house, put some pressure on her to see if she knows about any money, also see if Ray had been spending money lately, you know and looking a bit flushed'. Charlie nodded and again the pain throbbed in his head. Johnny looked across at Winston, 'Winston start asking questions in that club of yours, someone's bound to know something, after all your making lots of money out of me in that joint and I ain't seeing much of a return yet.'

Winston nodded, 'yes boss.

'Come on Charlie we're leaving, you're gonna need to get that head seen to, might need stitches in that if it carries on bleeding.'

Johnny lifted himself off the chair looking down at Charlie who was still sitting; Winston and his mate were looking at Charlie who could feel all eyes on him.

'Come on Charlie it was one bottle', Said Johnny again, 'you've had worse than that in your time, come on we've got work to do, are you ok to drive.'

Charlie looked up at Johnny, he could still feel the eyes of Winston and his mate on him as well as the bar staff who were still staring in disbelief.

'Yes boss, I'm ok to drive.'

'Well come on then you got a busy day ahead of you tomorrow, I need to know who's fucking topping my men and why.'

Charlie managed to get himself up out of the chair, he stood for a while to get his balance and to ensure he was ok, and then followed Johnny out of the bar and out of the stadium to the car park, and all the way, he felt the eyes of everyone piercing into his back.

Chapter 24

Sean Farrow was laying on his sofa day dreaming in his front
room, he was thinking through all the things that he had gone
through with Pete Murray. The plan was in place but he didn't
like it, Tina was insistent she had to be part of it and Sean was
beginning to feel like she was getting a kick out of the whole
thing. He was going through it all in his head and was starting to
panic but he knew he had a get out clause should it be needed,
but he was still worried and scared. Pete was right Sean thought,
Winston Scott was such a big guy and with his mental awareness
we had to have a robust plan where we could get close to him
without making him suspicious. He lay there looking up at the
ceiling going through it all in his head, the timings, and the
locations, what he had to do if it went wrong. He knew Tina had
the biggest part to play and he was so scared for her but he also
knew he owed it to her to take her part, and get rid of the anger
and demons deep inside her. Sean looked at his watch, it was
15:30, he looked out of the window, he could see from his
position that it was a warm day with some white clouds
occasionally blotting out the sun. He wondered about Tina, she
knew the plan well and he knew he would not see her now until
later tonight after she had completed the plan, Sean Farrow
wiped his brow, what the fuck was he thinking, he thought, why
is he allowing this to happen, if she fails he could also lose Tina.
He didn't want that to happen but her strength and persuasive

189

nature won the day as well as the confidence shown from Pete that this was the best way to get to Winston Scott. He looked at his watch again, 16:00, he knew he had to be at the location at 23:00 tonight and it's now only 16:00, fuck me time is going so slow, he thought. He raised himself up from the sofa, he knew what he had to do, he would take one more drive to Brixton, survey the area again, and he would park up and check out all the doors and alleyways one more time.

Brixton was fast becoming a no go area for many white people and Sean knew that, he drove passed the club several times getting the scene into his head as well as looking for access and exit routes. He parked up in a small side street with onlookers glancing over at him every now and then, he wasn't scared he had a local accent and has seen these streets before, but he knew these streets were starting to become more formidable then they had ever been before. Reggae music was bearing down on him from a local music shop as people went back and forth in whatever journey they were taking. Sean reflected on what Pete had told him again which didn't make him feel confident about tonight and made him even more nervous.

'Winston Scott revelled in his position', Pete had said, 'he was a well-known local black name as well as the main contact for the white gangsters of London. He was a tall well built man that had a distinctive mannerism in his body language that instantly showed fear in the eyes of every one he met. He was quiet, a mild mannered man but had a reputation to deal with issues in his life as well as requests and orders from those he worked for in a controlled professional manner. Winston Scott was very important to Johnny Saunders because it gave him close relationships with the drug dealers in Brixton and surrounding areas, it was a good relationship, one that Saunders respected, and he knew it was important for his financial gain.'

A controlled professional manner, Sean thought, again he was worried, again the reggae music bore down on him, and then there was a tap on the car window beside him. A large black man stood by the window grinning with gold teeth shinning from his mouth, Sean gripped the handle and undid the window, and the music instantly got louder filling the car.

'You after some Ganga, marijuana, some weed', the man said, 'something stronger or are you here in Brixton town for other reasons brother.'

'Weed, have you got any weed' Sean replied, knowing it was the only response he could give sitting in this street.

'Fuck me white boy you aren't a long way from home, you want weed go to Water Lane, there's weed at Water Lane, don't hang around this street, brothers are checking you out, thinking you may be the police or something', the man replied.

'Thanks for the tip, but I'm just here for weed' Sean replied and started to do the window back up, with the reggae music volume reducing at every turn of the handle. He started the engine and pulled away from the street taking one more glance at the club that he would re-visit tonight.

Chapter 25

The domino hit the wooden table with a smash and Winston
Scott smiled knowing that he had his opponent beat. Laughter
filled the air from all those watching the game, and those that
were congregating around the table had their backs slapped with
excitement. Winston's opponent looked baffled and upset that he
was beaten but took the light hearted banter well, until eventually
a big wide grin was seen across his face followed by him
swigging from his can of Red Stripe beer.

'Winston that is the first time you have beaten me in twenty
years, it's taken you that long to learn, you should be ashamed of
yourself', the man said.

' I'm not ashamed old man I'm proud, get this old fool another
drink, he needs one to wash away his woes'. Winston's laughter
again filled the air and those closest that could hear joined in
again.

Winston Scott was in a social club in Electric Avenue in the heart
of Brixton South London, his normal relaxing place where he
could drink enjoy friends and not worry about his back. It was a
warm day and he was happy. He had money in his pocket, he
was a lion in his own den, and he didn't have to worry about
anyone else, he was the king of the jungle and he knew it and
relished the tranquillity and how it felt, he didn't have a care in
the world. He paced up and down and spoke to those in the room
especially the women in the room, they all wanted a piece of
Winston, they all craved what it would be like to have that well

built man inside them, and if he had the time he would assist in that craving and then go home to his family. Winston Scott was also partial to a bit of white meat, as he called it, and there were often white girls that frequented the club because they enjoyed a bit of black meat, as they called it. The club was a haven it had drink, drugs, girls and the police were too afraid of any repercussions to raid the place, they were afraid of riots, being accused of racism and their ability to manage the population of Brixton. There was also the Northern Ireland issue, the government were too busy focusing on issues over seas rather then worrying what was happening locally, and it gave a license for those to exploit it, and this club knew that, and exploited it well, with Winston as lead role supported by Johnny Saunders.

Chapter 26

Streatham High Road was bustling, it was Saturday and the main shops were full with people busying themselves in the warm sunshine. Tina strode down the high street with a couple of shopping bags on each arm, she was alone and that's the way she liked it today, she wanted to be alone, she had some purchases to get with Sean's money that he had kindly given to her earlier. The hot pants would be fine she thought and the low cut top and knee high boots would be exactly the look that she was trying to achieve. The wig was the most expensive thing she had bought although she did manage to cut the price slightly suggesting that their was a flaw in the seams that just happen to be there by chance, Tina smiled to herself. The shop assistant was more than happy to help in the most expensive shop on the high street, as she did not want to get a bad reputation, the whole situation was made better by Tina knowing the shop assistant who even managed to get some money off with staff discount. Tina smiled again, she felt pleased with herself and even felt very horny when she looked in the mirror after trying on all her new gear in the fitting room, where's Sean when you need him she thought as she touched herself in the changing room, almost making her new hot pants damp. Naughty she thought, very naughty, considering what's happening tonight. On the way home Tina slipped into a phone box and dialled the number to Sean's flat, he answered on the fifth ring.

'Hello darling it's me', she said.

'Hello gorgeous how have you been?' replied Sean.

'I'm Ok, I've been shopping as you suggested and got myself some real horny gear, hopefully we can try it out later.'

'Yea hopefully babe, are you ok?'

'Yea I'm Ok I've been shopping, any girl that has been shopping is ok, I just miss you carrying my bags for me and telling me I look gorgeous in that outfit or pretty in that one.'

'You look hot in anything babe', Sean replied, 'apart from that new tank top you bought the other day, it was like shagging Donny Osmond, you could have removed it before we had it off.'

'It was you're tank top and I had nothing else on' you loved every minute of it'

There was a giggle from both ends of the phone, and then silence, Sean spoke first.

'Be careful tonight babe.'

'Of course I will babe' she replied, 'we have been through it loads of times and I'm confident I have everything in place, you just need to make sure you are where your supposed to be at, and at the right time.'

'I will be babe, just stick to the plan Tina, the next time you see me it will be done and we will be home before you know it, I just want you to be careful that's all'

'I will Sean, I love you so much that all I want is to come home with you and be safe in your arms, I should go now I'm running late and I have to get to Brixton, I love you Sean, don't worry, the plan will work.'

'Just be where you are meant to be as planned Tina', he said.

They both said their goodbyes and the phone went dead at Sean's end. He sat there and wondered how it would go, he still couldn't believe where this journey had taken him and Tina, he kept thinking to himself that they should pull out, but the urge of vengeance was deep inside him, deep inside his mind, body, soul and heart, and he knew it had to be finished for him to live. Tina left the phone box and continued along Streatham High Road before jumping onto a bus that led towards Brixton Town. She too was in a mind of her own, she thought of her mother, she thought of Sean and she thought of Taylor, she thought of her stepfather slain down by the same man as Taylor had been. The ticket inspector arrived, she paid him, and he turned his machine and gave her a ticket and moved on down the bus to collect more fares. Tina looked out of the window and watched the world go by, she had her shopping bags down by her feet, it had been a nice day, the evening may be different she thought, the sun shone and she could see people going from left to right either going home or to work. The stop was not far, the bus travelled down the hill towards the town hall and she knew she would need the next stop after the traffic lights, she left her seat and started down the stairs of the bus pressing the button on the handle to let the driver know she wanted the next stop, she felt scared but excited and then felt guilty about the feeling of excitement. She made her way off the bus and walked the streets of Brixton in the direction of the club, until she came to the street where the club was. She stood for a while looking at the entrance, she could feel people staring at her, but she ignored them, she continued to stare at the entrance until her legs moved without the sensation of her brain telling them too. She walked into the entrance of the club, she told the man on the door, an old man with a trusting smile, she thought, her name and he took her through to a relatively quiet hall where some men were playing dominoes, and then he showed her towards a set of doors to the left.

Tina noticed it started to get dark around nine o'clock, she could see the sky turn darker from the window in her new environment looking out of the window within the club. Tina sat there in front of the mirror putting on her make up with the other two girls in the room, that she had never met before. One girl was black a strong tall legged girl probably around twenty four Tina thought, and one that you would not want to end up in a fight with, she had that large arse that black men tend to love and go for in a big way. The other girl was half cast and very pretty, long dark curly hair and as skinny as a garden rake but with perfectly shaped breasts, you could see that she works out on a daily basis with the toned stomach and muscly legs. Tina looked at herself in the mirror again, the make up was nearly complete and the outfit was on, again she felt sexy but threw that away. She never danced in public before let alone in a black club in the middle of Brixton Town.

'So what's your name then cutie' said one of the girls behind her with a strong northern accent.

Tina was busy laying the last line of lipstick upon her lips when she looked into the mirror seeing lanky little miss ebony staring back at her.

'Melody, that's my name, I'm Melody, and what's yours' she replied.

'I'm Alison, that little cutie over there with a bit of white in her is Debby'

Tina looked up and could see Debby giving a quick glance in her direction while she was pulling up her stockings; she smiled and continued pulling them over her very beautiful legs.

Tina smiled back, turned and continued with her lipstick.

'So what brings you here tonight Melody' Alison said, 'white girl in a black club, not that I have a problem with that, I'm just giving a bit of advice, there's a few out there that might have a bit of a feel or expect one if you know what I mean'

'I need to get some money together for the bills, Tina replied, 'you know how it is, some fucker gets me pregnant and then fucks off.'

'Have you done this before Meoldy,' asked Alison, 'you know stripped in front of people before?'

Tina noticed that the other girl Debby, still hadn't said much, and looking back across at Alison replied.

'No never, this is my first time.'

A laugh came from Debby's direction. 'Bloody hell girl, you've never done this before and you choose a black club in Brixton to cut your teeth, what are you mental or something, you should have at least tried a few more pleasant locations or pubs before venturing into here', Jesus you are going to a need a friend tonight.'

'I'm, ok but thanks for the advice and the offer, I'm just going to dance, get paid and get out of here.'

'Your going to just dance, get paid and get out of here are you? Well good luck with that one sister', replied Debby.

Tina looked up, so the other one can speak, she thought. Tina watched as Debby opened the door and walked out laughing as she left. Tina and Alison watched as the faint sound of music started up, the sound of dance music and then the cheers from the hall within the club, butterflies churned in Tina's stomach, as she knew she was next to parade herself in front of a load of sexual animals.

'Pay no mind to her', said Alison, 'she's just been around a bit, knocked around with the wrong crowd and probably knows what you're letting yourself in for, I know she will end up in the private area later making a bit more cash, if you know what I mean, poor cow.'

No I don't know what you mean, what do you mean private area?'

'Dancing is one thing but this lot expect more and you being white you are going to be in demand, if you're lucky Winston will take a shine to you and take you upstairs on his own, he likes white.'

'Winston?' replied Tina.

'Winston is the club owner, well, keeper, he looks after it for someone a bastard called Johnny Saunders, do you know him?'

'No I don't believe I do', Tina said, and wondered if her poor acting skills gave her away.

'Well you don't want to meet him, he's a prick just out for himself. I've been to his house for parties, he likes to abuse women, but pays well.' Tina noticed as an embarrassed look came across Alison's face, she liked that; it made her look real and genuine.

'Winston runs around South London for him', continued Alison. 'You look good Mel, can I call you Mel?'

'Yes you can, can I call you Ally?'

'Yes you can call me Ally, unfortunately I don't want to be too friendly as I may not see you again after tonight, it depends on how you go down with the crowd and if you keep Winston sweet, I'm sorry Mel but you look like his type, just be careful is all I'm saying, have you got a new boyfriend, who can look after you?'

'No fuck them all, I seem to attract the wrong sort, only after one thing, I dropped my knickers too many times and then realised I was just being used, I have a child now that's my priority.'

'I like you Mel, we should stay friends', Ally looked towards the door, 'it sounds like Debby's dance is coming to a close, and she will be here in a minute moaning about the rabble outside.'

Tina's stomach turned, not because of the dance but because she wanted Winston to notice her, she wanted him to be all over her, she wanted him to take her to his private room. She knew she had to be brave, she wanted to be strong but she wanted it to also work for Sean, and most of all for her brother Taylor. That thought made her feel stronger and got the anger welling up inside her, she could feel it, she was scared by it, but she also welcomed it. With that the door burst open and music from the external room came bursting in.

'Big exciting crowd out there tonight Ally, most are drunk and trying to get on stage, filthy bastard's clawing at me, try and stay back as far as possible, I haven't even got my Fanny out yet just my tits, anyone would think they've never seen a woman before, Debby looked across at Tina, 'new girl, what was your name again.'

'Melody', replied Tina staring up at her.

'Stay to the back', replied Debby, 'you're lucky Winston is out there he will keep them at bay if he likes you, you are better off playing up to him so he can protect you' good luck.'

'Told you she wasn't all bad didn't I Mel,' said Ally, 'ok the music has started, go give it to them you sexy honkey bitch.'

That made Tina smile, she picked herself up from the chair, she felt nervous but confident, she looked once more in the mirror and left the room, leaving the two girls watching her leave with care in their eyes, she liked them she thought and wondered if she would ever see them again, probably not she thought and then the adrenalin kicked in.

She entered the lion's den and noticed the smell of beer, marijuana and stale sweat, at first she wasn't noticed but had to walk passed a few of them that were standing at the bar, and she walked tall, sexy with an air of arrogance. Very slowly the animals started to notice her and the wolf whistles and jeers began, she walked to the small stage and managed to get onto it at the right cue that she had been practicing for the last few days. It didn't take Tina long to notice Winston Scot in the audience, he had his long dread locks and a number of large men around him, they stared at her, some with broad smiles but she could see Winston had turned and was already showing interest in her, good she though with a fear of dread in her stomach. She continued to dance provocatively hoping that she didn't look too amateurish, it was then she slipped on her left foot as her high heel slipped from under her, which gained laughs from the

201

animals in the ring. Ignoring it she continued and couldn't wait for the song to finish, she hated every one of them, she thought and was starting to feel very angry inside, and that frightened her, but also gave her rare courage. She continued to dance and felt sick inside, these men staring at her every move, could she go through with this, she was never a great dancer but thought if she puts a bit of seductive movements in she might get away with it, 'bollocks' she slipped again, and again there was laughter, again she wanted to machine gun the lot of them down, she was getting angry but continued to move to the music. It would be a long song she thought and then a bottle went hurtling passed her right ear, there was a scuffle in the audience and she could see orders coming from the man they call Winston, he pointed, they reacted, and the man was beaten in front of her. She continued to dance, she was getting better she thought, and she started to feel more positive in every rhythm and note that she moved to. The man who threw the bottle and who was beaten in front of her was now closer to her, and on her last move she managed to kick him straight in the jaw with the toe of her boot, which also got another cheer from the animals in the room. The song finished and Tina stepped down from the stage, she started to head towards the dressing room when one of the men sitting with Winston grabbed her by the arm, she turned and struck him on his chin, he did not move, again laughter from the Den, she noticed Winston looking up at her, the man she hit pointed at Winston while rubbing his jaw, and she was beckoned by Winston to join him with a wave of his hand.

'Yes arsehole' Tina said.

'You're a very pretty white girl but a shit dancer and I now want you to sit here with me for the rest of the night.'

'Why?', she replied.

'As I said because you're a shit dancer.'

'It's my first time', she replied.

'Then it's your last, trust me it wont get better, now sit with me, you will be paid for the night and you don't have to dance.'

'Says who', she said looking down at him.

'Me Winston, I own the club and theoretically pretty white girl you are now working for me, what's your name?'

'Melody.'

'Sit Melody.'

One of Winston's minders got off his chair and made some room next to Winston; he pulled a chair from an adjoining table and placed it next to Winston.

'Ok for a bit' said Tina,' but then I have to leave, I have children at home'

'What do you want to drink?' he said.

She thought about the question, where she was, what she and Sean had planned to do and why she was there, could she do it, and would she need something strong to help her.

'Double rum' the answer came out of her mouth quicker than she expected, it surprised her she thought.

Winston smiled and she could see his white teeth and a couple of gold caps, it was a friendly smile she thought but also hiding menace within its features.

Another song started up and Tina looked to her left to see Debby rising onto the stage, it was her second dance Tina thought, it meant that something more would have to come off, the more dances the more erotic it got. Tina was now coming to the realisation that she would be spared from that part now, which was probably a good thing. Debby looked down and saw Tina with Winston, she acknowledged Tina with a look of astonishment and concern, and strange, Tina thought it looked like there was some care in her eyes.

Chapter 27

Sean met the police car as arranged and as the door opened he got into the passenger seat and said nothing as instructed by Pete Murray. The police officer in the driver's seat said nothing too, and never even met his gaze. That afternoon Sean had picked up his police officers uniform from his given location, a refuse bin at the rear of Tesco's food store in Streatham High Road, he got it home and tried it on, it fitted snugly but not enough to prevent his freedom of movement, the hat was a little to large for his small head so he stuffed an old t-shirt within it's inside straps to make it fit better. He looked at himself in the mirror, 'smart' he said to himself and started to tug on sleeves and front lapels to get it into shape after being stuffed into the package for gods knows how long he thought.

Everything was arranged by Pete or Pete's friends, either out of the force or some still in the force, there wasn't a lot of planning done by Sean and Tina this time which scared him, he was following someone else's strategy but he and Tina were the operators. He was going through it in his head, at this time I need to be here, I need to leave the house at this time, don't speak to the policeman in the car, when I get there move on my own terms, I am on my own when I get there, get her out, the police car you came in will be at this position with the doors open and the keys will be in my uniform jacket pocket. Do not speak to anyone else. When you arrive at your destination, there will be clothes for me and Tina in the police cars boot, Pete said, change clothes and throw everything in the boot and leave immediately. Sean left the house at the correct time after folding his police officers uniform into a large bag; he threw the bag into the boot of his car and headed towards Kennington. As he drove he continued with his thoughts in his head, and as usual they troubled him but continued to throw them away with ease. He headed towards a quieter street as he had planned, he chose a destination that he could park up and change into his police uniform without being spotted by anyone. He then went to the street where he was meant to meet the policeman in his car that Pete had arranged.

The policeman was to Sean's right in the drivers seat, and he still remained silent, it made Sean more nervous, Sean watched the police officer, he wasn't young, he thought, he seemed to be middle aged and appeared very experienced and professional and concentrating on his task. Sean wondered about him, was he a bent copper, why was he doing this, if Sean and Tina got caught it could jeopardise this policeman's career, Sean could sense his stare and thoughts were making the policeman uncomfortable as his grip on the steering wheel was getting tighter. Sean moved his head and felt the tension in the car subside almost immediately. The car did not move for at least ten minutes and the silence in the car was unmistakably spooky for Sean, he was relieved when the policeman looked at his watch for the fourth time and then eventually turned the key into the ignition and pulled away from the kerb.

Chapter 28

Tina looked at her watch, 'fuck' she thought the plan is well early, I'm already with Winston, I didn't even need to flirt with him and the raid is still another three hours away, what the fuck am I going to do with this black fucker for the next three hours. Tina thought harder at the time lines she had, dance, get Winston's attention, somehow get him to take me to his office by a certain time, kill the fucker and wait for the raid, fuck, kill the fucker, she thought, forgot about that part. The weapon, fuck the weapon, it's in my bag in the changing rooms, I need to get to the weapon, Tina felt a hand on her leg, she turned to face Winston and again noticed his broad smile with white and gold teeth staring back at her.

'You're away with the fairies missy, what up?'

Tina gulped back in her throat, she was all of a sudden taken back by the whole scene, she was in a black gangsters club in Brixton sitting with a gangster she was about to try and kill. She gulped again and realised that this probably doesn't look good; Winston will start to get suspicious. The man that shifted his seat to make way for Tina returned from the bar and put the double rum on the table in front of Tina, he put what looked like the same drink down in front of Winston and then moved away from the table. This gave Tina time to compose herself, she picked up the glass and downed half of it's contents before returning it to the table, and she sat back in her chair and managed to say something although in a garbled manner.

' I need to go to the toilet, and I need my bag.'

'Why missy you look scared, what in your bag you need so desperately?'

Again Tina stumbled for the words.

'Things just things, I need my things.'

She was losing it, it was all falling apart I am a failure, she thought, she felt deep depression growing inside her, it was her fault it's failing, fuck, fuck, fuck, she thought, until Winston spoke again.

'I have things here for you, you don't need your bag, what's in your bag is not as good as what I have here for you, it will make you happier then the cheap shit you have in your bag.'

Tina sensed a breakthrough with Winston's last statement but she still had the problem of getting away from him to get to the knife in the bag, until she remembered she told him she had kids.

'And where are these things you have for me?' she said.

'They are in my office' his smile broadened even more and even more menacing were his last words, but Tina couldn't believe how easy everything seemed to be going to plan but way too early, she needed to pause, take stock of the situation and ease on the gas pedal a bit.

'Your office?' she said.

'Yes my office we can go up there relax a bit and I can make you happy with things.'

'Things?' she said again.

'Yes things, the things that you want to go back to your bag for, things that will make you relaxed.'

'Oh those things, If I'm going to go to your office to relax, as you say, I will need to ensure my children are taken care of, so I will need to make a phone call, and I also need to piss.'

'Go and piss Missy, make your phone call but be back sharpish, I like you next to me, it makes me feel alive.'

Tina looked at him and inwardly smiled, she stood up and went to walk away when she felt a hard slap on her behind she turned to see the familiar broad smile, that was good she thought, it made her angry, I work better when I'm angry, she smiled at Winston and walked towards the changing room. From the corner of her eye she could see that the same man who moved the chairs and brought the drinks to the table was summoned by Winston to follow her.

Tina walked towards the changing rooms, she looked up at the stage, Debby was still dancing, she had no bra on and was busy pulling down her knickers erotically for the punters, and she noticed Debby took a glance her way. As she got to the changing room she could see that Ally was sitting at the mirror, she was next on stage and was preparing to go on.

'Fuck Mel you're already at his table, do you know what your doing girl' said Ally as she looked up at Tina.

'I do Ally yes, but I need to hurry I'm sorry, I have to call my kids.'

Tina started to go through her bag looking for change for the phone making sure Ally couldn't see the large knife wrapped in a cloth at the bottom of the bag, she didn't have any change, not that it mattered she wasn't gong to call anyone anyway.

'Have you got change for the phone Ally?' she said.

'Yes of course.'

When Ally turned to look in her purse Tina took the opportunity to retrieve the knife from the bag and slide it into her boot.

'Here you go Mel, said Ally, 'but listen be careful, I'm not sure you know what you are doing.'

The door opened and the chair and drinks man stood in the doorway just staring at Tina until Debby barged passed him telling him to 'get the fuck out of the way'

Tina left the changing room, she thanked Ally for the change and went down the stairs to the large darkened club room looking for a phone box, it took her a while to again adjust to the darkness but then saw in the corner of the room the public phone box. She was hoping someone was using it so it would kill a bit more time but no it was empty, it looked lonely standing there in the corner all by itself, It made Tina smile in a sarcastic way, all the times she has stood in the rain and cold waiting outside phone boxes for people to finish so she could call Sean for a five minute chat, and now she wants to wait she cant. She got to the phone and as best she could she pretended to make the phone call, with the chair and drinks fat oath behind her making sure she didn't do anything that would upset his boss. Tina returned to the table, Ally was dancing, Winston gave that same sick broad smile and put his hand on Tina's thigh, she left it there, it made her more angry, it helped her, it made her feel in control in some weird way.

'My kids are taken care of, when can I have some of those special things you say you have?' she said.

Winston turned and gave Tina his broad smile, 'soon Missy soon, I'm watching the dancing, enjoy your drink.'

210

Tina looked up; Ally was dancing away and doing a better job than she could, she thought. She moved her hand, she felt comfort in the handle of the knife just inside her boot, she remembered the day in the warehouse, the laughter, the noise of the punches, she wanted to stab this cunt next to her in the neck now, he was less then two feet away from her, easy, she thought, pull it out, stick in it his neck and run like fuck, she wanted to, she couldn't, she had to stick to the plan, she promised Sean and Pete. Tina looked at her watch, she was now on time, but needed to get to the room with Winston before the raid and kill him, she had less than ten minutes to get to the room, less than twenty minutes to kill the cunt, and thirty minutes time the raid will take place. The dancing continued, Ally had left the stage and Debby was now up there, she had her back to the audience, she was naked from the top down and started to slowly pull down her knickers, her long shapely legs started at her high heels and went right up to the start of her buttocks. Very slowly she peeled her knickers off revealing her moist pussy lips, Tina looked around, first time the lions dens was silent she noticed, and at the same time Winston's grip got tighter on her thigh.

'You're hurting me,' Tina said.

Again Winston turned, but this time no smile.

'You're hurting me,' she repeated.

Winston released his grip and then smiled, 'time to go to my office for some special things for you, missy, come lets go.'

Winston kicked the chair back, he pulled Tina up by her arm and started to walk away from the table, she pulled his arm off hers and followed him, leaving the others in the den staring at them as they walked off.

The room looked like any office, dark, and smelt of dust, there was a couch, a drinks cabinet and a small lamp on a desk that looked like it never gets used for any office activity. Tina looked at her watch; she was running out of time, change tactics she thought as she noticed Winston was locking the door.

'I've never slept with a black man', she said.

'Nor have I' replied Winston with a smirk.

'They say, go with a black, never look back, is it true', she said.

Winston looked like he ignored the remark, 'my friend out there, the one that followed you to the dressing room and the toilet', he said.

'What about him?'

'He said you never went to the toilet, but you told me you needed a piss.'

Tina fell silent, she didn't know how to answer, how stupid could she have been, I've made a mistake, she thought to herself, she was in a locked room with a fucking mental case and she didn't know what to say, she didn't need to say anything, because Winston spoke next.

'Do you still need a piss missy?'

'I do yes', she replied, 'I was so nervous of the dancing thing and all that, I just forgot about the piss bit, but now you mention it, I need to piss, where's your bog.'

Winston opened a draw from the desk; he pulled out a small packet, opened it, he made two lines of white powder on the table, rolled a ten-pound note and snorted them up both his nostrils.

'You want some missy, some of the special stuff, it will make you relaxed?'

'I really need to piss thanks.'

Winston left the desk, he moved across the room with an air of authority, he went to a corner of the room, grabbed a hook on the wall and pulled hard, pulling down a double bed from it's hidden wall.

'There missy, there is your bog.'

'What do you mean, there's the fucking bog?'

Now she was scared, she didn't know what the fuck he was on about, he was on drugs probably drunk and now he is saying the bed is a bog, she was confused and again looked at her watch for comfort, ten minutes, ten fucking minutes, she thought.

'I like piss missy and I like white piss, I'm going to lay on the bed and you are going to lean over me and piss on me, for an extra fee of course.'

Again silence in the room, he's fucking mad Tina thought, oh fuck what a fucking situation, I just need to get close and kill the fucker, she still didn't speak.

Winston went to a safe, he opened it and pulled out what he said was two hundred pounds.

'There you go missy, extra fees, special things, like I said, you just piss away and fuck good old Winston.'

Tina looked at her watch, seven minutes to the raid.

'I just piss on you fuck you and I get two hundred quid?' she said.

'Yes missy' Winston threw the money on the bed and started to undress, when he had finished she could do nothing but stare at length of his black manhood, he walked over and lay on the bed. ' Now take your knickers off missy, lay over me like the sixty nine and piss for England, or if not for England then for two hundred quid', he laughed.

Winston lay on the bed and was now lighting up a joint, puffing away on it, Tina could see that even the thought of what was about to happen was making him hard. How the fuck is she going to get out of this she looked at her watch again, five minutes to the raid, she thought about the situation further and realised that she will be very close to him at some point which should make it easier for her, she started to walk over to the bed. 'No knickers!' Winston yelled.

Tina stopped and started to remove her knickers, she pulled them over her boots making sure the knife was not dislodged in any way, she walked over to the bed, she was scared but ready, she stood by the bed. Winston was puffing away on the joint between his lips, she could smell the weed coming up into her nostrils, she felt sick and scared, she looked down, this fucker beat Taylor with a belt, she thought, she moved quicker, she climbed onto the bed, she opened her legs and straddled Winston's head, she peered down at his massive manhood. 'Fucking beautiful Missy, fucking beautiful', he said, 'now piss for Winston, piss all over me while I wank my cock in front of you.'

Tina was shocked, he was waiting for her, she knew the time was near for the raid, she had to move fast and do it well, she could not piss even if she needed to, what followed was swift and shocking to both parties. Tina moved her arm around to her boot, she didn't know where to stick the knife in, the plan was to go in his neck as Pete said, go for the jugular, she had the handle of the knife gripped in her hand now, her eyes could only see cock, she pulled the knife from her boot and she brought it down slashing from the right completely removing the cock from it's owner, there was no noise from Winston but blood spurted up into the room and all over Tina, her face and upper body. She came down again only this time leaning back sitting straight on Winston's face and stabbing deep into his heart with three constant stabs, still no noise but blood was now spurting out of his groin and his heart was pumping it out like a red fountain in timely spurts. Tina jumped off the bed onto the floor, she was covered in blood, she looked at the bed, there was still blood pulsating out of Winston, there was no sound from him, just the noise of blood hitting the wooden floor, she looked to her left, the penis was laying there about two feet away, it was just laying there like it was lost, she stared at it, stared again at the bed, no movement, she was alive and the cunt was dead, she still could not hear anything, as she lay there covered in blood.

Chapter 29

Sean joined the policeman breaking down the club doors, he joined them as they ran through the club shouting at people telling them it's a raid and for them all to stay calm, he looked for the stairs, to the right, to the right, Pete had said. Sean ran towards the stairs, the light was dim, he could see people running from left to right, he ran past the toilets where people were throwing stuff down the traps and hastily flushing the contents away. He got to the stairs just by the dressing rooms, he climbed the stairs, and he came across Debby and Ally, they dragged him back down the stairs, they were screaming at him, fucking pigs, fucking pigs, he tried to pull away, he kicked out and first caught Ally in the face and than Debby across her chest, they fell back, he ran again for the stair. He got to the top and found the office door, he tried the lever, it was locked, again the two women had caught up with him, they tore at his skin with sharp nails, they pulled at his hair, he punched Debby clean on the jaw, she went flying back down the stairs, Ally pulled away.

'Get the fuck away from me you fucking bitch!' he shouted at her.

Sean could not wait any longer, he pulled back from the door and gave one heavy kick to where he believed the lock was, it didn't give way, he tried again, and it still didn't give way. This time frustration made his adrenalin kick in more then it already was and he kicked at the door screaming, the door gave way, it smashed wide open. He saw red everywhere, and then he saw

Winston on the bed covered in blood, he looked dead. He could not see Tina so he ran into the room frantically searching, and instantly saw Tina behind the bed, and she was covered in blood. 'Tina, Tina, fucking hell Tina! He screamed.

He ran to her and cradled her in his arms 'are you ok, Tina are you ok, are you hurt', he saw the penis lying on the floor, 'fuck, fucking hell, Tina.'

Tina looked up at him, 'that's for Taylor Sean', she said, 'that's for Taylor, I'm ok Sean.'

Fucking hell, he thought, I didn't think she would be covered in blood, he looked around the room but he couldn't find anything to cover her with.

'You will need this' he heard from behind him.

Sean turned, he saw Ally standing at the door with a large coat, and he stared at her.

'If you want to get her out, you will need this' she said.

Sean grabbed the coat, picked Tina up and wrapped her in it and headed for the exit, they walked passed Ally who just stared at the pair of them.

'Thanks' Sean said, as he held tighter onto Tina.

'Walk with me Tina', he said, 'hold on to me and walk with me, keep your head close to my body, it's full of blood.'

They descended the stairs, Debby was still lying on the floor unconscious, but Sean could see she was breathing. There was still some minor commotion in the club, shouting and obscenities at the police, this helped Sean, he saw the policeman he recognised from the car, who pointed towards the exit. Sean held Tina close, there were some minor stares but the unknown policeman guided any interest away. They made it outside, it was dark, there was a crowd starting to gather, and they were making it clear it wasn't right for the police to raid their clubs in Brixton, they were getting curious restless and brave and Sean could feel it in the air. The police car was where it should be, they got in, the keys were where they should be, the crowd was getting closer, riot police were there but it didn't seem enough, bottles started to rain down everywhere, and the police had their riot shields out. Objects started to hit the windscreen and car roof as Sean started the engine and pulled away. The streets were dark and in the rear view mirror Sean could see fires had started in the area they had just been in, he got clear just in time, he could see and hear police cars and fire engines passing him going the other way flashing their lights and sirens towards trouble. He knew they had made it, 'it's ok Tina, he said as he looked down at her, 'we are going the other way, 'we are going home Tina', he said to her again, 'we are going home.'

Chapter 30

Johnny Saunders lifted his shotgun; he fired it once, then again, then lowered it down and passed it to the man next to him to reload. The man reloaded and passed the shotgun back to Johnny, this time he took a more careful aim, he didn't want to wound his target he wanted it dead and he hadn't killed for a while and wanted revenge. His aim this time was more accurate and after the second attempt he saw the dog run from out of the undergrowth and go to pick up his prize.

'Good shot Johnny!' shouted John Wall.

'Yeah got the bastard this time' shouted Johnny.

'I ain't had a hit all day!' shouted John Wall.

'That's because you're a copper John, coppers don't know how to use shotguns, they only know how to use truncheons, next time try throwing your truncheon at the fucking thing. I bet you get it right between the eyes', Johnny laughed hysterically, John Wall looked at him and wished he wasn't there.

The day was cold and Johnny was out pheasant shooting with john Wall and his accountant Chris Shultz, he needed to discuss matters with his accountant and also needed to have an update from John Wall the bent copper who was pursuing Johnny's requirements for information. A siren blew and the three of them walked off together towards the barn where hot drinks were being served.

'I'm telling you John I pay you good money to get me information from the street and the old bill, and you have come up with jack shit, when you gonna earn your money.'

'I'm asking questions Johnny, I think people are on to me, no one is telling me anything, you're right I'm getting jack shit at the moment.'

'Look John, Stan is dead, Ray is dead, my fifty grand is still on the fucking missing list, and you still ain't got a clue where the fuck Sean Farrow is, what are you a fucking thick or something? What about his bird, you know Tina Docherty, what about her, have you been asking questions about her? If you find her you find Sean Farrow.'

'I know that Johnny, give me a bit more time, I will come up with something, everyone has shut up shop. Johnny I need some more funds, you haven't paid me for a while and things are getting tough.'

Johnny stopped in his tracks, he looked at John Wall, and then he looked across to Chris Shultz.

'Chris have we got any money?' He asked.

'No boss' Chris Shultz replied.

Johnny started to walk again with the two following closely behind, with John Wall's boots sticking in the mud as he tried desperately to catch up.

'There you go John, the accountant says we have no money and that's what I pay him for, we will have money though when you get my fucking fifty grand back, until then fuck off.'

'Johnny, there is one thing' John Wall said while trying to catch his breath.

'What's that', Johnny replied, and again stops in his tracks with the delight of John Wall clearly showing on his face and his breathing.

'I've heard some rumours that the Met are also looking for the fifty grand, and if they get the money first, then they can get to you, the domino effect they call it. That's my option in finding the fifty grand, I've got some contacts in the Met that are leading that operation, if I can get to it before they do, and if I do, then maybe we can come to some arrangement.'

'Arrangement, what kind of arrangement', replied Johnny.

'Well I was thinking maybe we can come to some agreement on a percentage.'

'Do you know where my money is Wallsy?' asked Johnny.

John Wall cut in very quickly with both Johnny and Chris Shultz staring into his face.

'No Johnny, not at all, but I'm getting closer, a little incentive may get me closer as I may need to pay people off.'

There was silence in the fields around the three of them, apart from the sound of dogs being gathered by their owners near the barns where they were heading. Johnny Saunders took off again with a good pace towards the barn, there were pheasants on the table from the morning kill, Johnny picked one up, and looked at it.

'This looks like one of mine', he said as he turned to John Wall, he handed John Wall the pheasant.

'There you go', he said, 'payment for this morning's information which was fuck all, you're lucky to get anything at all with the shit you coughed up today', Johnny continued, 'and another thing any more fucking talk about arrangements and I will have your bollocks on a plate you got it Wallsy.'

John Wall looked at Johnny; he then looked at Chris Shultz who as usual had his poker face revealing fuck all, John Wall thought.

'Ok Johnny, I will see what I can get for next week or sooner if something comes up.'

John Wall turned and started to walk away, he had his prized pheasant in one hand and with his other he was fumbling around inside his jacket pocket for his car keys. He trudged off leaving Johnny and Chris Shultz busy sipping brandy and giggling like little children. One day it will be pay back time for that cunt, he said to himself, but he knew he needed Saunders, he knew he needed his money to help him pay for his mother's care. He noticed his boots were sticking deep into the mud as he trudged off towards his car, and he felt sorry for himself, he felt low and incapable of being a true police officer, was he bad, was he bad for what he was doing and giving information to people like Johnny Saunders. He thought about being a policeman and the money that he got for chasing villains who were earning a lot more then he was, he just needed to do it a bit more, well at least while his mother is alive. When she's passed away then he could stop what he was doing, if Johnny Saunders would allow it he thought.

'What you looking so fucked off about Wallsy?' he heard in front of him

John Wall looked up to see Charlie Allan looking down at him with a slight grin on his face.

'Bad shooting day that's all Charlie', he said, 'bad shooting day, anyway what you doing here?'

'I'm here to make Johnny's day even worse for him, he will probably look like you when I've told him what I've just found out myself.'

'What's that then' John Wall asked.

'You best get yourself out of here Wallsy, because I think you're going to be asked to snoop around a bit more then you currently are.'

Charlie Allan turned with that slight grin still on his face and headed towards the location where John Wall had come from, he moved with an air of arrogance with his long coat flapping in the wind leaving John Wall watching him leave and wondering what shit storm is about to come his way.

Charlie Allan knew this was going to be a bad day as soon as he heard the news from one of his team, he wondered how bad a day it was going to be, but he also wondered about his vulnerability now that he was losing his best men around him. Even worse

Johnny was starting to lose his grip on reality and potentially realising that there were younger people that were starting to show their faces around London. This was becoming a threat to Johnny's empire and there was still no news on the money, or who was topping his men, that was what scared Charlie, Johnny knowing that they were no nearer to discovering who or what was causing the problems lately. Charlie looked into the distance, he could see Johnny standing there with Chris Shultz who was obviously introducing him to some influential people that could help him or he could threaten. He never did like Chris Shultz, he thought, the brainy fucker who never smiled, had a weak handshake and probably took one up the arse at every opportunity, he laughed to himself as he approached Johnny. Johnny was laughing like a hyena, and patting someone on the back, who was talking like he had a frog in his throat, or a silver spoon stuck up his arse.

'What you looking so cheerful about', Johnny said looking up at Charlie.

'Wallsy boss I just passed him you must have given him a bit of an ear bashing as he looked like he's just lost ten grand or something.'

'You couldn't be any nearer the truth Charlie.'

Charlie looked down at Chris Shultz who was looking at him with that fucking Eton College stare, they shook hands and again Charlie thought it was like shaking hands with Alison fucking Wonderland.

'What you doing here, I don't remember calling for you', said Johnny.

'Got some news boss, we might want to go somewhere a bit more quiet.'

'Good news Charlie.'

'Not so good boss, no' replied Charlie.

Johnny turned to Chris Shultz, 'Chris take care of Mr Barrington here and make sure you care for all his needs I will be a few minutes', he turned to Mr Barrington, they shook hands and Chris Schulz escorted Mr Barrington away.

'Now what's all this shit your gonna bring my way today Charlie', said Johnny, ' I was having a restful time, are you gonna fuck it up for me, and don't tell me you're suing me for headaches', he laughed, Charlie didn't.

They moved far enough away from the table so no one could hear.

'It's Winston boss, he's been killed, it's a fucking sand storm, someone is out there deliberately targeting your men and we ain't got a fucking clue who it is.'

Johnny stood there and took in all the information that Charlie was telling him. Charlie could see the vein on Johnny's temple start to throb, a bad sign Charlie thought. There was silence between them and then Johnny pulled out a cigar, bit the end off and then waited for Charlie to light it for him. There was a hesitation, Johnny thought, months ago Charlie would have leapt with the lighter without hesitation, now there was a pause, Johnny didn't like that, was he losing his grip? Charlie pulled out his lighter and lit Johnny's cigar, there was still silence between them, and Charlie allowed his boss to respond.

'You see that man in there Charlie, with Shultz', that Mr Barrington bloke', Charlie nodded, 'that's our future, that man in there can make us more money then we can dream of. He's where we need to be going Charlie; he's a City gent and a banker who has some real good contacts, so we can move money around a lot easier. He's a poof though, so I've already started paying for rent boys for him, he cant get enough of them fucking shirt lifter.'

Charlie was looking at Johnny as if he had lost his marbles, was he starting to crack under the pressure, was he getting worried, but worse of all Charlie was starting to think if it was time for him to get out.

'And Winston boss?' said Charlie.

'Fuck Winston', Johnny said as he sucked on his cigar and blew the smoke into the air, he can be replaced.'

'There's a couple of things I need you to do Charlie, I've been thinking, you and the team, well what's fucking left of you, ain't come up with fuck all and as for fucking Wallsy, he's as useful as a fucking chocolate tea pot. I need you to find someone for me, someone who might be able to help us find Sean Farrow, I'm sure he's got my money.'

'We've tried that boss, not come up with anything.'

'That's because you ain't leant on them Charlie, not hurt them in any way, start with Patsy Docherty, then Pete Murray, they're not in hiding, they are bound to know where he is or have something to do with it.'

Charlie nodded and then went to turn and walk away, Johnny looked around to see if anyone was nearby and the cold air met his face.

'And Charlie!' Johnny called out, 'you can hurt Patsy to get her to speak but if Murray says fuck all, then you can kill the fucking pig.'

Charlie nodded again, turned and walked away leaving Johnny sucking on his cigar, he pulled his coat in tighter around his large body, getting fucking cold, he thought to himself, getting fucking cold.

Chapter 31

Charlie Allan left Johnny in the office cursing what was going on. He had given Charlie new actions for the day; we need to see if we can recruit new people into the team and who can take over from Stan, Ray and Winston, Saunders had said. Charlie had his ideas who he could recruit, there were people that were already working for him and they had started to show promise. Winston's friend seemed very experienced and Winston was gradually showing him the ropes and bringing him along to some of the meetings with him, so there was promise there, until Winston was killed. Charlie knew he had a good day ahead of him, he would be visiting friends and people that lived in his world, he would meet them in pubs, clubs, gambling halls and he would do this all day until he knew who he could rely on. But he also knew he would have to test them at some point. Charlie also had another task that he has not completed yet, and that was the order from Johnny that he needed to take care of Billy Boy, for the shit information on the dogs at the dog track. Charlie was hoping that Johnny had forgotten all about it, but no, every now and then Johnny would bring it up, so Charlie knew it was a job that would have to be completed soon. Part of today would be about who he can bring along to help him carry out that action of Johnny's, Charlie thought, he would choose right to make the task easier.

Charlie started the engine of his car and knew he would have to start the day driving around the streets of South London visiting pubs that he knew his colleagues would be in. At the end of the day he was hoping he would have people who could assist him in visiting Billy Boy as well as the potential to replace Stan, Ray and Winston.

After a long day meeting old faces and drinking heavily, Charlie Allan felt confident he had the right people with the right mentality to work alongside him. These were people he could trust but were also hard men with experience of inside and outside of prison life, something Charlie was looking for.

Charlie went back to the office hoping that Johnny would still be there, he parked the car and entered the building. When he entered the office he noticed Johnny was there and busy in a meeting with his accountant Chris Shultz. Johnny and the accountant looked up at him, Charlie nodded and went to the drinks cabinet and poured himself a whiskey and took a seat in the back office and waited.

'Charlie, Chris Shultz is leaving! He heard Johnny shout, 'come in here I need to know what's going on.'

Chris Shultz the accountant got out of his chair, to the relief of Charlie there was no handshake as he left the office, and Charlie entered the office.

'So what's going on Charlie?' Johnny said.

'No fifty grand boss and no Sean Farrow, but after our discussion I've managed to pull some people together to improve numbers, but they're talking boss, there's rumours that someone's trying to pull you down and that ain't good for business'

'Pull me down, what do you mean pull me down?'

'They know you have lost some of the boys and they think if they work for you they will go the same way, and not only that, they say you don't know who's doing it.'

'Right, I will sort that, and Billy Boy?'

'Tonight boss, I'm gonna deal with him tonight, how do you want it done, do you want me to warn him or hurt him?'

'Hurt him Charlie, we need to get our reputation back up, we also need people to know that we did it.'

'Are you sure boss? Ain't it better to wait until we have built our workforce up a bit.'

'No do it as I say and spread the word, where are you planning on doing it?'

'He's due in the pub tonight, so I was gonna go in there and bash some heads together, I've got Winston's mate with me and three others.'

'Three others, are you gonna need three others', replied Johnny

'I'm testing new people boss.'

'Are you taking guns with you' said Johnny.

'Yes boss.'

'Ok Charlie, do it tonight and report back tomorrow, and I want to meet these three others, are they trustworthy?'

'Yes boss, they have all the qualities you were looking for, I will see how it goes later and bring them here for a bit of an interview.'

Johnny looked at Charlie with a look of mistrust, it worried him that he was now feeling vulnerable, and the one he could always trust was now bringing doubt into his mind.

'Ok Charlie', he said, 'and what pub is it Billy Boy is going to tonight.'

'The Pheasant Arms boss', he replied.

Charlie left the office and made his way home, he prepared himself mentally for what would happen tonight. He ate some food, drank a little whiskey and prepared himself a line of cocaine on the table, he snorted it sat back and let the lines go through his brain. Charlie met his team at eight o'clock and they travelled towards Streatham where The Pheasant Arms was situated. They waited down a side street in the car until they saw Billy Boy enter the pub, he had two others with him, and Charlie and the team didn't see that as a problem as they were armed. The pub was large, and it was unusually busy for a midweek, and as Charlie entered, not many people took much notice. Charlie looked around, Billy Boy was looking up at him from a corner of the room, and he nodded at Charlie. Charlie and the team approached the table that Billy Boy was sitting at. Billy Boy and his two friends looked up, they could sense there was a problem.

'Evening Charlie, is there a problem?' said Billy boy looking up at him with fear and trepidation of what was about to potentially happen.

'Yes Bill, there is a problem, Johnny is fucked off with you, you gave him dead dogs the other day, he lost a lot of fucking money.'

'He's lost it Charlie,' replied Billy Boy, 'he's old School, you need to think about your future, I heard he bottled you at the dogs, is that how he repays you for your commitment.'

Charlie looked down at Billy Boy, Charlie could sense the atmosphere in the pub, he could feel the tension in his new crew he had with him tonight, he had to show face, and he had to deal with this man in front of him quickly, and he didn't want to waste time.

'Fuck you Bill, that's not how it is, I'm gonna fucking show you how it is', he said.

'Charlie pulled out his gun from his jacket, pointed at Bill and shot him in the leg, the others with Charlie pulled out their guns and fired at the three sitting there. One of the three tried to run, but he was shot in the back before he could get to the door, and one was killed as he sat in the chair. Billy boy lay on the floor screaming in pain from the bullet he received from Charlie in his leg. Charlie made the others stop shooting; it was over in seconds, Charlie looked down at Billy Boy.

'That's your fucking lesson Bill, learn from it.'

Charlie and his team turned and walked out of the pub, on exiting Charlie shouted out a warning to those still in the pub that if anyone spoke to the police they would be found and get the same. Those that were left stood and listened, and they watched them leave with astonishment and fear in their faces.

Chapter 32

Charlie Allan couldn't sleep, he was tossing and turning and he knew why. He was starting to mistrust everyone and everything, he even thought about Johnny Saunders and when the bastard smashed that bottle over his head at the dogs. Since that day he has been thinking about revenge, but knew it would be hard to get to him. He lay there in his room looking up at the ceiling rose dangling there in the dim light, he looked down at his watch, he pressed a button on the side to show a dim light, three thirty in the morning, there's no way I'm going to get to sleep now, he thought. He got up went into the kitchen in his pants and turned the kettle on. He stood in his kitchen, and thought how he had new problems, everyone around him was getting topped and he didn't know who it was, he was wondering if he was next, and was wondering where the fifty grand went to, and that Billy Boy will probably be wanting revenge. The kettle boiled and Charlie Allan poured the hot contents into a cup, he added two sugars, milk out of the fridge and stirred it looking out of the window. He was safe where he was, he thought, not many people know where I live, people in the pub will be too scared to talk to the police and Billy Boy will take a while to walk again, he felt better in himself. He moved into the front room and sat down on his chair to ponder a bit more and see if he could come up with a new strategy, maybe get away completely, go to Spain, I mean every other criminal is in Spain. I could settle down there learn the language and maybe open a bar. He smiled at himself being a bar owner, I'm only good at one thing and that's smashing people's heads in, I would be deported back to England in a week. He smiled again to himself and sipped on his hot tea, a dog barked outside in the street, he listened again, the dog barked again and was not stopping, it was barking at something or someone. Charlie got up and pulled back the curtain slightly, he waited until his eyes adjusted to the light and when they did fear went through his body, he could see police, he could see them coming up the path to his block of flats. They were carrying sledgehammers, and he knew why, they were there to break down doors, and possibly his.

Charlie Allan pushed the curtain back looked around his room, no time, he thought to himself, he ran to the rear of his apartment, he pulled the double curtains back and turned the key into the balcony door and just as he started to turn the handle he heard the first sledge hammer smash against his front door. He opened the door and ran onto the balcony, he knew the route well, he jumped onto the handrails and grabbed hold of the drain pipe that was adjacent to him, he gripped hard and leapt onto the drain pipe and started to slide down gripping on as hard as he could, he was on the second floor and he knew it was a long way down. He felt the cold against his naked body, he felt the cold from the cast iron pipes on his hands, he then heard the splintering of his front door give way and shouting policeman entering his apartment, not long now, he thought, another twenty feet, he looked up just as a policeman looked over his balcony, there was shouting and commotion. Charlie Allan looked down, another fifteen feet, he thought and decided to take a chance and jump, he did and landed on soft grass and rolled. He jumped to his feet and started to run in the direction that he had practised so many times before he knew he needed to get to the alley, he ran across the grass and down the alley hearing shouting behind him and now running footsteps. He could now see the end of the alley, once there he knows he can jump a small fence and run onto the railway line, cross over the track and then climb another small fence and enter his other safe house from the rear. He never made the end of the alley, he saw them too late but they came from the side not the rear, he felt the first truncheon hit him on the side of the head with full force, he felt the weight of about four coppers pounce on him, they hit him and hit him as hard as they could across his body. He heard them screaming at him as they hit, he then felt the arms go around his back and then the handcuffs locked on, it was then he blacked out as they continued to hit.

Charlie Allan was taken to court, he was bruised and battered but it was all down to him falling from his balcony as he tried to escape according to the police. He had no solution to his problem, Johnny Saunders weight in the community was slipping away with the loss of his closest gang members, and any legal team who used to work for Johnny could now refuse without major repercussions. He stood in the dock alongside the others accused of grievous bodily harm to Billy Boy and murder to the other two, and he was worried he may be framed for both. Those who were in the pub did have the bottle in the end to suggest who committed the assault; they either had the bottle or were getting off some of their crimes by helping the police. It didn't take the jury long, they convicted the other three with murder and would eventually get a life sentence, Charlie Allan was given attempted murder but a lighter sentence as he somehow convinced the jury he just fired a warning shot to Billy Boys leg and that he stopped the others from killing him. Charlie Allan was given ten years in prison and would only be eligible for parole after seven years. Charlie was escorted below the courts by two prison guards and as he walked he reflected how Johnny Saunders was nowhere to be seen throughout the case and Charlie Allan wondered if he would he ever see him again.

Chapter 33

Sean was sitting on his bar stool in his kitchen; he was thinking about recent times, and about how Tina and he had gone through a stressful time lately. They had to lie low and rely on any savings they had to buy food and provisions, for what they needed to carry out their agreed actions. It's not every day, he thought to himself, that you have to kill people occasionally, unless you're Jack the Ripper. He sat there reading a book of poems, unusual for him he thought. He would normally read the sport, gossip columns and basic shit in the newspapers, but he was drawn to a poem this morning as he sat there at the safe house he and Tina had. They had killed three men, Stan Smith, Ray Flynn and Winston Scott and they had heard that the fourth, Charlie Allan was safely locked up in Wandsworth prison, fortunately for him, unfortunately for them. They needed to kill the last one until this was over, and the fifth being the final prize, the ultimate reason why they started this journey in the first place. They were nearly there, but what would the ending bring, he thought, the woman he loves has been through a lot and has been very brave in all that she has done, and he knew why, they were from the same breed that will defend it's culture and family whatever the cost. He looked at the poem again; he read it, and Sean let it sink into his soul again.

A Man can only be a Man when he protects what he loves

A Man can only be a Man when he learns from those above

A Woman can only be a Woman when she trusts what her Man says

A Woman can only be a Woman when she guides family day by day

A Family will be happy, when they love and start anew

A Family will survive, when new family lives come through.

Sean reflected on the poem, he didn't know what it meant, he didn't know who wrote it, but he liked what it was suggesting. He thought it was suggesting peace and love as long as the man has the right woman, and as long as the woman has the right man. He was getting soft, he thought, maybe it's the whiskey he's been drinking for the last two hours, or maybe it's because he never really had a family because he lost them at an early age. He threw that one away, but the poem jumped out at him as if it was written for him. He took another swig of whiskey and allowed himself to think of his parents, which he rarely did because it left him with pain. He drifted to thoughts of them and his sister he never met, his sister that was cruelly taken away from him before he could kiss her on the cheek and welcome her to the Farrow family. He threw it away again; he was good at that, and he got better at it every day. He heard the key in the door, which took him away from his thoughts; he heard the rustle of plastic bags as they hit the floor and the door hitting the framework with the noise of the lock connecting keeping him safe inside. Then he heard footsteps climbing the stairs, the creak of the top step as weight made it's wood distort under pressure and then the squeak of the hinges as the door was pushed open by the woman he loves. She stood there with her wig on to disguise herself from the outside world, Sean sat there and looked at her, the woman he loves looked different, she looked as if she was pissed off, yes pissed off about something, he thought again, he smiled at her as she stood there.

'Bad day babe?' he said.

Tina pulled the wig off her head and threw it to the floor.

'Do you know what it's like wearing that fucking thing in this weather, I'm sweating like a rainforest's monkeys armpit, it's alright for you getting all your hair shaved off and having a skin head haircut to look different, I mean fucking hell Sean, you've gone from a rock freak to a skinhead over night and I have to look like fucking Lu Lu.'

Sean Farrow laughed, he laughed so much, that it made him feel human again, he couldn't stop laughing and the more he looked at Tina's expression the more he laughed. She was pissed off, and the more she was pissed off the more he laughed, she stood there looking at him and eventually she began to smile, she couldn't help it, because that's why she loved him, she loved him because he was a complete arsehole sometimes.

'Come and sit next to me babe you look exhausted', said Sean.

Tina wandered over and sat next to Sean, he put his arm around her and kissed her on the cheek, 'don't worry babe it will all be over soon and then we can relax and go back home.'

'Will we be able to go home soon Sean' she said, 'I mean will this all end, when we've finished all this, how do we know it's actually ended. We're going to need more money, and we know we haven't got too much of that.'

Tina was looking at Sean, he knew he was getting a bit of a bollocking but thought it was best to say nothing and let her have her say.

'And not only that Sean', she repeated, 'you need to get an honest job, you cant go around scamming like you used to do with Taylor, all that needs to end'. Sean continued to listen, he knew her too well he thought, just let her go on and in his head he only heard half of what she was saying anyway, he chuckled inside.

'Ok babe I know what you're saying, I can get a job when this is all over. There's plenty of work around, there's loads of building work in the city and they are looking out for decent labourers, Joe can get me some work easy.'

They both sat there quiet and reflecting on what Sean had said and cuddled each other. Tina had her head on his chest and Sean was stroking her hair. Sean noticed that the familiar tingle was stirring in his groin and he realised it had been a long time since they made love or even fucked. In his head he had already worked out why they had not been intimate, and he knew it was due to what they had been doing in the last few weeks and months, it's not every day that you kill someone and then come home and want to fuck, he thought.

'You ok babe', Sean said, are you ok in your head, you know, in what we have been doing?'

'We've been over this Sean, they deserve what they get, they deserve everything we do to them, it's just not built in us to harm anyone, but they aren't just anyone, these are the people that killed Taylor and my father and they're fucking horrible people. They don't give a shit about anyone but themselves, so yes I'm ok with what we're doing, and I'm ok to carry on until we have killed every last one of them.'

Sean looked down at Tina, he was worried about her and would always feel guilty for involving her in the project, but he knew deep inside that he will always feel more guilty about not helping Taylor when he needed him. That guilt ripped through him daily and the only way to get rid of the guilt was to do what he and Tina were doing, and he knew the guilt would stay with him, even when they had finished.

'I was planning on going to the warehouse', Sean said, 'I haven't been there since all this shit began and we dropped off Tony Clay's van, do you want to come with me? The suits should still be there, the ones he was picking up for Taylor and me, we can sell them off and get a bit of money behind us.'

'And what about Charlie Allan and Johnny Saunders?' said Tina.

'Charlie Allan is not our problem any more since he's been put away, we don't need to worry about him anymore, but I'm meeting Pete later, we can go through it with him, you can come with me.'

'Ok warehouse and then Pete, she said, so we have a plan, I like it when we have a plan, lets just sit here a bit longer though Sean', she said, 'it's been a long time since we had a cuddle, or a fuck for that matter.'

Sean smiled, so she's noticed too he thought.

'Well we can do something about that,' said Sean, and he got off his bar stool and wrapped his arms around Tina, picked her up and walked her to the door, he kicked it open with his foot and then walked her down the hall to the bedroom and threw her on the bed. They made love, they didn't fuck, they didn't feel the need or urge to fuck, lovemaking felt more needy after what they had been through. They kissed and caressed and held onto each other as if it was the first time they were together, they both needed it, it was sexual medicine that would heal how they felt and it bonded them together as if they were one.

Tina shifted her wig until it sat how she wanted it; she looked into the mirror and wondered if she would ever be a brunette again in the outside world. Sean was watching her and was pleased he didn't have to wear a wig and also felt lucky how quick his hair dried now as he hardly had any, he still fancied her, he thought as he watched her dress.

'Come on get up you lazy sod' she said.

They left the house and got into the Austin 1100, they did the same as usual and left by the back door and went down the side alley. The journey to the warehouse was again across town and when they got to the warehouse they approached cautiously not knowing if anyone was watching the warehouse. Even though Taylor and Sean never let anyone know where their warehouse was Sean still felt nervous on the approach to the warehouse and he constantly looked around. He unlocked the padlock and pulled the doors across on it's sliders, he then stepped inside with Tina following, he turned and pulled the sliding doors shut, and switched the light on which was on the side wall, and the warehouse lit up.

Tina looked around the warehouse, she had never been there before, she looked up and around and saw boxes stacked up and saw Tony Clays van with the back doors locked.

'The suits should be in the back of the van, I've got the keys here', said Sean

'What else is in all these boxes', she said.

Sean pointed at some of the boxes in the warehouse, 'those boxes over there are radios from China, those over there are shirts from Italy and those boxes over there are fancy dresses.'

'Fancy dresses?' said Tina.

'Yea fancy dresses open the boxes up and have a look.'

Tina walked over to the boxes; and pulled the sticky tape off and started to go through the contents in the box, Sean was opening the back of the van.

'Blimey, these look a bit posh Sean' she said, 'I'm having one of these', she pulled out a red dress with bows on it and immediately starting pulling it over her head.

Sean had the back door of the van open and could see the crates of suits that were to be delivered to him and Taylor by Tony Clay; he pulled the nearest crate towards him and looked around for a tool to open the crate up. He saw the crowbar on the far wall and asked Tina to pass it to him. He placed the crowbar underneath the lid and lifted it to see the Italian suits neatly folded and separated by soft paper tissue, he pulled one suit out and admired it's quality and then placed in back in the crate. He put the lid back on and counted how many crates there were, adjusting mathematically in his head how much he could get from his buyer.

'Why's that one got a cross on it Sean' said Tina while peering into the back of the van.

'What one', said Sean while turning around to see Tina standing there with her new dress on, that didn't go that well with her boots and jeans underneath? He smiled.

'That one there, it's got a cross on it', she said, 'a red cross, looks like it was done with a crayon.'

Sean looked across the van to see the crate with the Red Cross on it, 'I don't know' he said, 'probably put there during shipping or something.'

'Open that one up', said Tina.

'Why?' replied Sean.

'I don't know, I'm just curious, Tina replied, it might be full of new dresses, I'm just curious why that one has a red cross on it and the others don't.'

'You're just a nosey cow', said Sean you're not happy with one new dress are you.'

'Go on open the box Sean.'

'Anything for you my dear', Sean grabbed the crowbar and pulled the crate down towards him, he pushed the crow bar under the lid and prized it open, he threw the lid to the floor of the van and peered inside, 'more suits he said to Tina, more lovely expensive Italian suits', he picked a few suits from the top and turned to show Tina, 'see love we will get a few bob for these, they are quality these are, quality Italian suits. Tina smiled and Sean turned to put the suits back in, he stood there for a while and didn't continue putting the suits back into the crate, Tina was looking at him.

'What up Sean? He didn't answer, 'Sean what's up?' she said again.

'There's a briefcase in here.'

'A what?'

'A briefcase, there's a briefcase in this crate, it was under the suits.'

'Take it out Sean' she said.

Sean dropped the suits to the floor of the van and pulled the suitcase out of the crate and looked at it, it wasn't heavy, and he kept looking at it.

'Can you open it?' said Tina.

'I don't know but we can have a bloody good go, it's got a combination lock on it.'

Sean jumped down from the back of the van and then dragged the suitcase towards him, they both looked at it, Sean shook it, but there was no noise from inside. Sean went over to the tool chest that was in the corner of the warehouse and pulled out a club hammer and an old screwdriver. While Tina was watching he put the point of the screwdriver against the combination lock and with the hammer hit down on the screwdriver, it didn't budge, he tried again, and again it didn't budge, he adjusted the screwdriver and hit down on it for a third time and the lock snapped and a piece of metal went flying across the warehouse floor. they both looked at each other.

'Well open it then' said Tina.

Sean pulled the suitcase open but it didn't budge, he still needed to force it open, he hit down hard on the lock with the hammer and it snapped the lock further and the suitcase lid flew open. The contents exploded into full view, a case full of money taped up in bundles, they stood there and gasped at the sight in front of them, Sean spoke first.

'Fuck Tina this must be the money Johnny Saunders is fucking on about, the money that he's looking for, fucking hell there must be thousands here, what was it that Saunders said in the warehouse that day, he said fifty grand Tina, fifty fucking grand. Tina was still speechless until very slowly a smile appeared on her face, it got wider and wider until eventually she let out a streak.

'Jesus Christ Sean! What we gonna do with all this money, bloody hell, that's enough to buy a mansion for us.'

'Shit when you put it like that babe, that's a lot of money', said Sean, 'we need to talk to Pete and see what he advises.'

'What are we gonna do with it now, I mean we should keep it right?' said Tina.

Sean started to close the briefcase, 'fucking right we should', Tina stopped him shutting the case, 'take one bundle now and then we will hide the rest', she said.

Sean grabbed one bundle and started to count it, 'one thousand pounds Tina, it's one thousand pounds per bundle, count the bundles.'

Inside the suitcase was fifty bundles, they shut the suitcase and Sean got a strap from the tool chest and strapped the case up, they left the warehouse and locked it up securely leaving the suits behind, they carried the suitcase with them and Tina put it on her lap staring down at it while Sean drove to Pete's house.

Chapter 34

Pete Murray was sitting in front of his TV watching his favourite police drama a programme called Z Cars, he liked watching it, it reminded him of his past work and it made him wish he was still working. The adverts came on and he looked down at the paperwork in front of him, two sets of papers, one titled Charlie Allan and one titled Johnny Saunders, inside each file were descriptions dates, times, etc. of where they would be, what their favourite places were and where they lived. He picked up the Charlie Allan file and started to write something inside when the doorbell rang. He knew who it would be, but for safety and just in case, he picked both sets of papers up and put them into a draw in the side cabinet. He looked through the spy hole and saw Sean and Tina standing there, so he pulled back the two bolts and opened the door.

'Going on holiday are we', Pete said as he looked down at the suitcase.

'Put the kettle on Pete' said Sean and handed him a packet of Ginger nut biscuit's, 'this could be a long visit.'

Pete re-bolted the door and walked into the kitchen and put the kettle on the stove, 'something new then, something you need to tell me?' he asked.

'You could say that Pete, lets have a cup of tea first and talk about Charlie Allan and then we will share our news.'

249

'Oh yeah, Charlie Allan, well I have got some news, not good news but a bit of a bloody hindrance' Pete walked back into the front room to see Sean and Tina sitting on his sofa with Tina holding the suitcase on her lap, as if it was gold dust.

'You two alright', said Pete, 'only you look like you've just stolen from my cookie jar.'

'Yes Pete', said Sean, 'and Charlie Allan, what about him?'

'He's been nicked for trying to shoot Billy Boy's legs off, he got ten years, so we wont be seeing him for a while', Pete looked down at Tina, 'you sure you're alright Tina?'

'Yes Pete, I'm alright' she replied, 'we know about Charlie Allan, Joe let us know about it, I was disappointed, but me and Sean have discussed it' Tina could hear the whistle on the kettle start, 'your kettles boiling Pete,' she told him.

Pete walked into the kitchen, 'yeah, so he got caught because someone was brave enough to grass on him and was a witness at the court case. They identified him as taking the first shot, the others with him as taking the fatal shots so they got life, Charlie got off with murder because, he managed to persuade the jury that his shot was not to kill but to maim only. Saunders was nowhere to be seen but did get Charlie a good lawyer, but not good enough. Pete made the tea and put the cups on the tray alongside the ginger nut biscuit's that he had put on a plate, he walked into the front room to see the suitcase on his coffee table open fully, and what looked like an extraordinary amount of bank notes inside. He stood there staring at it and the tray started to wobble, Tina got up and took the tray away from Pete.

'I take it that's the missing money and the reason why you two are looking so sheepish tonight?' he said.

'Yes Pete, we think it's the missing money', Sean could not help but smile.

'Where did you find it?'

'It was in our warehouse, it looks like Tony Clay stuck the suitcase inside a crate that was destined for me and Taylor, he then got topped and no one knew what he did with the money. Taylor and me moved Clay's van to our warehouse after he was killed, we were covering his tracks and to make sure we got our suits.'

'What suits?'

Sean realised straight away he had made a mistake, 'oh just some suits Tony got for us, they were all legal.'

'Legal my arse', Pete replied, 'what do you take me for, I wasn't born yesterday, anyway, so what are you going to do with the money?'

'We were hoping you could help us with that Pete, a bit of advice.'

'How much is there?' said Pete.

'Fifty grand', said Tina.

'Fifty grand, bloody hell', said Pete while scratching his chin, 'where are you gonna hide that or even spend it without anyone being suspicious, you need to take a small amount out and bury the rest until we know what to do with it, you could always say you won the football pools.'

'What about Charlie Allan, and what about Saunders?' said Sean.

'This is why it's even more critical that we kill Saunders, we wont get to Charlie Allan, so you need to forget about him for the time being, he's gonna be tucked up nicely in Wandsworth Prison', replied Pete.

Tina closed the case and put it to one side, and they sat there drinking tea and dunking their ginger nut biscuit's. They discussed what their next move will be and that they need to forget about Charlie Allan. Tina said she still wanted him killed; 'he was there when Taylor was murdered and I won't rest until he's killed too', she said, but then reluctantly gave in to Sean and Pete saying that it can wait. They sat and looked at Pete's paperwork on Johnny Saunders, they looked at his favourite pubs, his favourite establishments, his two houses that he had and were trying to look at the best way to get to him. Pete also informed Sean and Tina that Saunders had started to surround himself with younger men, men that were not frightened to use knives and guns, and he was paying them well, he was starting to build a team around himself again after the loss of Stan Smith, Ray Flynn, Winston Scott and now Charlie Allan banged up in prison. When they knew what they needed to do about Saunders, and when, they discussed the money and the best place to bury it. Pete suggested burying it by a large Oak tree on the Common by the railway line in Tooting, 'bury good and deep' he said 'and put the turf back on top'. Pete then got up and got a bottle of whiskey from his side unit and opened it and poured Sean a glass. Tina who was now falling asleep on the sofa, was persuaded by Pete to go into the spare room and sleep, Sean said he would join her later and that they might as well stay the night. Pete and Sean discussed the current situation and spoke about the past, Pete spoke about Fiona and how he missed her, about his work and how he always liked the way he was allowed to break the rules sometimes so he could put scum bags inside, but now stupid human rights are allowing scum to walk the streets. The discussion did come up about the night Pete was called to the road traffic accident to find Sean's mum and dad inside the car, they skirted some of it as men do, but it got covered and then quickly vanished as quickly as it came into the room. They discussed the money and Pete suggested moving to the coast or even abroad, the difficulty will be getting the money out of the country. Eventually the discussions and the whiskey wore the two men down and they both retreated to bed. The next morning, Sean and Tina got up early before Pete woke; they placed five hundred pounds on his coffee table, and left the house.

Chapter 35

John Wall sat in his car impatiently waiting for Johnny Saunders; the heavy rain was hitting his car roof and front windscreen, which to him sounded like he was in a tunnel being bombarded by pellets of stone. He couldn't remember the last time it had rained that hard, he tried to look out of the windows and windscreen to see if he could see Saunders car arrive but it was very difficult to see anything in the heavy rain. John Wall waited another ten minutes and just as he decided to leave a car pulled up behind with the main lights on. When the car behind him flashed he pulled his coat up around his neck, he checked the rain again, which didn't give him any pleasure to get out into, he pulled his car door handle and ran out into the rain, he was soaked within seconds, but managed to get into Saunders back seat before being drowned further. Johnny Saunders was in the back seat, and there were two younger looking men sitting in the drivers and front passenger seats that John Wall didn't recognise. Johnny Saunders was looking at John Wall and the two in the front were facing forward.

'Jesus Wallsy you look like you've pissed your pants or something, damp out there is it?' Saunders said.

'Yes Johnny a bit fucking damp out there, I'm fucking drenched.'

Johnny continued to look at him with that disdainful look that he always showed when John Wall was in his company.

'What you got for me Wallsy?' he said.

John Wall, looked towards the front seats and at the two men sitting there, he noticed the driver was looking at him through the rear view mirror.

'They're ok' said Saunders, come on Wallsy I didn't come out all this way to dance in the fucking rain, what did you get me out here for?'

John Wall looked again at the two in the front seats and then turned back to Johnny, 'I've heard some chatter about a safe house, about a couple that are in there and that they are there on the quiet, not meant to be there if you know what I mean.'

Johnny listened to what John Wall was saying, he pulled out a cigar from his coat and lit it, sucked on the cigar and looked back at John Wall, 'and who are you suggesting that this couple might be and what interest is this information to me?' he said.

'The couple could be Sean Farrow and Tina Docherty Johnny, it's the information you have been looking for, it could lead to your money.'

Again Johnny sucked on his cigar, looked out of his car window and at the rain, the rain that was still heavy, with no indication of it ending.

'And what have you done about it Wallsy, have you checked out the authenticity of the information, and have you been to the safe house yourself?'

'No Johnny, I haven't been there because at the moment I'm not sure where it is, it's the bit of the information that I've not been able to get yet, that's where I thought you might be able to come in, because if I ask too many questions people will start to become suspicious.'

'And you want me to have a friendly chat with Pete Murray, is that where your going with this one Wallsy is it, and what about George Patterson, is he worth having a chat with too?'

'Yeah something like that, Johnny, both of them might be able to help you.'

'Johnny scratched his chin, and sucked again on his cigar, ' I think I might just do that Wallsy, you get yourself home now, your gonna need to dry off', he said with a smirk.

John Wall looked at Johnny with those puppy eyes as if he wanted a treat and Johnny took the bait.

'I'll pay you when, and if your information is correct Wallsy', he said.

John Wall was disappointed, his mothers help and support needed paying other wise it will stop, he looked up, the driver was still looking at him through the rear view mirror. He wondered briefly if he should reveal what he really knew but changed his mind, he needed a bargaining tool, so he pulled the door handle and left Saunders car. The rain hit him as soon as he exited, he got back into his car to see Saunders car pull away and pass him, and he sat there soaked to the skin, disappointed that he still had an empty wallet.

Chapter 36

Sean and Tina left the safe house, the house that had kept them secure over the last few months. They looked like any normal couple Tina with her long blonde hair and Sean with his short cropped hair style, they didn't look any different from those around them and they didn't feel it. But today would be different for them both Sean thought, when today is over it will be the end of all the mental pressure they have been under, and hopefully put an end to their sorrow and guilt, and he wanted it to end sooner rather than later. The plan was in place, they had discussed it over and over with Pete and they knew it was the best way to succeed in such short notice, but as usual the butterflies were starting to set in. They got into the Austin 1100, pulled away from the kerb and travelled to the end of the road, just as Sean was about to turn left he looked in his rear view mirror and spotted a car pulling into their road, but this car was different, he thought, because he had seen this car before, just before he and Tina hid behind the boxes at Tony Clays warehouse. He decided to say nothing to Tina and turned left out of their road. Sean checked his rear view mirror a few more times after, but the car was not following. He also thought about circling around to come up behind the car to see if his instincts were correct, but he decided against it and rightly so. Sean was driving but he was also thinking, he was thinking about the safe house and what was left there. Pete had always said don't have any photographs or any paperwork, do not leave any trace behind that anyone can use to find you, no addresses and no details what's so ever. Sean found comfort that he and Tina had done what Pete had said but he also took greater comfort that he listened to Pete and buried the money like he said and not put it under the floorboards like he was originally planning to do. He smiled to himself knowing that so far all is going well, but the smile went away when he realised they had left the house just in time, if what he saw, was the car. belonging to Johnny Saunders.

'At least the rain has stopped babe, that was some rain, I haven't seen rain like that in years' said Sean.

'I don't want to talk Sean, I just want to get this over with, we're not going fucking shopping or anything like that you know, it's not a day out.'

'Ok babe point taken, we wont talk now unless we have to, lets just stick to the plan', replied Sean.

The journey took them through South London as they both maintained their quiet moment, as they were both preoccupied with thoughts about what the evening might bring. The rain that had now stopped, was being taken over by the dark, which was starting to suffocate the car in it's envelope, Sean put the car lights on and brought some comfort to their surroundings. They knew where they were heading and they knew the location well, they were heading for Carshalton Surrey, once there they would park up near Carshalton golf course in a secluded alley. They would then get into the same dark clothing they used for Ray

Flynn; they would go onto the golf course and find green seventeen, which backs onto Johnny Saunders house. That was the easy bit said Pete. Sean thought, when Pete was explaining the situation, 'the hardest bit is wondering what to do if Saunders decides to lodge some protection in his house for the night, especially after what we have been doing to him recently.'

Sean continued to drive with his thoughts in his head about the night, he thought about the week before when he and Joe Swain played golf at Carshalton and how Sean deliberately hit the ball towards Saunders rear fence on the seventeenth green just so he could get a glimpse of the rear of his house. He even kicked the ball deeper into the bushes and undergrowth so he could look over the fence, he didn't feel that he accomplished much but at least the photographs he took and got developed by a trusted friend helped him and Tina get a feel for how they would try to enter the house. He had three more games of golf that week one of which was with Tina and at that time they deliberately lost golf balls around the undergrowth at the back of Saunders house. Sean pulled into the alleyway near the golf course, turned the lights off and looked across at Tina.

'You ok babe?' he said.

Tina was looking out of the window, the moon was not full, it was just showing enough light to make the trees glow at their peaks in the sky, it made her feel spooked by the whole thing. She felt herself tense inside and knew that she would feel a lot better if she had at least one drink inside her, she looked at her watch, they were early she thought.

'Lets go and have a drink or two Sean, we're early we don't want to be sitting here waiting, it will just freak us out.'

'We don't have to do anything Tina, we can just turn around a go home if that's what you want?'

'What I want is that fucker dead Sean and to make that a little easier, I just need to have a drink or two, I'm not going back now, we have planned this and it will happen, we're just too bloody early again.'

'Ok babe we will go and have a drink, there's a nice pub by the ponds in Carshalton we will go there' he said.

Sean pulled away from the alleyway and headed towards the pub, he knew it would be quiet this time of the evening and they may be able to get something to eat, he thought, as he pulled away.

The pub was a traditional public house and was overlooking the ponds of Carshalton, they entered the large car park and walked into the bar, although not too cold outside the fire was raging in the fireplace to give that old authentic country pub feeling. Sean went to the bar and Tina sat at a nearby table near the fire although she wasn't cold, she still felt a chill in her bones, Sean ordered two drinks, surveyed the menu on the bar and ordered fish and chips twice.

'Nice here isn't it', he said when he returned to the table Tina was sitting at. He put Tina's large glass of white wine on the table, and sat down and surveyed the bar further. Tina picked up the glass and took a gulp, Sean watched her intently, he was worried she may not be able to go through with it, but also hoping for his own sanity that she wouldn't. They sat in the corner of the bar by the fire looking out of the window and across to the pond, the moonlight was shining on the pond and it looked beautiful and peaceful Tina thought, she took another swig of her wine noticing it was going down nicely and the fire was starting to warm her bones.

'I'm looking forward to finishing all this', she said.

Sean looked across to Tina, 'me too babe, and you know these discussions we had about Spain, you know, running a bar or something, we can do that, we can start all over again and with the money we've got hidden we can also invest some.'

'All sounds very grand Sean, but you know what, I am looking forward to Spain, it's a bit of sunshine and being out of the rain and having a new start, do you think it will happen Sean?'

'Yes babe it will happen, you and me will make it happen, after tonight it will be a new start.'

Sean looked up quickly as a waiter came over with two portions of fish and chips; he put them both on the table, left, and came back with the condiments and a plate full of bread rolls.

'Bloody hell Sean how am I going to eat all this, you mad or something' Said Tina, 'I'm not going to be able to eat anything.'

'Don't worry I will eat what you don't eat, I'm starving', Sean left the table after seeing Tina had finished her glass of wine he went to the bar and ordered another large wine and another pint of lager, he turned to see Tina flicking her fork around the chips as if she was looking to see if it was edible. She looked vulnerable, he thought and wanted to hold her there and then, he wanted to take her to the car and take her away from all this shit that they have ended up with but now needed to finish, he walked back to the table with the drinks.

'I'm not sure I can eat this Sean', Tina said and carried on moving her chips around the plate.

'Don't worry babe just pick at it, leave what you don't want, I'll try my best to polish off both, anyway you can have lobster in Spain' he said and laughed.

'I've never eaten lobster', she said, 'I wouldn't know how to eat it, or what it even looks like.'

'I'm sure you can start to learn babe', he said.

Tina smiled at him and then lent over and kissed him on the lips.

Sean got stuck into his fish and chips and he was surprised how he was managing it considering what was to come, maybe he was trying to think about the next few hours by eating himself to death, he thought. Tina hardly touched her meal but managed to get through another large white wine, while Sean carried on consuming his meal, but eventually lost out to the giant cod and the three beers swigging around inside him. Sean looked down at his watch, it was time to leave, he didn't want to put it off any longer, he leant across to Tina and kissed her, 'I will be right back babe' and then headed towards the toilet.

Sean entered the men's toilet and went over to the sink, he looked in the mirror, he looked tired, he thought, he looked like he needed a good holiday, he rubbed his chin, he also looked nervous, he thought again, he could see it in his pupils in his eyes, he shook his head, pull yourself together Sean, he said to himself. He went over to the urinal and unzipped his trousers, he pulled out his penis, shook it and felt like he could piss forever, he started to urinate when he heard the door of the toilet open on it's very old hinges, he didn't look up but carried out with his task which seemed to be going on forever. He felt a presence next to him as a man joined him at the next urinal, as all men do there was an impulse to look up and Sean's personality dictated that that's what he wanted to do, but he resisted, for some reason, he thought to himself, he doesn't need to look up. He finished urinating before the new visitor in the room did; Sean shook his penis again and pulled his zip up, and at that point turned to the right to get a glimpse of the man next to him. His heart nearly jumped out of his body, the man also looked at him, Sean recognised him straight away from Pete's photo's but was hoping that Johnny Saunders did not recognise him. He continued with his move and that was to go to the sink and wash his hands, but his mind was racing, what should he do, should he attack him there and then, but he cant Tina is outside, he thought and Saunders may have men outside, maybe he hasn't recognised me, Sean thought, his brain and body was going to explode, he looked in the mirror, there was no movement from Saunders just the sound of piss hitting the pan, he decided that maybe he doesn't know who he is. He turned the tap on and started to wash his hands, he looked in the mirror and within seconds he felt Saunders behind him, he was looking at him through the mirror. Sean could feel the steel blade he had in his jacket pocket, it was very close and easy to get to, Saunders was also very close and easy to get to, his heart was racing and Saunders was watching him.

'Do I know you?' he heard Johnny Saunders say.

Sean turned to look at him, his hair was short almost cropped, his hair was always long, surely Saunders will not recognise him, he thought.

'I don't think so mate', he said, 'I don't recognise you, are you local?'

'No', said Saunders, 'only you look familiar.'

Sean moved away from the sink and passed Saunders who was still staring at him.

' I don't think so, maybe mistaken me for someone else, have a good evening'

Sean left the toilet with Saunders eyes burning into his back as he walked back into the main bar. To Sean's horror there were two men that are known to be with Saunders sitting at the table with Tina, he walked over and tried to be as calm as he could, before he got to the table, Tina stood up and said.

'There you are darling, I've been telling these men you must be having a shit because you've been so long, come on we're going to be late for mum's.'

Tina grabbed Sean's hand and they both went to walk out of the pub.

'You need to hang onto that one mate', said one of the men, 'she's a right sort, and if you ain't gonna give her a good time, I will.'

Tina and Sean could hear them both laughing as the pub door shut behind them. They ran across the car park, and got into their car and pulled away and out of the car park before any words between them were spoken. Sean continued back to the alleyway that they had left, he pulled into the alleyway and put his head back onto the headrest and let out a sigh.

'Fuck me that was close,' he said, 'I was fucking shitting myself, did you see him walk into the pub Tina?'

'I did,' she said, 'he just wandered in with the other two men, he went straight into the toilet where you were and the two idiots made a bee line for me, I couldn't move. I was so worried that he would recognise you and the whole pub would erupt, God Sean I was so scared, and when you came out of the toilet I was so glad to see you.'

Sean turned to Tina, 'did he look at you when he came into the pub?'

'He glanced my way but he didn't seem to notice much', she said, 'I looked up at him as he came in and I nearly wet my knickers there and then, but I think he was more interested in going for a piss, it was the other two who came over probably because I was on my own', bloody hell Sean how ridiculous was that.'

Sean looked away from Tina and looked out of the window, the moon was still showing the amount of light that it intended but he was lost in a world of darkness and he didn't know what to do next, maybe he should find a phone box and talk to Pete, he would know what to do, he looked back at Tina.

'Shall we call Pete babe, he would give us some advice, and he would know what we should do.'

'What do you mean Sean, what we should do, we just carry on with our plan, nothing has changed apart from he may be more suspicious if he did recognise any of us, so we should carry on with our plan and kill the fucker.'

Sean looked at Tina and inside his head he was hoping that was not what she was going to say, he was hoping deep inside that she would want to leave and just forget about the whole thing, but she didn't, he admired her for that, he looked into her eyes knowing he would follow her to the end of the world. He held her hand, he squeezed it and she squeezed his back, they were back on track, Sean thought, and he realised now they must still do this tonight, and there was no need to call Pete after all.

Chapter 37

Johnny Saunders left the toilet, he was still wondering about the man that left the toilet before him, there was something in those eyes he thought to himself, something in the way he looked at him in the mirror and he couldn't put his finger on it. He walked across the bar, his two colleagues were now sitting at the bar, they were drinking from a bottle of wine they had ordered, they looked up to see Johnny Saunders coming towards them. Johnny sat on the nearest bar stool and looked like he was trying to put two and two together; one of the men pushed a glass of whiskey towards him.

'There you go boss, a late night drink', he said.

Johnny picked the glass up and downed the contents, he pulled a cigar out of his inside jacket pocket, and as usual bit the end off, spat it onto the ground and waited while one of the men lit his cigar for him. Johnny sucked on his cigar, he looked like he was contemplating life and was not yet ready to share his thoughts, so the two men with him waited.

'Did any of you two see the bloke that came out of the toilet before me, skinhead hair cut about six foot, I cant see him in the pub anymore?'

The two men looked at him, one of them took the bottle of wine and filled the two glasses in front of him and the other one spoke for them both.

'Yes boss, he came over to us when he came out, we were talking to his bird, nice bit of stuff she was, sitting there all pretty on her own, they left very quickly as soon as he came out, why's that boss?'

'What bird', he said, 'was it the one by the fire, the one with long blonde hair, I saw her as I walked in?'

'Yes boss that's the bird, that's the bird he left with.'

Johnny Saunders sucked on his cigar again, something was playing on his mind, he didn't know what it was, but he was troubled by the man in the toilet and now the bird who also caught his attention when he walked into the pub, something was stirring in him and he couldn't put two and two together.

'Probably nothing boys, I'm just being paranoid', he said as he sucked on his cigar again and asked for another whiskey, he downed the second whiskey and started to think about fucking Isabel when he got home. That changed his thought process, and soon the stranger in the pub toilet became a part of his paranoia or was it the cocaine he had earlier and the whiskey that was starting to rule his mind, he thought. Johnny Saunders had three more whiskeys while he was discussing business with his two colleagues; they discussed how easy it was to get the information out of John Wall. Johnny always knew that John Wall knew more about where the safe house was and that he was holding back until he was paid, but Johnny wasn't going to play that game, he owned Wallsy and needed to control him. His decision to visit him instead of Pete Murray and George Patterson first played dividends, and finding out where Sean Farrow's safe house was, was a bonus to him, although it did cost John Wall some broken ribs. Unfortunately, thought Johnny, nothing came out of the visit to the safe house, there was no Sean Farrow and no money or any information found that could lead to Farrow or his money. Saunders and his men discussed their plan, they had already left one man watching the safe house and he would call, when and if Sean re-entered the house.

Johnny sat there with his two new colleagues, he was pleased with them, they were obedient, but probably because he had paid them well, he thought, but he still needed to test them and he was already trying to work out the best way to do that, he had already told them about Sean Farrow and they knew they had an action to find him to be able to get a nice little bonus, so that kept them eager. Johnny decided it was time to leave, he was thinking of Isabel again and he needed to empty himself, he raised himself from the bar stool and his two companions followed, they left the pub in Carshalton and drove the short journey back to Johnny's house which faced the seventeenth hole on Carshalton golf course. The two men drove Johnny to his driveway, they opened the door for him and he left the car, one of the men turned the handle on the car window and rolled the window down.

'You sure you don't need us to stay over night boss?' shouted one of the men from the car window.

Johnny Saunders reflected on the question, and he turned to the two men.

'No', he said, 'I need you to find Farrow for me, find Farrow for me and come back tomorrow, I want his head and my money, do that and you can have ten percent'. Johnny Saunders then turned and walked towards his house, he walked up his drive, put the key in the door and entered his domain.

Chapter 38

Sean and Tina watched the car leave the drive from their vantage point, they were buried deep inside the hedges and undergrowth at the front of the house, and they had been waiting there for some time until the car arrived.

'Fuck me, find Farrow for me and give me his head, Sean whispered into Tina's ear.'

'I know I heard' said Tina whispering back.

They were both pleased to see the car leave, this meant that Johnny would be on his own, they were cold but their black heavy clothing kept them from being frozen to the bone, as well as keeping them out of view. They had been there for about an hour, they had already made their way from the alleyway after changing into their new black clothing, they got onto the golf course and followed the route the same way that Sean had already done so on three previous occasions. They got to the back of the house by moving the fence panels near the seventeenth green that they had loosened previously on their golf days and then made their way across the lawn, bypassing the swimming pool and working their way round to the front of the house. They then found themselves watching Johnny Saunders entering his house with no protection, with them waiting outside to enter and kill him for the murder of their brother and friend Taylor Docherty.

Tina and Sean decided to wait that little bit longer for Saunders to settle in and hopefully fall asleep before they would try and enter the house. From their vantage point they could see where Saunders was going from room to room as he switched lights on and then off again, from what they had seen in the last hour there was no one else in the house, it seemed a bit easy to Sean, he thought, a bit too easy. When the lights seemed to stay off all together, and after about another thirty minutes lying on the cold and damp ground, they both agreed with some trepidation between them that they should try to enter the house.

Before they moved they both checked that they had their knives with them, Sean's was in his inside jacket pocket, he also picked up his small bag with the tools that he needed to enter the house, Tina's knife was still inside her left boot, they looked at each other; they kissed each other and slowly started to get to their feet still hidden and still well concealed in the undergrowth. They slowly walked through the bushes until they got to the side of the house, here they could re-evaluate their next move. They knew what they were going to do and Sean opened the bag that he had quietly put down on the ground, he pulled out a hand held manual drill known as a brace and a drill bit that was about one and a quarter inch in size, he placed the drill in the end of the brace and slowly turned to ensure there was no squeaking, 'well oil the brace' he remembered Pete saying, there was no squeaking, great, Sean thought. He took a measuring tape from the bag and a pencil, he measured and drew a circle on the back door lower panel about two feet in diameter, just big enough for them to get through one at a time. He looked across at Tina who was sitting on the ground watching every move he made, they didn't speak Tina nodded in agreement and Sean placed the drill bit on the back of the ply timbered panel on the lower part of the back door and started to make his first hole. There was no noise apart from the small low noise of metal cutting into wood, Sean was sweating with every turn and the first hole was completed in just less than three minutes after cutting into ten millimetres of plywood. He pulled the drill bit back out and removed the inch and a quarter piece of wood from the end of the drill bit, he listened for any noise from the house before he started his second hole. This method took them nearly two hours to get the two-foot diameter hole cut into the back door that was big enough for them to fit into. Sean slowly started to remove the panel trying to make as little noise as possible, there was the odd creak when certain sections of the ply was not cut right through so Tina was there to help cut those sections apart with a small hand saw. When the panel was out they again sat there in silence and listened for any noise coming from inside the house. Satisfied, Sean looked at Tina, who gave him that confident nod of approval, he placed the tools inside the bag and looked at her again, he whispered in her ear', 'no turning back now babe', he said, again she nodded.

Sean looked up into the sky the moon was low and clouds drifted across it disguising it every now and then and removing it from view, it seemed a peaceful evening he thought, but it was about to be shattered in some horrific way. Sean took a torch out from his inside pocket, he was frightened to turn it on, it was like some enemy, a traitor that would give his and Tina's position away, but he knew he needed to, to get some sense of where he needs to go when he enters the house. He turned it on and pointed it quickly inside the hole that he had just made, he could see where they had cut through was the correct room, he could see that inside was the utility room of the house, he quickly turned the torch off after seeing the door was at the far end and worktops were to his left and right and a sink at the far end. He put the torch back inside his pocket, he looked at Tina, again she nodded, and Sean thought, I wish at some point she would nod fucking horizontally instead of vertically all the time, he wished it but Tina was now focused on one thing, revenge. Sean got himself into a position that he could start to squeeze himself into the hole, they had always agreed he would go in first so he started to get his head in first, he then had his hands on Johnny Saunders floor, his shoulders were next and he had to get one shoulder at a time to be able to get in, the rest was easy once the shoulders were in. He slowly moved like a snake until one foot at a time was placed on the floor and then he stood up in the darkness of Johnny Saunders house. Tina followed Sean through and he managed to help her which was a lot easier once he was inside, they made no noise and when they were both in and standing, they again listened for any noise coming from inside the house. Satisfied again, Sean quickly shone the torch again so Tina could also get her bearings, and switched it off once he glimpsed the handle of the door, which would take them out of the utility room. This time Sean did not look for the horizontal nod from Tina, he knew

274

it would be the other way, so he pulled a small can of oil out of his jacket pocket and oiled the hinges, he slowly gripped his hand around the door handle and hoped there would be no squeaking from the handle itself, he turned the handle and slowly opened the door.

Chapter 39

Sean peaked outside the open door and saw what he thought was a large hallway to his right and a kitchen to his left that backed onto the rear garden. The hinges and the door handle made no noise as they both stepped out into the small corridor between the two big rooms, they stepped out and listened, nothing, still no noise. They both moved towards the right, as the large hallway would lead to other rooms and at every junction they would stop and listen for any noise. When they got to the hallway they could see a large staircase that led upstairs to other rooms, obviously the sleeping quarters, Sean thought, they made their way towards the staircase and got to the bottom step and again listened before making their next move. Sean motioned to Tina to stay at the bottom of the stairs and when he was at the top she should then climb the stairs behind him, she nodded. Sean started to climb the stairs very slowly hoping that none of them had a creaking piece of wood beneath his feet, when he got half way, he looked back down at Tina, but at that point a door was opened from upstairs and a streak of light entered the hallway above. Sean looked up quickly not knowing whether to go up or down, he looked down, Tina had gone, he looked back up and was frozen at the middle of the stairs, he listened and prayed that they would not see him. He heard footsteps upstairs somewhere, he heard another door open, and he saw more light come onto the above landing and then nothing until he heard a toilet flushing. Sean stood there transfixed on the noise and the light and didn't have the answers to his next move, he saw the light dim and he heard the door close, he heard footsteps that he prayed were going the other way, they were, he saw the light go out completely, he heard the door close, and then he felt his heart beating like he had never felt before. He looked back down, Tina was not there, he continued to look while darting his head back to the top and back down again. Eventually he saw Tina who had retreated to the nearest room and was now making her way back to the bottom of the stairs. Sean moved quicker this time to the top of the stairs the adrenalin, he thought, was now kicking in, he got to the top of the stairs and looked down at Tina, she walked with an air of confidence, he thought, as she climbed each step. When they were both at the top, they listened, again, nothing. Sean pointed to where the noise and light came from, that would be the direction, get in, do it quick and get out of the house. They walked now with speed and determination, it was like they were now on a free for all, the plan was definitely thrown to one side, the first door was opened quickly, Sean shone his light inside, it was a bathroom, fuck he thought, they are now making noise, the second door was opened, he shone the light inside, he saw Johnny Saunders laying in bed fumbling at his side draw, and it was nearly open. Sean threw himself inside and ran at Saunders who was now retrieving something from the draw, a shot rang out and the light and noise and smell of cordite filled the air, Sean launched himself at Saunders who was now getting ready for a second shot, bang, a second shot went off and hit the ceiling, plaster descended down on them as they rolled across the bed. Sean knew he needed to get the gun and was grappling with Saunders who was now cursing and screaming, Sean could not see Tina but was hoping she had not been hit by a bullet, they both rolled off the bed and onto the floor and Sean had time to quickly look up to see Tina who to his shock was not alone, there was another women with her and they too were gripped in a hand to hand battle, 'fuck' he thought what the fuck is going on and where the fuck did she come from. That short lapse in time gave Saunders the upper hand and he managed to roll Sean onto his back, the gun, which was first in his hand, was now across the floor and they both knew the battle would be won by the first to retrieve it. Sean looked to his left and right, there under the cabinet was a vase, he grabbed the vase when Saunders was looking at Tina and the other woman fighting, 'no! he heard Saunders shout, 'no Isabel, stop!'

Sean looked across to see a woman who was now clearly winning the battle against Tina, he looked up at Saunders, Sean felt the vase in his hand and smashed it against Saunders skull, he went down and was clearly knocked out. Sean pushed Saunders to one side ran over to the gun and pointed at the woman who was still pulling at Tina's hair and punching her as hard as she could, Sean shouted, he shouted again, the women turned and Tina threw a punch and caught the woman square on the chin, and she too went down and was out like Saunders. Sean and Tina stood there panting and trying to get their breath back, they looked around the room, a woman they had never seen before was laying knocked out on the floor and Saunders who they clearly knew was also laying there knocked out too.

'You ok babe?' said Sean panting.

'I'm ok yeah, I'm ok, that was a good punch weren't it babe? 'She said.

'Yeah a good punch, a cracker, now lets quickly tie them up.'

Sean grabbed a dressing gown that was on the bedroom door, he pulled the belt from it and tied Saunders legs, he looked in all his drawers and found his ties, he then bound his hands and left him on the floor, he then did the same with the woman. Tina was sitting on the bed, they looked around, a quick discussion between them made them move the woman to another room, they dragged her out into the hallway and then pulled her into an adjoining room and when they entered they could clearly see this was a woman's room, why were we not told about her, Sean thought. They picked the woman up and laid her on the bed, made sure she was breathing through the gag around her mouth and left the room. When they walked back into the room, Saunders looked like he was already coming around, Sean went over to him and looked around the room, there was a chair in the corner and he got it and placed it next to Saunders, Tina came over as she knew what Sean was planning, they both grabbed him and hauled him onto the chair. They looked at him, he looked a pitiful state, his hair was matted from sleep and his breath smelt of whiskey and blood was starting to fall down the side of his face, it took him a while to come round and they stared at him with hatred in their eyes.

Johnny Saunders looked up at Sean.

'You're the two from the pub', he said, 'the one that was in the toilet.'

Sean and Tina never said anything; they continued to stare at the man in front of them.

'Well what is it you fucking want from me, is it money, what is it, what the fuck do you want, and what have you done with Isabel?'

'She's ok' said Sean, 'we wont harm her, it's you we want, don't you recognise us?'

Johnny Saunders looked up at them both, 'yea I think I do, but I couldn't be certain in the pub, but you both troubled me I should have gone with my instincts. More blood dropped from his head onto the floor, and he looked down at it.

'So who are we then?' said Tina.

Saunders again looked back up at them both, he reflected what he should say, he's not in a good position he thought, so he decided to try and crawl his way out of it.

'You're Sean Farrow', he looked up at Tina. And I think you're Tina Docherty.'

Tina looked down at Saunders and pulled the blonde wig from her head. Her brunette hair dropped down below her shoulders. 'Correct', she said.

Johnny looked at Tina, he was right he thought, she is Tina Docherty, he then looked back at Sean.

'So what do you want?' he said.

'You killed Taylor Doherty, we were there in the warehouse', said Tina, 'we heard you do it, we heard you give the orders to your so called men, the men that we have gradually killed off one by one and ruining your life. You killed my brother and his friend and you also killed my stepfather, remember that you fucking cock sucker', she said, and then spat into his face.

Saunders looked at them both.

'You stole my fucking money', he said, 'what else did you want me to do?'

'We never stole your money you fucking idiot' Sean said, 'it was lost, but guess what we have found it now and we are going to spend every penny of it, why, because we need compensation you prick.'

'And me what about me?' Saunders said.

The room went quiet, all three were looking at each other, they all knew the answer, but Johnny was hoping that the truth was not going to happen.

'You can't kill me' he said.

'Why can't we?' said Sean.

Because if you do, you will have people looking for you all you're lives and you will never live a safe life, my men will hunt you down.'

'What the fuck do you care, your team, what team, you don't have any team or any influence any more, you're small fry now', said Sean. 'We saw to that, it's called revenge.'

Tina went into the next room, she wanted to check on the woman, she pulled the gag back to check her breathing; she was breathing ok, she was conscious now and was looking into Tina's eyes.

'We are not here to hurt you', Tina said, 'you will be safe here, as long as you just stay still.' She then left the room.

When she re-entered the room where Sean and Saunders were, she felt an urge to kill the man in front of her, she walked towards him and drew the knife from her boot, she could see the fear immediately enter his eyes, Sean looked up but didn't stop her, he knew she needed to do this.

'No stop!' shouted Saunders 'you can't do this, not you.'

'What do you mean not me you evil cunt', she said, 'what do you mean not me can't you stand a woman standing up to you', she lifted the knife to plunge it into him, when he shouted out again.'

'Cos I'm your fucking father, that's why, I'm your fucking father!' he shouted out

Tina stopped in her tracks; she looked at him, the pitiful man beneath her blade. She stopped before it entered him, she stood there glaring into his eyes, she looked towards Sean, his face showed it all, his mouth was open, he was as shocked as she was, the room again was silent. Tina's eyes moistened she could feel it, not through pity or anything else but for the sheer fact that she possibly shared this evil mans blood, she felt sick inside, she wanted to vomit there and then, she felt his evilness flow through her body. Johnny Saunders was looking at her, directly into her eyes, he looked across at Sean who stood there motionless, he looked back at her, she felt him looking into her eyes for passion hoping that she may change her mind now that she knew who he was. Tina looked into Johnny Saunders eyes and saw what she could never be, he looked pitiful, she thought, and she didn't want to share his blood. It was then she straddled the man that could be her blood father, the man that killed her stepfather and brother; it was then she slowly pushed the knife through his heart while he whimpered like a small baby looking up at her.

Tina stayed where she was, she was holding the blade deep into Johnny Saunders heart until Sean came over and helped her release her grip from the knife. Sean helped her take two steps back and they surveyed their surroundings and took in what they just did, what they saw and heard. Sean and Tina left the house after checking on the woman in the room, she was ok, and they promised her they would send someone round to untie her. There was no further talk throughout the journey home, a new home, and one they could sleep peacefully in. They left the house as they had entered, through the back door and onto the golf course on the seventeenth green. They got into their car in the alleyway but there was still no talk, Sean knew that would come later, much later, and not until after the shock of what they had just heard had sunk in.

Chapter 40

The digging was hard work, Sean thought, he knew he shouldn't have buried it so deep like Pete said, luckily there has been some rain so the ground is a lot wetter then usual. Sean Farrow was digging in the dark, he didn't want to have a torch light as it may prompt nosey bastards to see what someone was up to on the common at three o'clock in the morning. It was cold and there was a full moon, which at least gave Sean some kind of light to see with. He had been digging now for about one hour and was beginning to wish he hadn't buried it so deep when he hit the hard casing shell of the suitcase. He just had to dig around it now to be able to pull it out of the ground, he thought. After another twenty minutes he had enough ground out around the case to pull it from the grip of the earth, 'bingo' he said. Sean quickly undid the strap which was holding the case together, he pulled the case open and was pleased to see that the money was still intact and still dry due to the polythene wrapped around each wad of notes that he and Tina quickly did one night. Sean picked the shovel up threw the earth back into the hole, which was a quicker job then digging it out, he thought. He threw the clumps of grass back on top and stamped on it to make it level and make it seem that no one had been there, he was sweating and wanted to get the money out and off the common as quickly as possible. He picked the suitcase up and ran off to where he had parked the car under the railway bridge just by the common entrance, he got in his car and quickly locked the driver's door and pulled away. When he got back to the house, Tina was already waiting and pacing up and down the hallway, he had been gone longer then she thought and she was praying he was safe and that the money was also safe. Sean Farrow entered the house and Tina threw her arms around him.

'God Sean you were ages, why have you been so long?'

'It was bloody deep Tina, I buried it too bloody deep, I thought I was going to end up in bloody Melbourne.' They laughed as Sean threw the suitcase onto the bed.

'Is the money ok?' said Tina.

'Yes the money's ok, I checked it briefly, it's all still wrapped up in the plastic bags we did, and looks bone dry.'

' I want to have a look', she said and jumped onto the bed throwing open the suitcase. She looked at the money, it looked crisp, it looked clean, and it looked dry, but most of all she thought, it looked a lot, she couldn't help but feel her big smile getting wider on her face. Tina Docherty picked up about ten wads of notes tore the plastic off them and tore the paper bindings around them off, she threw them onto the bed, scattered them all over while Sean stood there and watched her laughing.

'Right come on Sean, if my mathematics are right that's ten grand on the bed', Sean was looking at her, 'that's ten grand and we're going to fuck on it',

'What?' he said still laughing.

'Me and you Sean, we are going to fuck on ten grand, or do you want to make it more then ten grand?' and Tina started to unwrap more notes.

'No Tina ten grand is enough' replied Sean as he started to pull his trousers off.

They made love and fucked on the ten thousand pound, it made them feel good it made them feel important, but it also made them feel relieved that it was all over. They lay there after a sex session that they had not had for some time, it was like a release from the pressures of what they did and wanted to do. They laid there all sweaty with notes stuck to their bodies, they laughed, then they laughed again while throwing hands full of money into the air.

'What's next Sean?' Tina said while she was peeling off notes stuck to her body.

'Pete's plan is what's next, we will move like he said we should do, but we will move further then you think, have you ever wanted to run a bar babe, because I have and we should do that but somewhere hot, somewhere like Spain, you know we have been talking about it.'

'Spain, bloody hell I thought you meant Brighton or something.'

'I've been talking to Pete about it, we can move to Spain, we can drive and get a boat over there, it's easier to take the money in and we can set ourselves out there, a lot of Brit's are moving there and making a new start in the sun.'

'What about mum Sean?'

'We can set ourselves up over there and then get her to come over, it will be ok babe, a new start and an honest living.'

Tina lay there thinking, she was taking in what Sean was saying, she had never thought about it before, she was too busy concentrating on what they had to do, she never thought about after it was completed. Sean got off the bed and went into the bathroom, he could tell Tina needed thinking time; he pulled a few notes off his body and stepped into the shower. Sean dried himself down with the towel, noting again how he didn't need to dry his short hair, he wrapped the towel around himself and walked back into the bedroom, Tina was still laying there amongst the money, she looked up at Sean.

'Ok', she said, 'but on one condition, mum is definitely coming over at some point, once we've settled down.'

'Of course babe, of course, Patsy will be coming over at some point, as you've said, once we settle down.'

Tina smiled; she got off the bed and started to tidy up the money and the ones stuck to her arse. She gathered them all up and placed them back into one thousand pound wraps and placed them back into the suitcase. Tina looked up at Sean; she caught him looking at her in that way and wondered if he wanted to jump back into bed.

'And when will this be Sean, when do we plan to move to Spain?'

'There's a few things we need to sort out, I need to meet with Joe, I'm going to give him the keys to the warehouse and tell him he can keep the contents, the lease runs out soon anyway. We then need to see Pete and then Angela Clay, we need to see that she is alright with money, and obviously we need to see your mum.'

Patsy Docherty was seen first, she was content and happy with the decision made by Sean and Tina, and she listened to them as they explained how they wanted a new start in a new country. Patsy of course new nothing about what her daughter had been up to, and of course didn't know that Tina now knew who her real father was, it was difficult for Tina, but after discussion with Sean she realised it was best to keep quiet about it and never bring it up. Patsy also jumped at the chance of going over to Spain as soon as they settled down, she was already planning how she could help out in the bar and cook home made British food. Tina and Sean left Patsy Docherty's house and felt rest assured that she would not tell anyone their plans. When they visited Angela Clay, they left her two hundred pounds and told her they were going away for a short while and would call her soon. Tina could not help feeling sorry for Angela, how lonely she looked in her home and how she was feeling, how she felt herself when she lost Taylor and how she would feel if she ever lost Sean.

Chapter 41

Pete Murray lit another match and threw it into the bin, he had all the paperwork that he'd gathered and written on over the last few months. He wanted it destroyed, he watched as it slowly caught alight and started to destroy the evidence of pre planned murder. He felt he had achieved something, at last after all his years as a policeman he had actually achieved something, but he knew he wouldn't have been able to do it without help from others still in the force, he knew that people took risks, but they also got something out of it, they too put the scum bags under ground. He looked across at the photo of Fiona on his sideboard; he spoke to her like he usually did sometimes and wondered if she'd approved of what he had done recently, although not done with his own hands but planned it in it's approach. He heard the doorbell ring and wondered who it would be, normally people would call before they visited him, it made him slightly worried, should he ignore it or should he check to see who it is. He heard the doorbell ring again within the five second rule only his friends knew about, he waited for the third, it happened before the five second rule again so he decided to peak through the spy hole, he saw Sean standing there with Joe Swain, he unlocked the two bolts and opened the door.

'Surprise visit boys' he said.

'Sorry Pete', said Sean 'should have called but couldn't get to a phone, bloody hooligans keep breaking them to get the cash out.'

'Yeah, I remember talking to you about that once Sean', Pete said with a smirk, 'what do I owe the pleasure for this visit then boys?'

'We wanted to keep you up to date with our plans Pete, that's all and hoping you might get your bottle of whiskey out', Pete smiled with that craggy face that seemed to be getting older and older Sean thought.

Pete turned and looked towards Joe Swain, 'and how are you then Joe, long time no see, you keeping yourself out of trouble?' he said.

Joe Swain was short of words as always but answered Pete with a smile that showed honesty and trust.

'Yes Pete, I'm fine and there's no trouble in my life.'

Joe Swain was a friend of Sean and Taylor; he grew up with them on the same estate and knew Pete well, he was a quiet individual, that never said much but was always a hit with the girls and knew how to handle himself whenever he needed to. He could be trusted and would be at your front door if trouble ever came your way to help in any way he could.

'That's good to know,' said Pete.

They all sat down, Pete poured three glasses of whiskey that he retrieved from the side cabinet, they clinked the glasses together and said cheers. Pete was an experienced policeman, he knew when to say something and knew when to say nothing, but he also knew that Joe had not been privy to the actions that he Sean and Tina had been carrying out recently. There was no reason to keep it from Joe, Joe could always be trusted and in some respect could have helped out, but it was personal, and they all agreed to keep it between themselves. Sean opened up and informed Pete about his and Tina's plans to move to Spain, he explained how they would drive down to Dover and get the boat over to France and then drive down to Spain. They would first look for a property to rent and then see if there was a bar they could rent out or maybe even buy. Sean's experience on taking money out of the country was nil and he wanted some advice from Pete on his best options. They also discussed about Joe looking after Sean's warehouse until the lease expired and could sell all the stuff off. Pete listened intently and spoke only after Sean had completed, he was calm and gave the relevant knowledge on how to move the money, but most of all he had a contact in Spain. He knew a policeman that could be trusted who lived and worked in Spain as part of a Met police plan with the Spanish Government on dislodging criminals who had moved to Spain with their illegal earnings. The last discussion was around Tina and how she has coped after what she has been through, Sean put Pete's mind at rest suggesting that she was fine and Spain would do her good.

'Pete' said Sean looking up at him with sincerity, 'Tina would like you to come over at some point and maybe even move over there yourself, she would like all her friends and family to come, even if it was just to visit, but even better to live there too.'

Pete scratched his chin, he thought about it as Sean and Joe Swain lifted themselves off the sofa to get ready and leave, they all shook hands and Sean threw his arms around Pete for what felt like a final embrace to him. They left Pete to himself who re-bolted his door, he sat back down and poured himself another whiskey, he looked back up at the photo of his deceased wife Fiona and was searching for approval or not, again.

Chapter 42

Tina closed the suitcase, she had everything now she thought, she looked again at her notes, and she checked them one more time. Yes, she said satisfied with herself that she had everything. She closed the suitcase and sat on it to get it down enough to be able to pull the straps round and buckle them up, satisfied she pulled the suitcase off the bed and onto the floor. She looked around her room, she was no longer in the safe house, the one that protected them from evil, she was back home with her mother and getting ready to depart for Spain. She looked around again, she was uneasy, there was something missing, she had forgotten something and it was playing on her mind because she didn't know what it was. Patsy Docherty walked into the room; she had something in her hand and was twirling it around her head.

'What about this love, are you taking this with you, if not I will probably find use for it?'

Patsy Docherty was twirling Tina's blonde wig around in the air, with a smile that went from ear to ear, that was it Tina thought, the bloody wig I knew there was something I needed to take with me.

'Give that here mother, that's coming with me', Tina chased after Patsy who ran out of the room laughing and ran down the stairs to get away from her daughter, Tina caught up with her and they both landed on the sofa laughing.

'I'm going to miss you darling', said Patsy.

'We're not going to be far away mum, you can visit when you want and who knows you might want to come over and join us one day, you know when we get married and have children you can come and baby sit.'

"Married, Sean Farrow has always shied away from marriage', said Patsy.

'No mum, Sean has said as soon as we are settled down, we will get married we will invite everyone over to Spain for the wedding, it will be like a new start and we can celebrate by getting married.'

'I will believe it when I see it' said Patsy.

'Oh mum your such a pessimist.'

'Tina', Patsy said looking uncomfortable.

Tina looked at her mum, she looked serious, and she looked like she was about to say something that Tina didn't want to hear.

'Yes mum', she replied.

'Remember that time you asked me about who your real father was, that time we went shopping in London, well do you still want to know? I've been thinking about it, you should know really, I've been selfish not telling you.'

Tina was shocked, she didn't know what to say and she just sat there thinking what she should say next.

'Well?' said Patsy, 'say something darling, you're making me all nervous.'

Tina was still sitting and thinking, but this time not too long for her mum to intervene.

'No mum it's fine I don't need to know anymore, it was a phase I went through, I needed to know at one point but I don't need to know anymore, it was me being selfish mum, not you.'

Tina could see the relief lift off her mothers face; she could see that the answer she gave was a good answer and one that would benefit them both.

'That's good' Patsy said, 'but I'm happy to if you ever change your mind love.,

'That's ok mum, I won't ever change my mind, lets not bring it up again mum, it's best for both of us.'

Patsy looked at Tina with a look of anger and a look that Tina had not seen before.

'Well that's good' said Patsy, 'because he's dead anyway, he got killed so good riddance to the bastard.'

'Again Tina was shocked, she didn't expect this to go on, but it looked like her mother wanted to get it off her chest, so she decided to allow her to.

'Go on mum', she said.

Patsy looked up at Tina. 'He was a bad man Tina, not a good man and you have come out with my genes thankfully and not his, and Tina', she said looking into Tina's eyes.

'Yes mum.'

'When he was killed everyone around here said, that whoever killed him, well they deserved a medal and if they ever found out who it was they would go up and shake their hand.'

'Popular was he?' said Tina with a smirk on her face.

Patsy looked up at Tina, with that sorry look on her face, ' Sorry Tina, I'm sorry love', she said.

'There's nothing to be sorry about mum, now come on no more about this, come and help me finish my packing, and give me my wig back, Sean's got a thing about that wig.'

'Dirty bastard' said Patsy, laughing.

Chapter 43

Sean left the bar at midnight, he left Joe Swain and the others still knocking back pints of beer and chatting up the local girls, he staggered a bit but was able to walk out with both feet pointing forwards. It was like a stag night for him but he knew he had to leave at a reasonable time as he had a boat to catch in the morning. He got himself home and didn't even have the energy to shower; he just threw himself straight into bed. When he woke up in the morning he had the typical headaches that he got when he was pissed the night before, he also woke with a hard on from heaven and wished that Tina was with him to enjoy it. He turned over and looked at the alarm clock on the side, shit he thought, the clock read 09:15, he jumped out of bed and then ran into the shower. As quickly as he could he washed and dressed, he grabbed all the bags that he thankfully packed the day before and headed for the door, shit the most important one, he remembered just before turning the front door handle. Sean turned and went back upstairs; he pulled the carpet back in his bedroom and pulled the crow bar out of the top draw and then started to ease the floor boards up in his bedroom, he saw the silver suit case with it's wheels and buckles around it to hold the case together, he grabbed the case put it to one side and then started to hammer the boards back into place, he then threw the carpet back over the boards. Sean left the house but not after looking back and taking one more glance at the house he had shared for some time with Taylor, 'Joe's now' he thought, that's good' Sean opened up the Austin 1100 boot and threw all his bags into it, he closed the boot and got into the drivers seat and started the engine, he pulled away from his house that he had shared with Taylor for the last time.

Sean pulled up to Patsy's house thirty minutes later than planned, he stood at the door waiting for Patsy or Tina to come and let him in. Patsy opened the door,

'What time do you call this you was meant to be here at eleven?' said Patsy, ' and look at the state of you, the Spanish police will take one look at you and deport you straight away.'

'Heavy night Patsy, it got a bit wild as usual, where's Tina?' he said.

'She's waiting in the front room, bags all packed and ready to go', she looked up at Sean, 'take care of her Sean' she said with love in her eyes.

Sean smiled kissed her on the cheek, walked into Patsy's house finding Tina as Patsy had said, sitting on the sofa with her bags beside her.

'Sorry I'm late babe it was a heavy night, I left early though and left them all to it, you all ready?'

Tina looked up at Sean and smiled, 'yeah all ready babe.'

"What's up, you look a bit sad, you haven't changed you mind have you?'

'No Sean just been having a few words with mum that's all, apparently I deserve a medal, I'm all set and ready to go.'

Sean looked at Tina not knowing what she meant and threw it away as women's chat, 'ok babe that's good', he said, 'there's one thing I need to do I didn't have enough time this morning, I will be five minutes.'

Sean went out to the car and grabbed the silver suit case from the boot, he then grabbed a blue rucksack that he recently purchased, he walked back into the house and ran upstairs to Tina's bedroom, he shut the door behind him and started to open the silver case. He pulled all the money out of the case and started to fill the blue ruck sack with the money, when he was finished, he zipped up the top pocket and pulled the two straps down and clipped them together. He pushed the empty silver suitcase under Tina's bed, picked the blue rucksack up and left the room shutting the door behind him.

He stood in the hallway waiting for Tina with the rucksack over his shoulder, he could see they were saying their goodbyes and he left them to it. When Tina came out of the front room he could see her eyes were moist, Sean gave Patsy a hug and made a promise to her that he would look after her daughter, and patsy made a promise to come and find him if didn't, and then they both hugged again. They both left the house and got into the car to travel to Dover, with Tina waving goodbye to her mum as they left.

They travelled across London onto the South Circular Rd and through Sidcup until they eventually ended up on the M20 motorway to Dover. The journey was quiet as they drove, Tina was busy looking out of the window watching the rain, which started to fall, the sky was going grey and they knew the sky was about to fall down upon them even more.

'We're going to be leaving all this behind babe, not much rain where we're going, just sunshine, even the winter wont be that cold, probably a bit like our summers', Sean laughed and Tina smiled.

'Let's hope so Sean, I never did like the rain.'

They left the motorway and pulled onto the main road that took them to the ferry port in Dover. Sean was starting to be concerned about the point where they will go through customs that will be there, but he was also hoping that they would not look under the back seats of the Austin 1100 where he hid the rucksack. The customs officers waved them through after a brief glimpse of their passports, they drove up the ramp, which took them onto the ferry. Once they were parked up Sean retrieved the rucksack from the hiding place and put it on his back and Tina ensured the straps were tight. They both agreed that this is how they wanted to travel, they wanted to make sure that the money was with them every moment of the journey until they found a safe place they could put it when they got there. They travelled up the stairs to find a bar where they wanted to sit and have a drink and wait for the ferry to depart. When the ferry started to depart, they left the bar and went to the rear of the ferry and watched the white cliffs of Dover disappear, they wondered when, and if they would ever see them again.

1988

Chapter 44

Sean Farrow didn't move, he was sweating, and he was scared
and tense. The blade was now closer to his throat, he tried in
vain to stop it but then it glided across his jugular once again
with professional ease from ear to ear. He felt the cold steel
against his throat and realised it was still not over as the owner of
his turmoil bared down on him from above once more. Sean
could do nothing; it was inevitable that the man above him with
his professional grip would come back for another pass to ensure
the job was finished.

Jose wiped the residue off of Sean's face and placed a hot towel
over his neatly shaven chin, this was the best bit Sean thought,
hate that bloody razor, though it does always gives a cleaner and

fresher feel. Jose then gave Sean that traditional Turkish massage to his shoulders and head, Sean felt good, and at ease and probably the happiest he has been for a long while. Yet he was still troubled and often thought of Taylor and his past, which occasionally still comes up and haunts him.

'There you go Sean, as soft as a bambino's bum', said Jose the Spanish barber

'Thanks Jose', replied Sean.

The Turkish shave was over for another week, Sean enjoyed the pampering but still couldn't get used to the cutthroat razor gliding across his throat, and he understood why. Sean left the barbers and felt refreshed; he put on his sunglasses and surveyed his surroundings. A golden beach in front of him, the blue sea calm and reflective, people splashing and swimming in it's tranquil and warm waters. He looked across at the long promenade that housed bars and cosmopolitan restaurants along the front, he knew them all, he knew the owners and those that frequented them, after all he thought, I also own one of them. He spoke good Spanish but often didn't need it, most locals spoke good English but he tried to speak Spanish as often as possible, not just to impress the locals but also out of respect for the new country he now called his home.

He is respected in Marbella, the town that he and Tina first started to settle in ten years ago; in that time he had become a local respected businessman and well known to put money back into the town for improvements as well as sponsoring local charities. Sean continued along the promenade and let the fresh air fill his lungs and flow through his newly cut hair and fresh face. He stopped, and again took in his surroundings, he was pleased with his choice, he waved at a local that he knew on the beach with his family enjoying a barbecue in the sun. He crossed the road and walked up a side street beside a Spanish tapas bar and waved to the owner, he made his meeting with his accountant on time and entered the air-conditioned office.

'Can we do this in Spanish Miguel', he said as he entered, 'it keeps up the practice for me.'

'Sure, no problem Sean', replied the man sitting there with the fan on cooling his body.

Sean listened intently to his Spanish accountant while he gave a precise account of his financial matters. His assets were still secure, he still had one and a half million pounds in the bank, he had one restaurant that was doing very well and profitable with exceptional bookings. He had an apartment block called Singleton Villas with eighteen two bedroom flats that were fully booked for most of the high season with some apartments having guests living there full time. He had his five-bedroom house overlooking the harbour and marina where he stored his twelve-birth yacht called 'Tina of the Seas' that was also profitable and booked throughout the year. He had a bar that was well respected and frequented by rich locals who knew nothing of his past and never questioned it either. The accountant continued and assured him that he is in a very safe financial position, all assets were doing well and his income was still outstripping his outgoings.

'There is one thing Sean', said Miguel, 'the three apartments in Singleton Villas that you do not receive any income from, is there any move on that?'

'No Miguel, I will not be getting any income from them unless the properties become empty for some reason, the people in them are special to me, they do not need to pay any rent to Farrow enterprises', replied Sean.

Sean thanked Miguel and told him to come to his house tonight with his family for the barbecue. He left the office and started to walk towards the Marina, the sun was still burning hot and he enjoyed the heat on his tanned body. Mario a local friend and husband to Angela Clay was washing down the decks of Tina of the Seas getting it ready for the next guests. Sean positioned himself in a familiar bar at the quayside and said hello to the waiter who looked pleased to see him, he ordered a large cold beer. He thought of the past, his upbringing, the friendship with Taylor, the bloody unfortunate mistake with the money, the horror of Taylors murder and the killings that followed, he thought of Tina and how she had coped very well with her part in the pay back rituals they achieved. He knew he would never be free from those memories and they would always haunt him even in his new life in the sun. That was all ten years ago now and he still wondered if his new life can amend his past.

Sean Farrow sat at the bar and reflected on what he had achieved since he arrived there ten years ago. The quick cash purchase of his first bar, which quickly became a popular place to visit, then his first apartment purchased with a good down payment, then his first boat and then a second apartment. Tina and his life had exploded very quickly since they arrived, he was happy with how it was going so well, but still his past troubled him and he secretly knew why. He felt her presence like a dragons flame on his neck.

'Penny for your thoughts Sean' he heard Patsy Docherty say behind him, and he turned to face her.

'Nothing major Patsy, just remembering the past and analysing what I have now, I miss him.'

'I miss him too but he wouldn't want you being all sad you twat, so don't sit here all day getting pissed like yesterday, you bought me this bar but I can't afford to give you free drinks two days in a row. Besides you have a barbecue at seven o'clock at your gaff and you have to take home the burgers and buns, Tina will go nuts if you're late and pissed.'

Sean looked up at Patsy from his bar stool and feeling the wrath from her telling off on his newly shaved face.

'You don't change do you, you old bag, but I still love ya', he replied smiling.

Patsy kissed Sean on the cheek, he swigged his beer down and left the bar hearing Patsy screaming orders at the bar staff behind him.

Sean entered his property, the large entrance door swinging open to expose the large interior hallway and staircase to the next floor, he threw his keys on the side table and looked around at his home, so much bigger then the council flat he grew up in with his uncle, he smiled to himself as he remembered how friends would knock on the door and ask if he was coming out to play. He heard children's laughter; his nostrils smelt a lit barbecue and he decided to go where his senses told him his family was. He saw Tina coming from the kitchen holding a tray of plates and cutlery, she saw him and smiled at him, he kissed her full on the mouth and then took the tray from her and they kissed again, Tina looked into his eyes.

'You ok?' she said.

'Yeah fine love, I take it the kids are in the pool?' he replied.

'Yes, Taylors teaching Megan how to swim, Pete has started the barbecue, did you get the meat and buns?'

Yeah, and I only had one beer at your mums bar before she threw me out.'

'She told me you were dancing on the tables last night.'

Sean smiled with a guilty frown, yeah, a few of the boys were in the bar, and it got a bit wild.'

Sean saw Pete Murray sitting on the patio and quickly moved over to him.

'Hi Pete, how you doing?' he said as he gripped ex Police Sergeant Pete Murray's hand with a firm handshake, noticing the Spanish sun was starting to age his old friend.

'Fine Sean, I started without you, hope you don't mind, the kids were getting hungry.'

'No problem Pete.'

Sean turned to the pool; he saw Taylor, his dark hair and bronzed skin from the Spanish sun splashing around with Megan. He looked at his boy who was ten years old today and wondered how time had flown by since they had been in Spain.

'Look dad she's swimming, she's swimming', shouted Taylor Farrow.

Sean smiled, he felt proud, passion and love but also loss, but he smiled and told Taylor what a fantastic job he was doing. 'Happy Birthday son', he shouted.

Tina noticed there was something sad about Sean today and broke the oncoming silence before it arrived.

'Angela, Mario and Sam are coming over and mum will be coming later about nine with some regulars from the bar.'

'Great' Sean replied.

The night was like any other birthday barbecue, with friends and relatives, drink and food, the evening was warm and the conversations were jolly. Pete Murray would always thank Sean for giving him a new start, allowing him to stay in The Singleton Apartments rent free for the rest of his life, Sean would always wave him away and say he didn't need thanking, but Pete persisted. Pete had a new life in Spain and although he missed Fiona he was now living the life of an English eccentric gentleman, dating older ladies who needed a bit of male company. He did odd jobs for Sean and often baby sat when Sean and Tina went out for the evening. Sean was giving something back to Pete, he liked that, because Pete was a massive influence on his early life and was always there when Sean needed him after Taylor's death. Sean would always know that it was Pete's hard work and detail that was beneficial for him and Tina to be able to complete what they did in a safe and precise way, to kill Saunders and his men, the bastards that killed Taylor. Pete was like a father figure to them and they respected that. Sean did the same for Patsy and Angela Clay; they all lived in The Singleton Apartments rent free, he didn't need the money; just knowing he was doing people a favour was good enough for him. They all had a new life in Spain, Pete was enjoying his retirement from the police, Patsy had her new bar generously given to her by Sean and Tina and there was Angela Clay, who when settled in to her new life met and married Mario, a local fisherman who Sean respected and now looks after his boat. Sean was on the veranda with Pete Murray chatting for a while; he enjoyed these chats because Pete would listen intently and would guide him through situations on everyday problems, he gave a calm guiding influence, which Sean often followed and respected.

'How are you Sean?' asked Pete.

'I'm fine Pete', he replied.

'Are you sure?' Pete repeated the question, as he was not happy with the first answer.

'Yeah why?'

'Tina says you're getting drunk a lot.'

'I am Pete, but it's nothing major, sometimes the past catches up with me, I have everything now but there is something missing.'

'You do have everything, Tina, Taylor and Megan, you don't need anything else, what is it you believe is missing?' Said Pete searching for the truth.

Sean looked across the veranda, at his children, his wife and then out across the sea, the boats and the lights of the bars and restaurants at the quayside.

'There's one more Pete, it won't go away', he said.

'One more what?' Replied Pete.

'There's one more who was at Taylors killing, we couldn't get to him he was in prison, remember, Charlie Allan Pete, they're releasing Charlie Allan.

Pete sat in silence and then sipped on his whiskey before he spoke.

'I remember, throw it away Sean, it wont do you any good.'

'Joe has been in contact and told me he's getting out of prison and going to live with his brother in Vauxhall.'

'Does Tina know?' said Pete.

'No, I'm keeping her out of it.'

'Keeping her out of what Sean?'

'My thoughts, that's all Pete, just my thoughts.'

'You're safe here Sean, there's nothing you need to do, it's over, don't waste what you have here.'

'Pete, if I don't do anything, he may come looking for me, that's my fear.'

'Wait a few days, let me make some enquiries and get back to you, I can contact some old colleagues, we can do something just by staying here.'

Tina walked onto the veranda, 'what are you boys talking about?'

'About how beautiful you look tonight Tina' Pete replied.

'Flattery gets you nowhere you old goat' she replied, 'come on you two we are bringing the cake and candles in for Taylor.'

'Ok love we will be in shortly' replied Sean.

When Tina left the veranda Sean looked at Pete with a troubled and concerned look, 'Pete, three days for some info, but then I'm going to be telling Tina I need to go to London.'

Tina was in her bed in her comfort zone, she had her head on Sean's chest and was stroking his arm, which she always did when she was scared and needed comforting. The sun shone through the patio doors, and the thin curtains moved slowly with the slight breeze coming through the ventilation gap. She continued to stroke, Sean could feel Tina's worries, he could sense it within her, they had discussed it the night before, what he needed to do, although he worded it in a way to not make her worry too much. He had an early flight and they lay there together thinking. Sean's worries were about what he was going back to do and Tina's fears were about whether she would see her husband and her children's father again. Tina was not silly, she knew something was not quite right and why Sean had to leave them to go back to London. What was drawing him back to London, she thought, now of all times, now when life has been cured and was very peaceful for them all.

'I don't want you to worry too much babe' said Sean, 'I will be gone one week, and Pete has set it all up for me, to meet people who can help us while we are in Spain.'

'You're not telling me the truth Sean, your not being honest.'

'Babe I am going to London to solve issues that will make us more financially safe here, it's a government tax thing honest, as I've said already, Miguel has warned me I need to do this.'

'I'm just scared Sean that's all.'

'Trust me babe, I will be safe, it's not going to be dangerous in any way, it's just a meeting with some people.'

'I know Sean, of course I trust you, but can you do one thing for me before you go?'

'What's that babe?' he said.

'Will you make love to me before you leave?'

'Of course I will babe, I will be delighted to', he said with a smile.

Tina and Sean made love like they always did with passion, but this time Tina was gripping on harder then normal, she didn't want him to leave, she didn't want him to go, he is her world, her soul mate and life without him was not what she would ever be able to cope with. Sean felt it inside her and when she cried it was like she knew what he was leaving to do but could not stop her man doing what he believed was best for her and his family. Sean showered and dressed as he knew Miguel would be there soon to take him to the airport, he went into the kids room and smiled at their innocence while they were asleep, he wanted to pick them both up as he went into each room, he wanted to smell them and hold onto them for eternity but instead just kissed them both on the forehead and closed the doors slowly behind him. They had coffee together on the veranda with the sun slowly rising, the pool was alive with lights from the patio and the sun gleaming across it's surface, it was calm and quiet and they held each other.

'Do you know Sean, since we've been in Spain we have never been apart for one night and now you're going away for one week, do you understand why I feel the way I do?'

'I do Tina, believe me I do', he replied.

'Come home safe Sean Farrow?' she said while looking into his eyes.

'I will Tina Farrow, I will', he said as he held her in his arms.

Sean collected his bags just as Miguel was arriving at the door, he took one more glance into the children's room and kissed Tina goodbye. He left the house looking back one more time as he got into the car, for the journey that would take him away from his loved ones for a short period of time, and then the car pulled away.

Tina waved to him until the brow of the hill took her man away, just as the sun was rising for the start of a new day.

Chapter 46

Charlie Allan looked out of his cell window, he could see the clouds dispersing in the morning breeze, he knew in a short while he would be feeling the wind on his face for the first time in a number of years. He spent his time within the walls of Wandsworth prison as a respected prisoner, but within a short period of time some of his friends and colleagues, and then his boss Johnny Saunders were brutally killed. His reputation changed, as after that short period in his life his protection was eradicated, and had to work very hard to keep himself respected within the prison walls. He listened to the whispers within the prison, he listened to the assumptions, the chitter and chatter about how each of his colleagues were killed one by one, and then made his plans that he would carry out on his eventual release. He lay there pondering his future, he knew his plans well and he had a very robust strategy as soon as the doors released him from the shit hole he was in. He still could not understand how amateurs could carry out what they did and if they had finished, will they be waiting for him outside these walls, will they want to complete what they started all those years ago. He didn't care too much about that, what he cared about was how his life got worse in prison, and they created that by destroying his protection, he needed to attack before being attacked, he needs to come off the ropes before they look for him. He didn't need the information written down, it was all in his head; all the information that was given to him while he was inside, and it was imbedded deep into his brain.

Charlie lay there on his cell bed knowing the guard will soon come for him, he had already shaved, showered and packed, he was in his own world and preparing himself for what he had planned for ten years now and was recalling all the detail of the past before he ended up in jail.

Tony Clay was killed, and the fifty grand has gone missing, the money is still missing and Johnny is going mad, he doesn't know who is responsible. Taylor Docherty was killed and the money is still fucking missing. Stan was killed, burnt alive, Ray was killed; the whole thing is falling apart. Johnny is looking for Sean Farrow, he's gone missing, and they think he has the money. Winston was killed, they cut his fucking cock right off him Charlie, still no money and still no Sean Farrow, and Johnny is starting to lose it.

Charlie was laying on his cell bed reflected all that went on ten years ago and then he ended up in prison for shooting Billy Boy. He remembered when he heard that Johnny had been killed, he had been found dead, tied up and stabbed through the heart, and it was then Charlie knew he would find it harder in prison.

Charlie Allan continued to reflect, Mitch Reddy was the new boy in the prison after Johnny's death and his first contact with him would always be remembered.

'No friends now you ponce', Mitch Reddy had told him, 'you don't own fuck all now, I want all the incoming now, all the trade and influence inside this nick and your gonna work for me now, your old school now you cunt, now that Saunders is dead.'

That was the last thing that Charlie Allan recalled in his head, that conversation with Mitch Reddy. From that day Charlie recalled how Mitch Reddy, who was already an established gangster and hard man, as well as an up and coming daddy within the walls of Wandsworth Prison made life hell for him. He worked for Mitch Reddy from that day when Johnny Saunders was killed; after all it was all he knew on the outside and now he could use his experience on the inside too. Charlie would carry out the normal running around roughing people up and controlling the inmates, but he also knew he would have to work for a new boss on the outside on his release but that could wait, he thought, he had a new priority first. From the day the deaths of his colleagues started, his power started to diminish, and on the death of Johnny Saunders it was eradicated completely, he wanted pay back and the only one still alive through it all was himself and Sean Farrow. Charlie heard the key in the cell door, he didn't move, he still commanded some respect from the screws, he smiled to himself and prepared himself mentally.

'Come on Charlie time to go, you're a free man' said the guard.

'Ok Mr Jennings, just laying here for the last time', he replied.

Charlie Allan swung his legs around from the bed and raised himself up, he picked up his bag and kissed the poster of Rachael Welch full on her lips, 'bye babe' he said. He followed the guard outside of his cell and walked along the corridors, some inmates who were on a break shook his hands, some patted him on the back, and others just stared, including Mitch Reddy.

He continued to the exit of the prison, signed a few papers and was handed his belongings he had to hand over when he first arrived. He was taken through a number of locked gates and was eventually taken to the main exit of the prison, the guard opened the gate with his bundle of keys, it was then the sunlight caught Charlie's eyes, he shook the hand of Mr Jennings the guard, turned and walked out of the gate. At first due to the early morning sunlight he could not see who it was that was there to meet him, but once his eyes were adjusted to the light he could see that the person that had come to meet him was John Wall, the bent copper from all those years ago.

'Hi Charlie you look like shit', said John Wall.

'I feel like shit Wallsy, it's been rough in there, have you got what I asked for?'

'I have Charlie, new passport, false name, some money, Pesetas of course and an address, but I don't suppose you want that now, it's time to party, it's been a long time.'

'Keeps me focused Wallsy, it keeps me focused, I need to get out of this country now, what about the flight ticket.'

'Fucking hell Charlie, you need to chill out a bit first, I didn't get the ticket I thought you would want to take your time, learn about the new world first.'

'I asked for a flight ticket Wallsy, that's what we agreed on, passport, money and flight ticket.'

'Times have changed Charlie there's new people new territory new people to work for, I did the things you asked for out of old times and respect but the ticket I thought you could get yourself in your own time.'

Charlie looked at John Wall with disdain, he wanted to throttle him there, right there outside the walls of the prison he had just come from, but thought better of it in the circumstances and the location. Charlie looked into the sky, he felt the cool breeze on his body, his scars had hardened inside and he felt the breeze sting his face, he was calming himself down, he had a prick in front of him and wanted to do him right there, he looked back down at John wall.

'John, I will ask this question once, where can I buy myself a fucking plane ticket and will you take me there and then to the airport?'

John Wall looked at Charlie Allan, he was looking at him in a confused way, he could quite easily tell him to fuck off and leave him right there but knew Charlie still had some clout and knew a lot about his past. He could help him now; get him out of the country and carrying on dealing with the new bigger people in Town.

'Ok Charlie, I will take you to the travel agents and then the airport dependent on what flight you can get and when.'

'It's today Wallsy, I want to go today.'

319

'Even better Charlie, even better.'

John Wall and Charlie Allan travelled to a travel agents in Balham High road; Charlie purchased a plane ticket, which was leaving Gatwick airport at six thirty that evening, he did not purchase a return ticket. Charlie was taken straight to the airport on his request; John Wall did not mind this, as he was getting rid of Charlie quicker than he thought. The journey was quiet apart from the odd chat about the deaths of Charlie's colleagues and Johnny Saunders, Charlie didn't want to discuss what he was doing although John Wall had a good idea as it was him that provided the detail that Charlie wanted. The journey ended at Gatwick airport drop off point, Charlie retrieved his bag, there was no handshake, he shut the door behind him and John Wall pulled away from the kerb. It was early Charlie thought, still early and a long wait to his flight, time to plan he thought to himself, maybe grab a beer and a bite to eat and plan.

Chapter 47

After successfully going through immigration with no issues at Malaga airport Sean Farrow boarded the plane; he hadn't been on a plane for a number of years, and he wasn't surprised to feel a little nervous. Things had improved slightly, he thought, the airhostesses looked smarter and it all looked a bit more modern then he remembered. He found his seat and put his luggage in the overhead locker, he sat down and fastened his seat belt, he still didn't like flying, he thought, never did like the uncertainty of a heavy lump of metal traveling across the sky when it wasn't meant to. To get over the fear he downed a few pints of Spanish beer in the airport lounge earlier and was now glad he had an aisle seat, knowing he would probably need a piss soon. One of the air hostesses smiled at him with that glint in her eye, he still had the looks, he thought, even at his age, but now had a tan to go with it, he smiled back at her adjusting himself in his seat.

The flight over was smooth and Sean took the advantage of the aisle seat and took that piss at least three times he knew that he would need. The flight was due to land mid afternoon and as they approached Gatwick airport it gave Sean a chance to look down again at the country he loved and respected. The flight started it's approach and Sean could see the Surrey Hills, the green farmlands and the big main roads that he didn't remember from before, cars were going back and forth to wherever they needed to go. As the plane landed one thing came to his mind and that was the entry into his own country, he knew that Pete had done some work before they went to Spain but was unsure if things had now changed, was he wanted by the police, will he be under suspicion when he arrives, will anyone be waiting for him? Sean was now beginning to think this could all be a big mistake.

The plane landed and Sean Farrow grabbed his bag from the overhead locker, he didn't have to go to the luggage hall, he had all he wanted in his bag he had with him. He left the plane noticing the air hostess smiling at him again, he returned the smile noting her smile was warm and caring just like Tina's, he left the plane and walked down the steps. When he got to the bottom, he looked at the tarmacked floor; he wanted to kiss the floor but decided not to in case eyes were watching him. He headed towards the airport across the tarmac, went into the airport main building and headed onto immigration. Travellers and airport workers were everywhere going back and forth, he looked around and thought how he didn't remember the airport being this busy years ago. The immigration line was long, he waited with his bag over his shoulder, the line moved slowly and his bag was getting heavier, he decided to put it on the floor and kick it with his foot along the line. When he was about five deep away from the immigration officer he picked his bag up and placed it back over his shoulder, it will be his turn soon and he really wanted to turn and run. When it was his turn he tried to look as calm as possible, in front of him another officer arrived, was there a problem, Sean thought, the other officer had come to the immigration desk in front of him, they both looked along the line, the original officer stood up and left his seat, the new officer sat in his seat and started to arrange paperwork, Sean was conscious that he was starting to sweat. The new officer continued to arrange paperwork when he looked up and raised his hand to Sean, Sean approached the desk and handed over his passport, the officer scrutinized each page, looked up at Sean and then back at the passport, he seemed to be taking more time over his passport, he wanted to run but had no idea where to.

'You've been away a long time sir?' the immigration officer said.

'Yes, I have my own business in Spain, I have family issues back here I need to help with so I needed to come home.'

'Where will you be staying sir?' repeated the officer.

'With friends and family, I will be staying for about a week.'

The officer was looking at Sean, he looked at the passport again, and he closed the passport and handed it back to Sean.

'Have a good trip sir, welcome home, and I hope you sort your family issues out',

'Thanks', replied Sean.

Sean took the passport and headed towards the exit of the immigration hall, he went straight through the 'nothing to declare' line and was not questioned. He went to the first bar he saw in the airport and ordered a whiskey and soda. He downed the whiskey and soda and ordered a second one as he watched the people go by. He felt more relaxed now as he waited for his next drink, he looked around the bar, everyone was just waiting for flight arrivals or relaxing before they went through to departures. His second drink came, he turned back to the bar when he felt a man stumbled into him, he turned round to see a large man standing there, make a fumbled apology and then turn to exit the bar. Sean took more time with his drink this time; he sipped at it feeling his calmness returning as he watched the big man stumble out of the bar.

Charlie Allan was sitting in the airport bar before going through to departures, it was still too early, and he was free but bored. He was on his fourth pint of beer and as it's been his first taste of alcohol for some time he could feel it starting to have an impact. He decided to stop at the fourth and get some food inside himself before his flight. Charlie Allan left his seat; he walked towards the exit noticing he was not too good on his feet, he tripped on something on the floor and bumped into a man at the bar, he cursed himself, he turned to the man who had his back to him, the man in front of him turned round, they looked at each for a short while, Charlie managed to fumble a sentence, get some stability back into his legs again, turned and stumbled out of the bar.

Chapter 48

Sean contemplated his situation, he had things to do, he didn't want anyone to know he was here; he needed to do what he had to do and then fly back home. He had the information he needed, Charlie Allan was being released from Wandsworth prison today, and he would be taken to a house where he will stay with his brother for a while, he would need to sign in to a police station every week and he will have to see his parole officer, he will have no passport and would not be allowed to leave the country. It was going to be easy to find him, Sean thought, he had the address of Charlie Allan's brother, Mick Allan, he knew who the parole officer was, where the parole officer's office is, and where the police station was that Charlie Allan had to visit weekly. Sean gathered his thoughts and remembered the past, it wasn't that easy then and maybe it wont be as easy again now. Sean Farrow left the lounge bar and headed for the exit of the airport, he needed to catch a train into London, go to the house that Pete set up, relax and sleep for the night.

The train journey brought him back home; he saw the country he knew from the windows of the train, although faster then he remembered. He relaxed himself into the journey as the train rumbled through the Surrey countryside and then into the London suburbs and into Victoria Station which looked bigger now with far more advertising boards than he remembered. He left the station and went straight to the nearest phone box to ring the number he was given by Pete. This contact was an old friend of Pete and was there to ensure things would run smoothly for Sean, as well as give him the keys for the house he would adopt for the next week while he carried out his plan. He dialled the number and put the coin into the slot when required, there was no answer, and he tried again, again no answer. He waited in the phone box for another hour trying every few minutes, this was the only contact he had, he tried his house number in Spain to speak to Pete, again no answer, Sean was confused, this is not going as smoothly as he thought. He left the phone box to gather his thoughts as there was a queue forming outside and they looked like they were getting restless. Sean decided to walk, after all he knew the area to head to and when he sees another phone box he will try again. He walked for another ten minutes when he spotted another phone box further down the road in Vauxhall. He entered the phone box and tried again, he dialled the number he was given by Pete and waited to drop the coin in when and if it was answered, the phone was answered and Sean dropped the coin into the slot.

'Hello' said Sean.

'Who is that' came the reply.

'It's Pete Farrow' Sean said the name Pete told him to say when the call was answered.

'Is that Sean Farrow?' Sean heard the man reply.

'Yes it's Sean Farrow.'

'For fucks sake' said the man on the end of the phone, 'I've been trying to call Pete in Spain, there's no answer and I can't get hold of him, you don't know who I am, just listen, what was the password Pete gave you to give to me'

'Singleton', replied Sean.

'Ok Sean just listen, I know why you're here, but things have changed, Charlie Allan was released as expected, but we didn't anticipate what he would do next, I kept an eye on him as instructed by Pete and he was right to tell me to do that.'

'Why?' replied Sean.

'Because Charlie Allan didn't go to his brothers as instructed, he went to Gatwick airport; he bought a flight to Spain, Malaga. I watched him and found out that he met John Wall a well known bent cop, I lost them both at one point but caught up with John Wall later in the evening, after I threatened him a bit with informing the Met about him he gave me the detail about Charlie. I've been trying to get hold of Pete ever since, probably why you haven't been able to get hold of me.

'Are you telling me that I've come over here the same time that he's gone over to Spain, what's he gone to Spain for?'

'That's not the bad news Sean, the bad news is I think he's gone looking for you, I didn't get too much out of John Wall but I think Charlie Allan may have your address in Spain.'

The phone went silent, Sean didn't know how to respond, shock had entered his body and there was not enough adrenalin to combat it, the fear was too intense.

'Sean, Sean are you still there? Sean!' the man was shouting down the phone.

It took a while for Sean to respond, 'yes, yes I'm still here, I need a plane ticket quickly, can you arrange it for me, and why have you not been able to get hold of Pete?'

'You're better off going straight back to the airport Sean and trying to get a ticket, I will try and get hold of Pete on the number I have for him, I don't know why I can't get hold of him, it's like there's a phone issue or a failure on the line, normally I can get hold of Pete easy.'

'What time did he get the flight out of Gatwick?' Sean asked.

'All I know is he was dropped off around midday and didn't seem to be in a rush, I don't even know how the fuck he got a passport, John Wall was being very protective and would only offer so much, he's a bent cop but he also has information on me, so I could only deal so far, get going Sean I will continue trying to get hold of Pete.'

'I don't know your name' said Sean, 'but I'm thanking you for your help, but I need your help more then ever now for the sake of my family, as soon as you get hold of Pete warn him about what you know and that I am on my way back.'

Sean put the phone down and exited the phone box, he searched the street for a black taxi, none to be seen, he ran back the way he came from, his mind was at breaking point, he saw a black cab coming along the opposite side of the street, he ran into the road to haul the cab down, the cab saw him and pulled over to the kerb.

'Fuck me mate your in a rush ain't ya' said the cab driver.

'I need to get to Victoria Station, or even better how quick can you get me to Gatwick airport?'

'Victoria Station is cheaper but all depends how quick you want to get to Gatwick, this time of night I can get you there pretty rapid but I will have to break the law to do it, with an additional fee of course.'

'Gatwick airport it is then I need to get there pretty rapid.'

'Ok jump in, what's the urgency?'

'Drive mate, I will fill you in on the way', replied Sean.

Sean jumped into the cab and the cab driver pulled away, Sean knew the route well and was keeping an eye on every street that the driver was taking, he was so far taking every turn correctly and with good speed so Sean started to settle into the back of the cab.

'You gonna fill me in then mate?' said the driver through the glass panel.

'I need to get to Spain urgently my mother has been involved in a road traffic accident, I want to be there if you know what I mean.'

Sean didn't know where that answer came from, he had never spoken about his mother and father's accident since the tragedy years ago and why it came out now baffled him, it was the only thing he could think of to say.

'Ok mate I understand, I will get you there as soon as', replied the cab driver.

The cab fell silent apart from the screeching of brakes at every corner the cab took until eventually the cab got onto the A23 main route towards Brighton and Gatwick airport, and then all that could be heard was the wind whistling passed the windows. Sean was in a prison cell he couldn't get out of, his only friend was time, and he knew he had to have time on his side. He could not contact anyone until he was at the airport, he doesn't even know if the guy on the end of the phone managed to get hold of Pete, yet Sean Farrow felt useless unable to do anything but sit and rely on the unknown taxi driver. At one point he heard a bang from the back of the taxi, his mind was racing, are nuts and bolts or whatever piece of car machinery falling off the taxi, and will the taxi suddenly stop or breakdown, he was at the mercy of so many things and he was desperate to take control again. He saw a sign for Gatwick airport and the taxi seemed to be flying along.

'Soon be there mate', said the cab driver, 'another couple of miles, I'll get you right outside the departure lounge, you can get tickets there, stick ten quid through the window now, you're going to want to jump out when we get there, I've let you off the legal fees as I never got nicked, good luck mate.'

Sean pulled ten pounds out of his wallet and passed it through the cabs partition window, he thanked the driver and started to prepare to exit the cab. The cab pulled off the A23 main road and headed towards the airport, skidding around roundabouts like a racing car at Brands Hatch. On arrival at the flight departures the cab pulled into the set down point and Sean exited the cab, he thanked the cab driver one more time and ran to the entrance.

Sean looked at his watch, it was 19:35. He didn't know what time Charlie Allan left for Spain but he knew he needed a ticket fast, he would get the ticket first and then try calling home. He ran towards the ticket office, lucky he thought, not much of a queue, he looked for the line where he could get tickets to Spain, bloody typical he thought no signage indicating which line, he pushed through a line of people to the front apologising en-route.

'Tickets to Spain, where can I get a ticket to Spain! He shouted at the first lady he could see with a uniform on. The lady at the desk looked up at Sean, 'this line Sir but you will need to join the queue.'

Sean thanked her and re-joined the back of the queue.

'Are you in a rush Sir' Sean heard from behind him, he turned and to his astonishment the air hostess from his flight over was standing right behind him with that familiar smile.

'I saw you enter the airport you looked in a terrible rush', she said.

'I am in a rush, I need to get back to Spain urgently', he replied.

'I'm afraid there are no more flights this evening these people are queuing for tickets for tomorrow I believe, let me find out.'

The airhostess walked to the front desk and Sean watched as a conversation was carried out between the two women, which made the people in the queue get irritated even more.

'I'm sorry Sir I am right', she said on her return, 'there are flights tonight but they are all fully booked this queue is for flights tomorrow.'

Sean looked at the airhostess he could not believe it, that pain of feeling useless ripped through his body again.

'How urgent is it sir?' the airhostess said pulling Sean away from the queue of people.

'It's very urgent', Sean replied, and again he told the story of the accident with his mother and how he needed to be in Spain sooner rather then later.

'The air hostess listened intently, 'leave it with me' she said, 'my flight goes in two hours I will see if I can get you on it, it's going back to the same airport, is that ok?'

'Yes', said Sean, not believing his luck.

'Go and sit over there for a while sir, you will need to give me your passport, I will then come and get you if payment is required.'

Sean handed over his passport to the air hostess and went to sit down, he looked up and noticed the line of people were looking at him as if he was a piece of shit on their shoe, he looked away.

The wait was unbearable for Sean and in that time he thought of the taxi driver and the airhostess, where did they come from, they appeared when he needed them, he threw the thought away when the airhostess returned.

'I've got you on the flight, it was full but we have what is known as a crew seat, not very comfortable but it will get you there, you need to get back in the queue to pay the lady at the desk, she has all your details from your passport.'

Sean let out a sigh of relief, his energy returned, he was now in a position to fight back, and he was feeling back in control.

'How can I thank you, you've been terrific, I can't thank you enough, you've saved my life honestly, what is your name?' said Sean.

'My name, my name is Sarah. I will see you on the flight Peter Farrow, you don't need to thank me, as my father always said, it's a good thing to make someone smile everyday.'

'Well you have certainly done that Sarah' thanks again, and yeah, I will see you on the flight.'

Sarah turned away with that familiar smile and headed towards departures, Sean watched her leave and again wondered where she came from.

Sean headed towards the queue again, when he got to the front, as Sarah suggested the woman at the desk had all his details and the ticket was ready, he handed over the money and she apologised for the cabin crew seat, he smiled at her and told her it's a miracle he has a scat anyway and thanked her. He headed to the nearest phone, he first tried his home number in Spain, nothing no dial tone just like what the man said it's as if there is a technical fault. He then tried the phone number for the man again, there was an engaged tone, this gave him some hope, and maybe he's talking to Pete, Sean thought. He waited at the phone box trying several times to make contact with his home and the man, but still there was the technical fault and the engaged tone, time was ticking by and he had to make contact, or at least know if Pete is aware of the situation, he looked at his watch, he will need to board soon, he tried one more time, still the same situation, he left the phone box and headed towards departures, hoping there was another phone box en route. He looked up; 'shit' he said to himself I have to go through security again, he wanted to turn round but knew he had to press on, again the long line to get checked, he waited, again the check of the passport, again the look up into his eyes, again the flipping through of the pages in the passport, these fuckers know how to get your blood pressure up he thought.

'You've just arrived Sir?' said the immigration officer.

'Yes, a family tragedy, I've just found out about it and I need to return urgently'

Again his passport was checked by the immigration Officer, fucking IRA, Sean thought, increased security is a good thing but having a name like Farrow does have it's problems. He stood and waited.

'Very well sir have a safe flight, good luck', the officer handed the passport back to Sean and waved him on.

Sean tried a few more times on a phone box in the departure lounge but still the same issue, he decided to make one last try while watching the board above his head indicating his flight was boarding, this time he made contact with the man.

'It's me Sean', he said in an erratic voice.

'Sean I've been trying to get through to Pete, I've found out there's a Spanish telephone issue in the area where you live, no one can get through, they're still trying to fix it, and did you manage to get a flight?'

Sean didn't speak, he thought for a moment, he doesn't know who this man is, Pete does, but sometimes you have to go with your instincts, he then decided on his answer. 'No I can't get one till tomorrow, all fully booked, I'm going to stay here at the airport for the night, fly first thing in the morning.'

'Ok good luck, I will keep trying Pete to let him know, call me every hour to see if I've managed to get through.'

'Ok, thanks', Sean put the phone down and looked around departures, he looked up at the board, his flight was boarding, and he left the phone box and headed towards the gate. He joined the queue for the plane and kept his eye open for Sarah, he wanted to thank her again for what she had done for him, but she was nowhere to be seen, maybe she is on the plane he thought. He boarded the plane showed his boarding pass and was shown which cabin crew seat he was in by another air hostess; he thanked her and sat down pushing his bag under the seat. When he was settled in his mind started to race and was hoping that the man had got through to Pete, he again felt trapped, he couldn't do anything, he decided to try and relax, think about his next move and hope the plane takes off on time.

Chapter 49

Charlie Allan caught the plane, which left thirty minutes later then expected. This made him get more frustrated, as he wanted to get away from the airport; he needed to get away from England before they even knew that he had vanished, he knew full well he would now be a fugitive. He had never flown before and the four beers he had in the lounge bar helped with his nerves for the flight, although it made him a lot drunker than he realised it would after so many years inside. The plane was due to land soon and he wondered what he would do when he got there, he had his plan and the plan was to find and kill Sean Farrow tonight or as soon as possible depending on the difficulty of the situation. Once that was done he could relax down in sunny Spain, he knew many criminals that have retired there, he would soon find his feet and new friends. There is no need to follow a plan so soon, he thought, after all he's just got out, he could wait, relax for a bit enjoy Spain, after all he had time on his hand, or did he? He questioned that last thought in his head, did he have time, his own father always taught him to strike while the iron was hot, if you wait, it will happen without you and hurt you, he would say. Charlie Allan sat thinking as the plane started to descend, he grappled with his decision and decided to take his fathers words and strike while the iron was hot, and he will do it tonight.

The plane landed smoothly as Charlie looked out of the window, he had never been abroad before and the dusty landscape looked different from the damp grounds of England. The night was just starting to draw in, he left the plane through the exit door and started to descend the stairs, he instantly felt the hot climate attach itself to his face and upper body. As this was all new to him he decided to follow most of the passengers across the tarmac, they all looked like they knew what they were doing as they headed towards baggage claim and passport control, he followed along like a lost sheep and did exactly what they did. After retrieving his case from the conveyor belt, he went through to passport control, there was a short queue, Charlie didn't even think about passport control and they didn't seem to notice him either, they looked at his passport, looked up at Charlie, stamped it and waved him through.

After exiting the airport he knew he had to look for transport for his onward journey; he approached the taxi rank and asked the cab driver to take him to a hotel in Marbella. En route Charlie was surprised to see the difference between his country and Spain, England seemed to be a bit more organised and cleaner he thought and Spain seemed a little bit out-dated and a bit more in the past, however the weather must make up for it. He thought of the criminals that he would have to meet soon to make him feel more at home and help him settle in easier. Charlie Allan was taken to a hotel, he paid the cab driver after trying to work out what each bloody foreign note meant, he didn't know if he'd been ripped off by the cab driver or not. Charlie Allan took a cheap room, one bed a shower and a cupboard to hang his clothes in, he looked around, this was the first room he'd had that had a shower in it for some years, he stood for a while to gather his thoughts. After a quick shower, which he relished and noting he was alone without another inmate standing next to him, Charlie Allan got dressed and left his room. He brought a small bag with him, which he threw over his shoulder; he felt the contents hit his back, a small cosh, a length of rope, and a map of Marbella. He walked along the main street and noticed small bars starting to get busy, along the main promenade he noticed some shops selling bigger coshes than the one he had in his bag, better ones, spring loaded made with heavy metal, there were knives on sale, big knives, flick knives, any sort you required which would have been illegal in England. Charlie entered one shop and came out with a spring loaded metal cosh and a large hunting knife, that he thought had an excellent grip for his size of hands, he dropped them into his bag. He found a square with street lights and a bench, he sat on the bench, pulled the map out of his bag and started to familiarise himself with the streets around him and the streets he needed to go down to get to his destination. He kept looking up at the bars and wondered again if he should enter and have a few drinks before he did what he wanted to do, but his father was on his shoulder with those familiar words 'strike while the iron is hot son, strike while the iron is hot'. He threw the thoughts away and looked back at the map, he calculated that he needed to go along the promenade until the end then walk up to a dirt track that would take him up into the hills, he would have to take a left then two rights until he got to a small town, known as

Castillo de Castellar, he would then need to go through the town take a right at the end and there was about five properties that overlooked the sea, one of the properties was the one he wanted. Charlie Allan calculated that it would probably take him about an hour to get to his destination; he folded the map and put it into his bag, got up from the bench, and threw the bag over his shoulder again. He noticed that the bag felt heavier, with his new weapons that were tucked away neatly inside.

Chapter 50

Tina sat on the patio over looking the sea, the children were in bed, she was relaxing with a glass of Spanish red wine, she looked out to sea, the waves below were crashing onto the rocks that made their way up to her veranda and patio. She felt relaxed but scared, she wondered how Sean was and why the phone had not rung for while, she knew he would have called her as soon as he got to England he would have made sure of that, she checked her watch, he would have been there a few hours already, he would have had time to call. Tina stood up and walked towards the veranda edge and looked out further to sea, the wind blew into her hair, she looked down onto the marina that she knew well, the lights were on, the bars and restaurants were busy she thought. She took another gulp of red wine and made her way to the kitchen, she looked across at the phone on the wall and again wished it to ring, and it didn't ring. She walked out into the hall and entered both the bedrooms one by one, the kids were fast asleep, they looked peaceful and happy, she thought, she smiled and again walked into the hallway and back into the kitchen, she looked at the phone on the wall and again wished it to ring and again it didn't. She poured herself another red wine and went back onto the veranda, something is not right, she thought, something is not working out as it should, she would have heard by now if he was safe or even if something was not going to plan, she could feel the panic starting to well up inside of her. Tina sat back on the patio chair and again looked out across the sea, what was she looking for out there, an answer to her situation? She didn't know, but she knew she needed to do something or at least get some kind of communication from someone. She decided to take the initiative and find out for herself, Pete may know something, Sean may have contacted Pete, she thought. She took one more sip of wine and decided to call Pete.

Tina got up from the patio and walked back into the kitchen and over to the phone on the wall, again she wished it to ring but it didn't. She picked it up to make that call to Pete. She put the receiver to her ear but could not hear a dialling tone, there was a sharp crackling that she had not heard before, she placed the receiver back down on the cradle and picked it back up, the same crackling, was there a problem with the phones she thought, is that why she had no phone calls? She pressed the phone switch a few times but still the same crackling. The phone line is dead, she thought. Tina placed the phone back on the receiver again and walked back onto the veranda, she didn't know how she felt, she was relieved that the phone was dead as that would explain why she had received no calls but maybe that would also suggest that Sean was ok and that maybe there is no problem with Sean, he just can't get through. Tina looked out at the sea again she watched as a large cargo ship drifted across the curvature of the earth, with it's light from it's main tower blinking, she watched it as it vanished beyond the cliffs to the left hand side of where she was. She turned away and sat on the patio chair and took another sip from her glass, she started to think if there was something she should be doing but there wasn't anything to do, Sean had specifically told her he was just going to sort out financial stuff back home in England, there's nothing for her to fear here tonight. Tina got back off the chair and decided that she was being paranoid and what she is best to do is go to bed early and finish her book that she had been engrossed in for the last week, she walked into the bedroom and had a shower, she then put on her unflattering but comfortable pyjamas and settled down in bed with the side light on to help her read.

Tina woke with a start she heard a noise, like a bang, god she thought, I must have dosed off, she listened again, she could hear a faint noise coming from the front room, she looked to her left, Megan was fast asleep next to her, Tina didn't remember her getting into bed with her, but pleased she was there and safe. Tina jumped out of bed, still slightly disorientated from the sleep and the wine, she listened again, this time with her ear against the bedroom door, there was a faint noise, she waited while her brain was trying to make the next decision. Decision made she turned the handle to the bedroom door and slowly opened the door, she looked around to the left along the corridor and then the right, she didn't see anything, but there was still a faint noise coming from the front room area. She walked into the hallway and along the corridor towards the noise, she entered the main front room and noticed the veranda patio door curtains blowing in the wind, she looked to the floor and saw that a vase had smashed on the floor obviously blown over from the wind, she thought, she cursed herself for not shutting and locking the patio doors. She closed the patio doors and locked them, she pulled the curtains across and turned to see the mess the wind had caused, the vase had shattered and needed to be cleared up before the kids got up. Tina walked back out of the main room into the corridor passing her room, she glanced at Megan who was still fast asleep in bed, she walked further along the hallway and opened the door to Taylor's room, his side light was still on and she could see him lying there asleep, covers tossed to one side as usual due to the heat. She walked back into the front room to see Charlie Allan sitting on the main chair, and holding a large kitchen knife.

Chapter 51

Sean wrestled with his anxiety on the plane, he couldn't, settle during the flight and wandered along the plane back and forth from the toilets, he was agitated and again felt useless. He was wondering during the flight how he had never seen Sarah the air hostess that managed to get him on board the plane, after all, he thought, she said she would be on the flight, he wanted to thank her again, but she wasn't anywhere to be seen. He decided to ask one of the of air hostess but she'd said that all the crew on board are the ones that were expected to be on the flight, it baffled him but he came to the conclusion that she had to change flights at the last minute. Sean looked at his watch, another thirty minutes or so and then he will be landing, he would try and rush through immigration and customs and get a cab as soon as possible, he knew he needed to get home to make his family safe. The rest of the journey went by slowly and Sean was glad when the airhostess told the passengers to get back to their seats ready for landing. The flight landed on time and Sean pulled his bag from underneath his seat, he thanked the air hostess and left quickly descending the stairs. He walked across the tarmac noticing he didn't feel the need to kiss the ground, he walked quickly through to the immigration hall where he once again had to join a queue, although it was shorter than the one in England. When he got to the front of the queue the Spanish immigration officer looked at his passport, he spoke to Sean in Spanish, Sean understood what he was saying and answered in Spanish explaining the short time he had left the country. Once again had to explain about family matters that brought him back home so quickly within twenty four hours, the Spanish immigration officer did the same old, I'm fucking important look up and down from his passport, back to Sean, and then waved that fucking hand again waving him through. Sean could not stop himself thinking what a load of wankers these immigration officers are, but was pleased to be let through again. He threw his passport into his bag and ran to the exit of the airport looking for the nearest taxi rank. On the way he saw a phone box and rushed into it to try his home number, he heard the dead tone again, he tried Pete's number again, again a dead tone, he left the phone booth and headed towards the taxi rank. He got into the first taxi in the queue and gave the taxi driver his home address and settled into the back seat, he wondered what he would find, but what he really wanted was to find his family safe and well. He would wake them up and take them to a hotel for a short period until he sorted all this out, find a safe house in Spain somewhere, maybe get a bodyguard for the kids, his mind was racing with how he could protect his loved ones. The taxi made it's way along the major roads and Sean could see the signs showing they were getting nearer to his destination. The taxi driver was quiet, which made it easier for him to think, it was then he realised that he had no weapons, no way of protecting himself or his family, he just had clothes in his bag, he was going to get his weapons to kill Charlie Allan in England. He decided he just needed to get home first make sure his family was safe, move them, then decide on his next move, he directed the taxi driver to the other side of Castillo de Castellar, it was dark and it was getting late.

Chapter 52

Tina stood still, she did not move, she just looked at Charlie Allan, he was sitting there with a broad smile. She decided to stay where she was because where she stood was the entrance to her children, and she would protect them at any cost.

'Hello Tina, it's been a long time', said Charlie Allan.

Tina did not answer, her mind was racing, how could she protect her children with Sean out of the country, she stood there and then decided to answer.

'What are you doing here?' she said.

'I've come to see your husband, he owes me fifty grand, and he looks like he's done very well out of it.'

'We don't know anything about any money, anyway he's due back soon, can you come back tomorrow?' she said with fear clearly showing in her voice.

Charlie Alan laughed, and put the knife away inside his jacket pocket.

'I know he's not in the house', he replied, 'I've already checked, you're all on your own little lonesome until he gets home. Apart from the kids, that is.'

'You fucking go near my kids and I will fucking kill you', she shouted.

'What like you killed, Stan, Ray, Winston, oh and your old man, you know, your own dad don't you? Johnny Saunders, to be honest with you I can see the resemblance now', Charlie Allan said with a grin across his face.

Tina looked into Charlie Allan's eyes, but stood her ground at the entrance to where her kids were, she said nothing.

'To be honest with you love, my plans have changed slightly since I've seen your gaff and the lifestyle you have, you see I've been in the nick all this time with you pair of cunts living like Spanish fucking royalty, well that's really pissed me off, so I'm thinking about the past and come up with a conclusion. I think Sean and Taylor nicked Johnny Saunders money, sorry daddies money, and then your brother Taylor got topped by daddy, you got scared and decided to top everyone before they topped you and then run away to sunny Spain, very ingenious and very brave if I do say so.'

Again Tina stood her ground and said nothing but erratically in her head she was planning out her next move, or if there was any move she could make to protect herself and her children. She decided to answer.

'Sean and Taylor would never have had the bottle to do any of that, they were made suspects by', she went to say the name but couldn't bring herself to say it, 'you know who I mean, and I certainly wouldn't get myself involved in anything like that.'

'You're forgetting one thing love', he replied.

'What's that?' Tina said.

'You've got Johnny Saunders blood in you, you're capable of anything, I was there when he fucked your mum, she was drunk, she did try to resist, but you know Johnny, always got his way, she had to lie there and take it otherwise he would have hit her again.'

Tina was looking at Charlie Allan taking in everything that he had just said, she was wondering why her mum could never tell her the truth, she would have understood. She would have believed her mum if she had said she was raped, maybe there was some reality in it now that she was a mother herself, and as a mother Patsy would have been protecting her daughter from the disgusting reality of where she came from.

'Anyway, back to my change of heart', said Charlie, 'it's obvious that you ended up with daddy's fifty grand that went missing.' I will walk away now if you can find it and give it to me, because I know everything, I can quite easily tell the whole fucking story and bring your happy little Spanish life down around you, what do you think?'

'What do I think about what?' Tina replied.

'About the money you idiot, where is it?'

'I don't know, Sean deals with the money, I haven't got a clue about any money and you should get out of my house now or I will call the police.'

The room went quiet, they both stared at each other, Tina felt the mistake she had made run through her body, she knew what she said was a load of bollocks and that she had allowed herself to get angry and she did not want to get this man angry, it was then she felt the tug on her pyjamas. Tina looked down to see Taylor standing there wiping his tired eyes.

'What's all the shouting mummy?' he said.

'Nothing son go back to bed, it's ok.'

'Who's that man?' asked Taylor.

'He's a friend of your daddy's, he's here to see daddy.'

Taylor wiped his eyes again, 'but daddy's in London.'

Tina quickly turned Taylor around and took him back to the door to his room, she told him to go back to sleep 'daddy will be home tonight son' she said, 'he will be home tonight' she turned back to go back to the front room hoping and praying to God that what she had just said would be true.

'London eh', said Charlie.

'He's home tonight'' said Tina.

'Then we shall wait for him together, I need to speak to him about the money, unless you can pay me some money now?'

'How much?' Tina replied.

Charlie Allan looked into her eyes as if he was searching for the best figure, and one that he would be happy with to walk back out of the door.

'Twenty five grand', he said.

'I haven't got twenty five grand, and if I did I wouldn't keep it in the house.'

Charlie got off his chair and walked over to the drinks cabinet opened the cabinet doors pulled out a bottle of whiskey and poured himself a large measure. He sat back down and looked up at Tina.

'Well make yourself comfortable, how long have we got to wait?' said Charlie.

'Look why don't you leave and come back tomorrow, he will be here tomorrow I will tell him you came by', she said without trying to sound too sarcastic.

It was too late, she knew she had made him angry she could see it in his eyes and his facial expression, she waited for his next response with feared anticipation, and then it came.

'Shut up you fucking idiot, I'm making all the rules here, do you know where I have been while you two have been swanking around in fucking Spain, I've been in the fucking nick. I've had no alcohol and no sex, do you know how that makes a man feel, no you fucking don't so sit fucking down and relax, sit fucking down!' Charlie shouted again.

Tina sat down at the nearest chair to the hallway like a an endangered animal protecting her young. She felt scared, intimidated and needed to calm him down and not make him angry again, and she was annoyed at herself. She tried to think if there was any money in the house, she cursed herself for allowing Sean to manage all the finances, the only money she knew about was what she has, which is very little, and will not make Charlie Allan go away, she cursed herself again.

'Ok so you have made your point, we have to wait for Sean to get back or I give you money to leave which I haven't got, so we have to wait, she said, praying it was the right thing to say.

Charlie Allan got off his chair and started to walk towards Tina, 'then wait we shall do', he said.

Tina felt the fear inside her increase as she gripped the arms of the chair tighter, and she was not expecting it but he punched her in the face, which hurled her backwards and onto the floor, she then felt herself being picked up quickly and put back onto the chair. Charlie Allan was moving around her quickly, the pain in her head was intense as she tried to get herself back into reality. When she managed to get her senses back, she felt the blood on her lips and the banging in her head, she also sensed that she could not move her arms or her legs, she knew instantly she had been knocked out and then tied up by the man in her house.

'What are you doing?' she managed to say through her damaged lip.

'This gives me more bargaining power', he replied, 'you tied up, and your kids in the bedroom, when he comes home, he will be more like a pussy cat when he sees the situation in his home, your best to shut the fuck up and wait like a good little girl.'

Tina felt helpless, she thought of her children, she thought of Sean miles away, she didn't have an answer, no one will come to the house tonight, and she has at least eight hours until somebody would or need to, she cried inwardly.

Chapter 53

The taxi driver turned to Sean and gave the price from the airport
to the quiet deserted road that Sean had been dropped off at.
Sean paid the taxi driver who then had to turn around on the quiet
road to go back the way he came from, Sean noticed he had a
look in his eyes as if to say why are you being dropped off in the
middle of nowhere? Sean had decided in the cab that he may be
better off being dropped a short distance from his house and then
approach by foot, he didn't know why he came to that conclusion
but he went with it anyway. He turned around to see the taxi
drive out of sight at the bottom of the road they had just come
from, and he watched as the taxi's lights vanished into the
distance. Sean turned and started to run up the road towards his
house, he had about a half a mile to run but he was comfortable
with that as he often ran these roads in the daytime to keep his
fitness up. He approached the drive to his house, all the front
lights were off, he went around the back by going down the side
of the house, he carefully took his time as he knew there were
bit's of builders material in the alleyway at the side of the house
and he didn't want to make a noise. He approached the rear of the
house and noticed there was a light on at the rear, his first
thoughts were that maybe one of the kids had left the light on as
usual, he worked his way slowly along the back until he could
get to a window so he could see inside the house. What he saw
made his heart beat with a ferocity that he had never felt before,

his eyes adjusted and he peered through the window again, he was right, he could see his wife tied to a chair in his house, but he could see no one else.

He wanted to move fast, he wanted to solve it there and then, he moved again and went around further to the back of the house, he moved too fast, and kicked a large bucket that went clattering down the alleyway, he cursed himself, as he squatted down to listen, he heard nothing, got up again and carried on around to the back of the house. He crept low and went round to the side of the house towards his children's windows; he saw that Taylor was fast asleep in his bed, he went to Megan's, he peered inside but she was not there. He then moved onto his and Tina's room window, the bed was empty, he didn't know where Megan was and this made him more anxious. He went back to the rear of the house and squatted down again. He was sitting in his garden in Spain with his wife tied up in his house his, ten year old son asleep in bed and his six year old daughter missing, he didn't know where she was, he could see no one else in the house but someone had to be in there, someone tied Tina up and it wasn't Taylor or Megan. He had to make a decision; he couldn't go for anyone else, it may be too late, so he went with his instincts. He crawled along his patio until he came to where he kept his garden tools, the shed was not locked, he picked out what he wanted, and then sat for two minutes before deciding it was now or never. He lifted himself up and ran towards the rear doors of his house, when he got to the double doors he lifted his right arm and smashed the club hammer as hard as he could against the windows, it smashed with the force of his swing and he followed through the windows with his own body weight. He landed on the floor and rolled over quickly jumping to his feet, he saw Tina first, whose eyes looked like she had just seen an alien from outer space. He quickly looked around the room, to his left he saw Charlie Allan who was getting to his feet and going for something in his jacket pocket, Sean ran at him screaming with the club hammer still in his hand, they clashed very quickly and both fell to the floor with the impact, smashing into the far wall. Sean jumped to his feet, he could see Charlie Allan pulling a knife out of his jacket pocket while he was still on the floor, he started to slash at Sean's legs but was missing with every lunge, Sean was jumping back to miss each slash which gave Charlie the chance to get to his feet in time as Sean came in with the hammer. Charlie felt the force of the hammer hit his left upper arm as he protected his head with his arm; Charlie pulled his right arm up and gripping the knife went to stab into Sean's kidneys but Sean was already bearing down again hard with the hammer, this time catching Charlie on the side of the head, Charlie went down still griping the knife, he swung as he went down and caught Sean in the thigh slitting open his jeans and his skin and muscle. The pain hit Sean hard, but he knew he had to continue, he could not stop, if he stopped his opponent would counter attack, Charlie had collapsed in front of Sean but Sean could see he was starting to get up again, Sean clubbed down hard with the hammer across Charlie Allan's head, this time the noise of metal on flesh and bone reverberating around the room. Sean knew he had made good contact; he hit him again and again

356

until the weight of the club hammer took it's toll but had completed it's work. Sean Farrow collapsed on the floor with exhaustion, his breathing was uncontrollable, and he knew he would take him time to get his breath back, it took a while for him to be able to raise his head, but when he did he wished he hadn't. He looked across the room to see Tina, who was still tied to the chair, looking down at him with tears in her eyes. He saw Taylor untying the ropes from around her, and he saw Megan hugging on to Tina, staring down at him.

Chapter 54

Pete Murray looked out to sea; the Marbella sunshine warmed his old face as he watched the fishing boats in the distance busy at work catching their fresh fish for the day. He wondered about his life in the police force and he thought about Fiona his deceased wife and he was thinking about Spain, Sean, Tina and the children. Pete realised he was fighting against himself, did he do wrong in suggesting there should be pay back for Taylor's murder and did he do wrong in suggesting Sean and Tina should be involved, it niggled away at him, it niggled away deep in his kind soul. He didn't have the answers but he knew one day he might be judged for what he helped do, he was right he thought, but he didn't expect certain things to happen, and he didn't expect the children to see such an awful thing.

The day started early for Pete, he got up and showered, he had his normal breakfast, tea and toast with jam and then cereal set out on his balcony looking out to sea. He then walked down to town and spoke to all his local friends; he walked towards the front and found himself looking out to sea. He should not be so deep, he thought to himself, after all the entire world is a better place without the scum that were eradicated, he just wished it didn't impact such young lives. Pete thought about that impact and what they had witnessed, he knew how quickly Tina reacted when she was untied and managed to get a sleeping tablet into

Megan and take her back to her bed very quickly, and to this day she miraculously believes it was a nightmare she had. He remembers Tina telling him what happened, how she found Charlie Allan in her house, how he hit her and then she found herself tied to a chair and the entire room exploding when Sean came through the patio doors screaming at the top of his voice. She saw Sean quickly get up and look around to see Charlie Allan getting to his feet and then she felt the kids run to her side. Oh God she thought, they must have been woken by the noise of Sean coming through the doors, and then she saw the killing of Charlie Allan, and she couldn't protect her kids from the same sight.

Pete was glad Megan was not harmed by it, apart from the nightmares she sometimes gets, he was also glad the young boy was getting the professional help that he needed, he knew with time wounds would heal for the young boy and girl. Pete thought about Taylor and what he saw at such a young age and how brave he was to be part of the plan that they should never mention anything in front of Megan and in time her nightmare will fade away. Pete nodded in his own agreement that Sean and Tina did the right thing in getting a recommended psychiatrist for Taylor and one that will be partial, discreet and trustworthy, being respected in the community amounts to a lot he thought. Pete came to the conclusion that the right thing was done, his last thought about respect did that, Johnny Saunders got things done through fear and violence, Sean Farrow gets things done through respect and love, there's a big difference. Pete felt better in himself because to him and all those around him that share his world, that will always be the answer, how to lead your life, by respect and love.

Pete looked out to sea again and in the distance could see a boat near the spot that brought back memories on the day it happened. He knew he had a hard job that day and that was to get rid of the body of Charlie Allan, this was completed by putting his body into a van, taken down to the harbour where he was placed onto Miguel's fishing boat. Charlie Allan was then taken out to deep waters; he was tied to heavy rocks and then dumped over board for the fish to feed on.

Pete Murray walked away from the harbour wall and started to walk towards town, he knew he had a lunch meeting with Sean and the family and friends, and it will be busy he thought, it's Saturday and tourists and locals will be mingling together in the sunshine.

When Pete approached the meeting point, he could see that Sean was sitting at the bar with Miguel, but was also surprised to see what looked like Joe Swain sitting with them. Tina and the kids were sitting outside in the sunshine; he could hear Latin music playing throughout the bar and they looked like they were waiting for everyone else to turn up, Pete crossed the road from the beach side and approached Tina, Tina looked up.

'Hi Pete' she said, 'Sean is inside with Miguel and guess what, Joe has come over to see Sean, isn't that great,'

'Hi Tina, yeah that is great I will pop in and see them, he said and turned to look at the kids. 'Hi kids how are you doing, what are you up to?'

'Hi Uncle Pete', Taylor and Megan shouted back while continuing to run around outside with other local Spanish and English kids, they looked happy, and he liked it, it made him feel like he was right with what he was recently thinking.

He looked down at Tina and kissed her on the cheek, 'how's things Tina?' he said

'They are good Pete; I'm just sitting here with the kids waiting for the others to join us. And yourself?'

'I'm ok Tina, the kids look happy.'

'They are happy Pete, I think they are getting better by the day, Megan doesn't ever mention it anymore and Taylor is doing really well with the doctors, it's hard but he's getting through it, he understands that what he saw was his daddy protecting his family.'

'That's good Tina' Pete replied, 'and you and Sean?'

'We are Ok Pete, we are doing really well, still madly in love and we have really settled into the new home, it's better not looking out to sea for obvious reasons, it's really peaceful looking out into the mountains.'

'I will go in and see Sean and the others, do you want a drink?'

'I'm ok Pete; I've got a jug of Sangria, I'm going to wait for Angela and mum to join me when they get here.'

Pete walked into the bar, he took a seat next to Miguel at the bar and shook his hand, he turned to Sean and did the same and then turned to Joe Swain, he put his arms around him and hugged him like he hasn't seen him for years, which he hadn't, Joe did the same, in his shy way.

'Good to see you Joe, you here long?' said Pete.

'I'm here for a couple of weeks Pete, to see Sean, Tina and the kids, and I knew I might bump into you at some point you old codger, you ain't changed have you, just a bit more craggy around the face', Joe Swain said with a smirk on his face

Pete laughed and so did Sean; Miguel smiled but took a little longer as usual due to the London dialect used by Joe.

'How's London?' said Pete.

'Not the same,' said Joe.' Not been the same for years, so many changes, too many bloody foreigners now, you lot did the right thing coming over here when you did, but it's still the best City in the world.'

'We have the same thing here too' said Miguel.' All you bloody foreigners coming over here spending money and making Spain great again, we should send you all back.'

They all laughed, and this time Miguel laughed with them at the same time. At the end they all smiled, they were so much happier in Spain; they were all doing well, thanks to Sean and his growing businesses. But they still thought of London occasionally, they still discussed it on a regular basis and were still interested in it's politics, and, of course, the football, and with Pete and Sean's support for different teams it sometimes became an interesting debate.

'Whiskey, Pete?' said Sean.

'No Sean I'm going to have half of lager, it's a warm day and I've got a thirst on.'

The day was beautiful, the sun was shining and once everyone had arrived it stayed the same through to the evening, with everyone enjoying the weather and the company of friends and family. Angela Clay, who was now Angelina Santos turned up with Patsy Docherty and helped Tina with the Sangria. The kids ran around while the adults sat discussing life, politics, sport and religion and any other topic that came up. Sean insisted that Spanish Tapas was ordered and was delivered to the table throughout the day and drinks flowed until the music managed to eventually get them all up dancing including the kids. Everyone smiled, everyone laughed and everyone was happy.

When the evening ended they all walked along the main harbour wall, the wind was blowing warm air across them, they continued to laugh and joke until one by one they all went their separate ways home. Joe was the last to leave as he walked off towards Sean's boat Tina of the Seas, he was staying there for the duration of his stay, he liked the quietness and to be able to have the ability to launch her off and in no time be in the middle of nowhere. This left Sean, Tina and the kids walking alone the rest of the way home, the kids ran in front of them laughing and giggling and playing chase while Sean and Tina walked along holding hands.

'Joe's a nice man' said Tina.

'I know babe, do you know he's never married we might have to pair him off while he's over here', they both laughed, 'he asked me about work, and asked me what it was like to live in Spain, I told him I could get him work, although he only knows building work. I'm sure I can sort him out, he wants to get out of London, I suppose a bit like we did, although ours was a had to, not a need or want to.'

Sean and Tina stopped again by the sea wall.

'This is our home Tina', Sean said, 'it feels like our home and we have made it our home.'

They looked out to sea, the air was still warm, they were holding hands, and then they both turned and looked at Megan and Taylor running across the sand with the moonlight shining down on them making them look like angels.

'I love you Tina, I've loved you from the first day I set my eyes on you.' Said Sean.

Tina turned to him with that smile that has always attracted Sean to her.

'I love you too Sean.' she replied with happiness clearly in her voice.

'Have we achieved our goals Tina?' Said Sean.

'What do you mean Sean? She replied, 'what goals?'

'I mean, have we done what we were meant to be here for, you know life as we know it and all that jargon.'

'Yes Sean, we have achieved it, we have conquered it, and we have two beautiful children from it, with beauty in their hearts, you've done it and I have supported you.'

'Do you think so Tina?' said Sean.

They stopped and both looked out to sea again, Sean put his arm around his wife and kissed her on the neck, the kiss made Tina tingle when the wind hit the moisture left by his lips.

'I know so Sean, I know so', she replied.

'I think we had other support around us babe' said Sean.

'I know', she said, 'we couldn't have done what we did without Pete and the others.'

Sean looked into Tina's eyes and then started to tell her about his journey to London, he told her about the taxi driver and the air stewardess and how they seemed to be there when he needed them. He told her about his pain and frustration at not being able to do anything because he was so far away, and that he will never be far away from her or the kids again.

Tina smiled and kissed him on the lips, 'angels on your shoulders Sean' she said, 'they were angels on your shoulders.'

Sean smiled back, he kissed her and they let it linger there until they felt Taylor and Megan wrapping their arms around them and shouting in playful disgust at mummy and daddy snogging in front of them, they laughed, they all laughed, and together, they walked home laughing.

Printed in Great Britain
by Amazon